THE NORSEMEN
IN THE WEST

America Before Columbus

R.M. BALLANTYNE

Frontispiece by John Betancourt. Based on a painting.

THE NORSEMEN IN THE WEST

America Before Columbus

R.M. Ballantyne

WILDSIDE PRESS

THE NORSEMEN
IN THE WEST

INTRODUCTION

Robert Michael Ballantyne (1825–1894) was a Scottish author who published more than 100 books. He was also an accomplished artist and exhibited some of his water-colours at the Royal Scottish Academy.

Ballantyne was born in Edinburgh, the ninth of ten children (and the youngest son), to Alexander and Anne Ballantyne. His father was a newspaper editor and printer in the family firm of "Ballantyne & Co" based at Paul's Works on the Canongate. His uncle, James Ballantyne, was the printer for Scottish author Sir Walter Scott. A banking crisis in 1825 resulted in the collapse of the Ballantyne printing business the following year with debts of £130,000,which led to a decline in the family's fortunes.

Robert Ballantyne went to Canada at the age of 16 and spent five years working for the Hudson's Bay Company. He traded with the local Native Americans for furs, which required him to travel by canoe and sleigh to the areas occupied by the modern-day provinces of Manitoba, Ontario, and Quebec—experiences that formed the basis of his novel *Snowflakes and Sunbeams* (1856). His longing for family and home during that period impressed him to start writing letters to his mother. Ballantyne recalled in his autobiographical *Personal Reminiscences in Book Making* (1893) that "To this long-letter writing I attribute whatever small amount of facility in composition I may have acquired."

In 1847 Ballantyne returned to Scotland to discover that his father had died. He published his first book the following year, *Hudson's Bay: or, Life in the Wilds of North America*, and for some time was employed by the publishers Messrs Constable. In 1856 he gave up business to focus on his literary career and began the series of adventure stories for the young with which his name is popularly associated.

The Young Fur-Traders (1856), *The Coral Island* (1857), *The World of Ice* (1859), *Ungava: a Tale of Eskimo Land* (1857), *The Dog*

Crusoe (1860), *The Lighthouse* (1865), *Fighting the Whales* (1866), *Deep Down* (1868), *The Pirate City* (1874), *Erling the Bold* (1869), *The Settler and the Savage* (1877), and more than 100 other books followed in regular succession, his rule being to write as far as possible from personal knowledge of the scenes he described. *The Gorilla Hunters: A tale of the wilds of Africa* (1861) shares three characters with The Coral Island: Jack Martin, Ralph Rover and Peterkin Gay. Here Ballantyne relied factually on Paul du Chaillu's Exploration in Equatorial Guinea, which had appeared early in the same year.

The Coral Island remains the most popular of the Ballantyne novels still read and remembered today, but because of a mistake he made in that book—he gave an incorrect thickness of coconut shells—he prioritized research on his subjects for later books. For instance, he spent time living with the lighthouse keepers at the Bell Rock before writing *The Lighthouse*, and he spent time with the tin miners of Cornwall while researching *Deep Down*.

In 1866 he married Jane Grant, with whom he had three sons and three daughters. He spent his later years in Harrow, London, before moving to Italy for the sake of his health, possibly suffering from undiagnosed Ménière's disease. He died in Rome in 1894 and was buried in the Protestant Cemetery there.

One of the young men influenced by Ballantyne's novels was Robert Louis Stevenson (1850–94). Stevenson was so impressed with the story of *The Coral Island* (1857) that he based portions of his most famous book, *Treasure Island* (1881), on themes found in Ballantyne's classic novel.

—Karl Wurf
Rockville, Maryland

CHAPTER I.

The Curtain Rises and the Play Begins.

One fine autumn evening, between eight and nine hundred years ago, two large hairy creatures, bearing some resemblance to polar bears, might have been seen creeping slowly, and with much caution, toward the summit of a ridge that formed a spur to one of the ice-clad mountains of Greenland. The creatures went on all-fours. They had long bodies, short legs, shorter tails, and large round heads.

Having gained the top of the ridge they peeped over and beheld a hamlet nestled at the foot of a frowning cliff; and at the head of a smiling inlet. We use these terms advisedly, because the cliff, being in deep shadow, looked unusually black and forbidding, while the inlet, besides being under the influence of a profound calm, was lit up on all its dimples by the rays of the setting sun.

The hamlet consisted of one large cottage and half a dozen small cots, besides several sheds and enclosures wherein were a few sleepy-looking sheep, some lean cattle, and several half starved horses. There was active life there also. Smoke issued from the chimneys; fresh-looking women busied themselves about household work; rosy children tumbled in and out at the doors, while men in rough garments and with ruddy countenances mended nets or repaired boats on the shore. On a bench in front of the principal cottage sat a sturdy man, scarcely middle-aged, with shaggy fair and flowing locks. His right foot served as a horse to a rapturous little boy, whose locks and looks were so like to those of the man that their kinship was obvious — only the man was rugged and rough in exterior; the boy was round and smooth. Tow typified the hair of the man; floss silk that of the boy.

Everything in and around the hamlet bore evidence of peace and thrift. It was a settlement of Norsemen — the *first* Greenland settlement, established by Eric the Red of Iceland about the year 986 — nearly twenty years before the date of the opening of our tale — and the hairy creatures above referred to had gone there to look at it.

Having gazed very intently over the ridge for a considerable time, they crept backwards with extreme caution, and, on getting sufficiently far down the hillside to be safe from observation, rose on their hind legs and began to talk; from which circumstance it may be concluded that they were human beings. After talking, grinning, and glaring at each other for a few minutes, with gestures to correspond, as though on the point of engaging in mortal combat, they suddenly wheeled about and walked off at a rapid pace in the direction of a gorge in the mountains, the head of which was shut in by and filled up with cliffs and masses and fields of ice that overtopped the everlasting hills, and rested like a white crest on the blue sky. Vast though it seemed, this was merely a tongue of those great glaciers of the mysterious North which have done, and are still doing, so much to modify the earth's economy and puzzle antiquarian philosophy; which form the fountain-head of influences that promote the circulation of the great deep, and constitute the cradle of those ponderous icebergs that cover the arctic seas.

From out that gloomy gorge a band of more than a hundred hairy creatures issued with wild shouts and upraised arms to welcome back the adventurous two. They surrounded them, and forthwith the nation — for the entire nation was evidently there — held a general assembly or parliament on the spot. There was a good deal of uproar and confusion in that parliament, with occasional attempts on the part of several speakers to obtain a hearing at one and the same time — in which respects this parliament bore some resemblance to civilised assemblies of the present day. There was also an immense amount of gesticulation and excitement.

At last there uprose a man clad in garments that had once belonged to a seal, and with a face that was quite as round and nearly as flat as a fryingpan. He stood fully half a foot higher than the tallest of his fellows. Like the adventurous two he had a tail — a very short tail — to his coat; but indeed this might be said of all the men of the tribe. The women's tails, however, were long. Perhaps this was meant as a mark of distinction, for their costume was so very similar to that of the men that their smaller size and longer tails alone marked the difference. To be sure there was additional presumptive evidence of their sex in the fact that most of them carried babies in their hoods; which hoods were made preposterously large for the express purpose of containing the babies.

To the tall man with the flat face the assembly listened with eager looks, bated breath, and open mouths. What he said — who can tell? His language was unintelligible to civilised ears. Not so, however, his actions, which were vigorous and full of meaning, and comprehensible by all nations. If there be any significance in signs at all he began by saying, "Hold your stupid tongues and *I* will speak." This drew forth loud and prolonged applause — as consummate impudence usually does. When he pointed with both hands to the women and children, and spoke in tender tones, instantly thereafter growling in his speech, gnashing his teeth, glaring fiercely, waving one hand at the surrounding hills and shaking the other, clenched, at the unoffending sea — he was obviously stating his grievances, namely, that the white men had come there to wrest from him his native hills and glaciers, and rob him of his wife and children, and that he defied them to come on and do their worst, seeing that, in regard to the whole assembled white world in arms he did not care a button — or a walrus-tusk, for buttons were unknown to these creatures at that time. When, suddenly changing his manner and tone, he seized a spear, hissed his sentiments through his teeth with great volubility, and made a furious plunge that caused the assembly to gasp, and the man nearest the spear point to shrivel up — what *could* be his meaning save that nothing short of a hole right through the body of a Norseman could appease the spirit of indignation that caused his blood to boil? And when, finally, he pointed to the setting sun, traced a line with his finger from it downward to the centre of the earth under his feet, then shook his spear wrathfully toward the sea and wound up with a tremendous Ho! that would have startled the echoes of the place had there been any there, it was plain to the meanest capacity that an attack — impetuous and overwhelming — was to be made on the strangers at midnight.

Whatever were his sentiments, the assembly heartily appreciated, applauded, and approved them. They cheered and shouted "Hear, hear," after their own fashion, and then the whole band rushed back into the mountain gorge — doubtless with the intent to gorge themselves with raw blubber, prepare their weapons, and snatch a little repose before issuing forth to battle.

But let us return to the Norsemen, over whose innocent heads such awful prospects were impending.

The sturdy man with the fair shaggy locks was Leif, the son of Eric the Red of Iceland. The boy with the silken curls, who rode on his foot so joyously, was his son Olaf.

Eric had died several years before the date on which our tale opens, and Leif inherited his cottage and property at Brattalid in Ericsfiord, on the west coast of Greenland — the hamlet which we have already described.

"Come now, Olaf," said Leif, flinging the child from his foot to his knee, and thence to the ground, "give me your hand; we shall go see how the boats and nets get on — Hey! there goes a puff of wind. We shall have more presently." He paused and scanned the seaward horizon with that intent abstracted gaze which is peculiar to seafaring men. So long did he gaze, and so earnestly, that the child looked up in his face with an expression of surprise, and then at the horizon, where a dark blue line indicated the approach of a breeze.

"What do you see, father?" asked Olaf.

"Methinks I see two ships," replied Leif.

At this there came a sweet musical voice from the cottage: — "Ships, brother! Did I not tell you that I had a dream about two ships, and said I not that I was sure something was going to happen?"

The speaker appeared in the doorway, drying her hands and arms on a towel — for she had been washing dishes. She was a fair comely young woman, with exceedingly deep blue eyes, and a bright colour in her cheeks — for women of the richer class were remarkably healthy and well-made in those days. They did a great deal of hard work with their hands, hence their arms were strong and well developed without losing anything of their elegance.

"You are always dreaming, widow Gudrid," said Leif, with a quiet smile — for he was no believer in dreams or superstitions, in which respect he differed much from the men and women of his time; "nevertheless, I am bound to admit that you did tell me that 'something' was going to happen, and no one can deny that something *is* about to occur just now. But your dream happened a month or six weeks ago, and the 'something,' which you are pleased to assume is these two ships, is only happening today. See, now, I can be a more definite prophet than thou: I will prophesy that Yule is coming — and it will surely come if you only wait long enough!"

"You are an unbeliever, brother-in-law," retorted Gudrid, with a laugh; "but I have not time to reason with you. These ships will bring strangers, and I must prepare to show them hospitality — Come, Olaf, help me to put the house in order."

Thus summoned, Olaf followed Gudrid into the house with alacrity, for he was passionately fond of his pretty aunt, who stood in the place of a mother to him, his own mother having died when he was an infant.

"But, aunt," said Olaf, checking himself in the doorway and looking wistfully back, "I want to see the ships come in."

"You shall see that, my son; I will not keep you too long."

This was quite sufficient. Olaf thoroughly believed in his aunt's truthfulness and wisdom. He set to work to assist in clearing away the confusion — part of which, in the shape of toys and chips — was of his own creating — and became so busy that he almost forgot the ships — at least if he did remember them they did not weigh heavily on his mind.

"Now, Olaf," said Gudrid, going to the window when the preparations were nearly completed, "you may run down to the shore, for the ships will soon be on the strand."

The boy waited no second bidding, you may be sure. He flew out of the house, and to his great surprise beheld the two ships — which so lately had appeared like sea-birds on the horizon — coming grandly up the fiord, their great square sails bulging out before a smart breeze.

All the men of the little colony were assembled on the shore — all, at least, who chanced to be at home at the time; but many of the inhabitants were absent — some fishing, some gone to Iceland, and others on viking-cruise. There were probably about thirty men on the sands, besides a good many women and children.

It must not be supposed, however, that this was the whole of that Greenland colony. It was only the part of it that had settled at Brattalid in Ericsfiord. There was another portion, a few miles distant, named Heriulfness, nearly as large as that of Ericsfiord, which had been founded by Heriulf a friend and companion of Eric the Red. Heriulf had soon followed his friend Eric to the grave, leaving the management of the colony of Heriulfness to his son Biarne.

Biarne had not been present when the two sails were first observed, but he chanced to come over to Brattalid just before their arrival.

"What, ho! Biarne," shouted Leif, as the son of Heriulf went down to the beach, "come up hither."

Leif stood on an elevated rock apart, and Biarne, a good deal excited, went up to him.

"Why, what ails thee?" asked Leif.

"Nothing," replied Biarne, "but I think I know whose ship that first one is."

"Ay! is it the ship of a friend or a foe?"

"A friend," replied Biarne — "at least he was a friend when I knew him in Norway, nigh twenty summers past, and I did not think him changeable. You and I, Leif, have often sailed these northern seas together and apart, but I do not think that in all our wanderings either of us has met before or since a finer man than Karlsefin, though he was a mere stripling when I knew him."

The Norseman's eyes flashed as he spoke of his friend, for, besides being a strong and handsome man, he possessed a warm enthusiastic heart. Indeed, he had been noted in the settlement for the strength of his affection for his father Heriulf, and his dutiful conduct towards him as long as the old man lived.

"Karlsefin," repeated Leif, musing; "I know him not."

"Yet he knows you," said Biarne; "when I met him in Norway I told him all about your discovery of Vinland."

"Nay, thine own discovery of it," said Leif.

"Not so," replied the other, with a blush, in which a frown mingled; "I did but look upon the land — you went ashore and took possession."

"Well, if I did so I have not retained it," replied Leif, with a laugh; "but say, how know you that this is Karlsefin's ship?"

"I know by the cut of her figurehead and the colour of her sails. Karlsefin was always partial to stripes of white and blue."

"Well, it may be as you say; we shall soon know." Thus saying, Leif descended to the beach as the vessels approached and ran their keels straight on the sandy shores of the bay. There was great bustle on board, and there were many men, besides some women, who could be seen looking over the bulwarks with keen interest, while Leif's men brought planks with which to make a gangway from the ship to the shore.

The ships which had thus come to Greenland were of the quaint build peculiar to the Norse vessels of those days — a peculiarity of build, by the way, which has not altogether disappeared, for to this day the great central mast, huge square sail, and high prow may be seen in the fiords of Norway.

Each of the vessels which now lay beached in Ericsfiord had a high fore-castle and poop, with figureheads on stem and stern-posts that towered higher still. The ships were only half decked, with benches for numerous rowers, and each had a crew of sixty men.

When the gangway was laid to the leading ship the first man who descended to the shore was of striking appearance. It was not so much that he was tall and strong enough to have been a worthy foeman to the stoutest colonist in Ericsfiord, as that his demeanour was bland and courtly, while there was great intellectuality in his dark handsome countenance. Unlike most Norsemen, his hair and beard were black and close-curling, and his costume, though simple, was rich in quality.

The moment he landed, Biarne stepped forward, exclaiming, "Karlsefin!"

The stranger's face lighted up with surprise and pleasure.

"Biarne!" he said, seizing his hand, "I thought you were in Iceland."

"So I was, but now I am in Greenland, and right glad to be the first to welcome my friend."

Hereupon the two shook hands fervently; but, not content with this, they seized each other in an embrace, and their bearded mouths met with a hearty masculine smack that did credit to their hearts, and which it might have gratified the feelings of an affectionate walrus to behold.

CHAPTER II.

Strong Emotions are Succeeded by Supper, and Followed by Discussions on Discovery, which End in a Wild Alarm!

When Karlsefin had been introduced to Leif Ericsson, the former turned round and presented to him and Biarne his friend Thorward, the captain of the other ship. Thorward was not a tall man, but was very broad and stout, and had a firm yet pleasing cast of countenance. Both Thorward and Karlsefin were men of about thirty-five years of age.

"Are you not on viking-cruise?" asked Leif as they walked up to the house together, while the male members of his household and the men of the settlement assisted the crews to moor the ships.

"No; my friend Thorward and I are not men of war. We prefer the peaceful occupation of the merchant, and, to say truth, it is not unprofitable."

"I would that more were of your way of thinking," said Leif. "I do not love the bloody game of war, and glad am I that we have got into a quiet corner here in Greenland, where there is small occasion for it. Biarne, too, is of our way of thinking, as no doubt you already know."

"He has often told me so, and, if I mistake not, has feathered his nest well by merchanting."

"He has," answered Biarne for himself, with a laugh.

While they thus advanced, talking, little Olaf had kept walking in front of the tall stranger, looking up into his face with unbounded admiration. He had never before seen any man so magnificent. His father and Biarne, whom he had hitherto regarded as perfect specimens of mankind, were quite eclipsed. Looking backward and walking forward is an unsafe process at any time. So Olaf found it on the present occasion, for he tripped over a stone and in falling hit his little nose with such violence that it soon became a big nose, and bled profusely.

Karlsefin picked him up and set him on his legs. "My poor boy, don't cry," he said.

"No fear of *him* crying," observed Leif; "he never cries — save when his feelings are hurt. When you touch these he *is* addicted to blubbering. Run, lad, and Gudrid will wash you."

Olaf bounded into the house, where he was carried off to a sleeping-room and there carefully sponged by the sympathetic Gudrid. "Oh! —" he exclaimed, while his face was being washed.

"Does it pain you much, dear?" said the pretty aunt, interrupting him.

"Oh!" he continued, enthusiastically, "I never did see such a splendid man before."

"What splendid man, child?"

"Why, Karlsefin."

"And who is Karlsefin?"

"The stranger who has come across the sea from Norway."

"Indeed," said Gudrid.

Whether it was the sound of the stranger's voice in the adjoining room, or anxiety to complete her hospitable preparations, that caused Gudrid to bring her operations on Olaf to an abrupt termination, we cannot tell, but certain it is that she dried him rather quickly and hastened into the outer hall, where she was introduced to the two strangers in due form as widow Gudrid.

She had no difficulty in distinguishing which was Olaf's "splendid man!" She looked at Karlsefin and fell in love with him on the spot, but Gudrid was modest, and not sentimental. It is only your mawkishly sentimental people who are perpetually tumbling into love, and out of it, and can't help showing it. Cupid shot her right through the heart with one powerful dart, and took her unawares too, but she did not show the smallest symptom of having been even grazed. She neither blushed nor stammered, nor looked conscious, nor affected to look unconscious. She was charmingly natural!

But this was not all: Karlsefin also fell in love on the spot — over head and ears and hair, and hat to boot; neither did he show sign of it! After the trifling ceremonies usual on an introduction were over, he turned to continue his conversation with Leif and paid no further attention to Gudrid, while she busied herself in preparing supper. It is true that he looked at her now and then, but of course he looked at everybody, now and then, in the course of the evening. Besides, it is well-known what is said about the rights of the feline species in reference to royalty. At supper Gudrid waited on the guests, Karlsefin therefore, necessarily paid her somewhat more attention in accepting her civilities, but Thorward was quite as attentive as he, so that the most sharp-witted matchmaker in the world would have failed to note any symptom of anything whatever in regard to either of them.

Gudrid felt this a little, for she was accustomed to admiration from the young men of Ericsfiord and Heriulfness, and, you know, people don't like to want what they are accustomed to. What Karlsefin thought, he did not show and never mentioned, therefore we cannot tell.

Now, good reader, pray do not run away with the notion that this love affair is the plot on which the story is to hinge! Nothing of the kind. It ran its course much more rapidly, and terminated much more abruptly, than you probably suppose — as the sequel will show.

During supper there was not much conversation, for all were hungry, but afterwards, when cans of home-brewed ale were handed round, the tongues began to move. Leif soon observed that Karlsefin merely sipped his beer, but never once drank.

"You do not drink," he said, pushing a large silver tankard towards him; "come, fill up."

"Thanks, I drink but sparingly," said Karlsefin, taking up the large tankard and admiring the workmanship.

"In good sooth ye do," cried Biarne, with a laugh; "a mouse could hardly slake his thirst with all that you have yet imbibed."

"I have been so long at sea," rejoined Karlsefin, smiling, "that I have lost my relish for beer. We had nothing but water with us. Where got you this tankard, Leif, it is very massive and the workmanship such as one seldom meets with save in kings' houses?"

"It belonged to a king!" replied Leif, with a look of pride. "Good King Olaf Tryggvisson gave it to me on an occasion when I chanced to do him some small service. Many winters have passed since then."

"Indeed, Leif! then you must be a favourite with King Olaf," exclaimed Karlsefin, "for I am the bearer of another gift to you from his royal hand."

"To me?"

"Ay. Hearing that I meant to sail over to Greenland this summer, he asked me to bear you his remembrances, and gave me two slaves to present to you in token of his continued friendship."

Leif's face beamed with satisfaction, and he immediately filled and quaffed a bumper of ale to King Olaf's health, which example was followed by Biarne and the guests, as well as by the house-carls who sat on benches in various parts of the hall drinking their ale and listening to the conversation. Even little Olaf — who had been named after the king of Norway — filled his tankard to the brim with milk, and quaffed it off with a swagger that was worthy of a descendant of a long line of sea-kings, who could trace their lineage back to Odin himself.

"The slaves," continued Karlsefin, "are from the land of the Scots. Wouldst like to see a Scotsman, Gudrid?" he added, turning to the widow who sat near him.

"I should like it much. I have heard of the Scots in Iceland. 'Tis said they are a well-favoured race, stout warriors, and somewhat fond of trading."

Leif and Biarne both laughed loud and long at this.

"In good truth they are a stout race, and fight like very wildcats, as Biarne and I can testify; as to their being well-favoured, there can be no question about that; though they are rather more rugged than the people farther south, and — yes, they *are* good traders, and exceedingly cautious men. They think well before they speak, and they speak slowly — sometimes they won't speak at all. Ha! ha! Here, I drink to the land of the Scot. It is a grand good land, like our own dear old Norway."

"Brother-in-law," exclaimed Gudrid, reproachfully, "do you forget that you are an Icelander?"

"Forget!" exclaimed Leif, tossing back his yellow locks, and raising the tankard again to pledge his native land; "no, I shall only forget Iceland when I forget to live; but I don't forget, also, that it is only about 130 years since my great-grandfather and his companions came over from Norway to Iceland. Before that it was an unpeopled rock in the Northern Sea, without name or history.[1] 'Twas as little known then as Vinland is known now."

"By the way, Biarne," said Karlsefin, turning to his friend, "the mention of

1   Iceland was colonised by Norsemen about the year 874.

Vinland reminds me that, when you and I met last, you did not give me a full account of that discovery, seeing that you omitted to mention your own share in it. Tell me how was it, and when and where was it? Nay, have I unintentionally touched on a sore point?" he added, on observing a slight shade of annoyance pass over Biarne's usually cheerful countenance.

"He *is* a little sore about it," said Leif, laughing. "Come, Biarne, don't be thin-skinned. You know the saying, A dutiful son makes a glad father. You had the best of reasons for acting as you did."

"Ay, but people don't believe in these best of reasons," retorted Biarne, still annoyed, though somewhat mollified by Leif's remarks.

"Never mind, 'tis long past now. Come, give us the saga. 'Tis a good one, and will bear retelling."

"Oh yes," exclaimed Olaf, with sparkling eyes, for the boy dearly loved anything that bore the faintest resemblance to a saga or story, "tell it, Biarne."

"Not I," said Biarne; "Leif can tell it as well as I, if he chooses."

"Well, I'll try," said Leif, laying his huge hand on the table and looking earnestly at Karlsefin and Thorward. The latter was a very silent man, and had scarcely uttered a word all the evening, but he appeared to take peculiar interest in Vinland, and backed up the request that Leif would give an account of its discovery.

"About twenty summers ago," said Leif, "my father, Eric the Red, and his friend Heriulf, Biarne's father, came over here from Iceland. [A.D. 986.] Biarne was a very young man at the time — little more than a boy — but he was a man of enterprise, and fond of going abroad, and possessed a merchant-ship of his own with which he gathered wealth, and, I will say it, reputation also — though perhaps I should not say that to his face.

"He was a good son, and used to be by turns a year abroad and a year with his father. He chanced to be away in Norway when Heriulf and my father Eric came over to Greenland. On returning to Iceland he was so much disappointed to hear of his father's departure that he would not unload his ship, but resolved to follow his old custom and take up his winter abode with his father. 'Who will go with me to Greenland?' said he to his men. 'We will all go,' replied the men. 'Our expedition,' said Biarne, 'will be thought foolish, as none of us have ever been on the Greenland sea before.' 'We mind not that,' said the men — so away they sailed for three days and lost sight of Iceland. Then the wind failed; after that a north wind and a fog set in, and they knew not where they were sailing to; and this lasted many days. At length the sun appeared. Then they knew the quarters of the sky, and, after sailing a day and a night, made the land.

"They saw that it was without mountains, was covered with wood, and that there were small hills inland. Biarne saw that this did not answer to the description of Greenland; he knew he was too far south, so he left the land on the larboard side, and sailed two days and nights before they got sight of land again. The men asked Biarne if this was Greenland, but he said it was not, 'For on Greenland,' he says, 'there are great snowy mountains, but this is flat and covered with trees.' Here the wind fell and the men wanted to go ashore, 'Because,' said they, 'we have need of wood and water.' Biarne replied, 'Ye are not in want of either;' and the men blamed him for this — but the season was far spent, he knew not how long it might take him to find Greenland, so he had no time to spare. Was it not so?" said Leif, appealing to his friend.

"It was so," replied Biarne, nodding gravely.

"Well then," continued Leif, "it must be told that he ordered them to hoist the sail, which they did, and, turning the bow from the land, kept the sea for three days and nights, with a fine breeze from the south-west, when a third time land was seen, with high snowy mountains. Still Biarne would not land, for it was not like what had been reported of Greenland. They soon found it to be an island, and, turning from it, stood out to sea, when the breeze increased to a gale, forcing them to take in a reef; so they sailed for three days and nights more, and made land the fourth time. This turned out to be Greenland, and quite close to Heriulf's dwelling at Heriulfness. Biarne then gave up seafaring, and dwelt with his old father as long as he lived; but since his death he has been sometimes at sea and sometimes at home. Now, these lands which Biarne discovered, were what I have since called Vinland."

"Yes," exclaimed Biarne, with a look of indignation; "and when I afterwards fared to Norway they blamed me for not going on shore and exploring these lands — as if I, at the end of autumn, could afford to put off time in explorations, when it was all I could do to make my port before the winter set in!" He finished off by striking the table with his fist, seizing his tankard, and draining it to the bottom.

"I have often observed," said Karlsefin, quietly, "that people who sit by their firesides at home, and do nothing, are usually very severe and noisy in their remarks on those who fare abroad and do great things; but that arises not so much from ill-will as ignorance."

"But what of your own doings, Leif?" said Thorward, breaking in here impatiently.

"Well, I didn't do much," replied Leif. "I only took possession, and didn't keep it. This was the way of it. Fourteen years after this voyage of Biarne,[2] I was seized with a desire to see these new lands. I bought Biarne's ship from him, set sail with a good crew, and found the lands, just as Biarne had described them, far away to the south of Greenland. I landed and gave names to some places. At the farthest south point we built huts and spent the winter, but returned home in spring. I called this part Vinland, and this is the reason why: We had a German with us named Tyrker, who is with me here still. One day Tyrker was lost; I was very anxious about him, fearing that he had been killed by wild beasts or Skraelingers,[3] so I sent out parties to search. In the evening we found him

2   About the year A.D. 1000.

3   Esquimaux or savages, probably Indians

coming home in a state of great excitement, having found fruit which, he said, was grapes. The sight and taste of the fruit, to which he was used in his own land, had excited him to such an extent that we thought he was drunk, and for some time he would do nothing but laugh and devour grapes, and talk German, which none of us understood. At last he spoke Norse, and told us that he had found vines and grapes in great abundance. We found that this was true — at least we found a berry which was quite new to us. We went off next day, and, gathering enough to load our boat, brought them away with us. From this circumstance I called it Vinland. Two years after that my brother Thorwald went to Vinland, wintered three years there, was killed by the Skraelingers, and his men returned to Greenland. Then my youngest brother, Thorstein, who was Gudrid's husband, went off to Vinland to fetch home the body of our brother Thorwald, but was driven back by stress of weather. He was taken ill soon after that, and died. Since then Gudrid has dwelt with my household, and glad we are to have her. This is the whole story of Vinland; so if you want to know more about it you must e'en go on a voyage of discovery for yourself."

"I should like nothing better," replied Karlsefin, "if I could only —"

At that moment the door was burst violently open, and a man with blood-shot eyes and labouring breath rushed in exclaiming, "The Skraelinger! the Skraelinger are upon us!"

CHAPTER III.

Dark War-Clouds Lower, but Clear away without a Shower — Voices and Legs do Good Service.

"Up, carls, buckle on your war-gear!" cried Leif, rising hastily on hearing the announcement with which the last chapter ended.

"Run, Thorward, call out our men," whispered Karlsefin; "I will stay to learn what Leif means to do. Bring them all up to the door."

Thorward was gone almost before the sentence was finished. Leif and his house-carls, of whom there were ten present at the time, did not take long to busk them for the fight. The Norse of old were born, bred, and buried — if they escaped being killed and cut to pieces — in the midst of alarms. Their armour was easily donned, and not very cumbrous. Even while Leif was giving the first order to his men, Gudrid had run to the peg on which hung his sword and helmet, and brought him these implements of war.

"My men and I shall be able to render you some service, Leif," said Karlsefin; "what do you intend to do?"

"Do!" exclaimed Leif with a grim laugh, as he buckled on his sword, "why, I shall give the Skraelingers a tremendous fright, that is all. The rascals! They knew well that we were short-handed just now, and thought to take advantage of us; but hah! they do not seem to be aware that we chance to have stout visitors with us tonight. So, lads, follow me."

Biarne, meanwhile, had darted out on the first alarm, and assembled all the men in the settlement, so that when Leif, Karlsefin, and the housemen issued out of the cottage they found about a dozen men assembled, and others running up every moment to join them. Before these were put in array most of the men of Karlsefin's ship, numbering forty, and those belonging to Thorward, numbering thirty, came up, so that when all were mustered they were little if at all short of one hundred stout warriors.

The moon came out brightly at the time, and Leif chuckled as he watched Biarne put the men hastily into marching order.

"Methought you said that war was distasteful," observed Karlsefin, in some surprise.

"So it is, so it is, friend," replied Leif, still laughing in a low tone; "but there will be no war tonight. Leave your bows behind you, lads," he added, addressing the men; "you won't want them; shield and sword will be enough. For the matter of that, we might do without both. Now, lads, follow my leading, and do as I bid you; advance with as little noise as may be."

So saying, Leif led the way out of the little hamlet towards the extremity of the ridge or spur of the mountains that sheltered Ericsfiord from the north-west.

Towards that same extremity another band of men were hastening on the other side of the ridge. It was a band of our hairy friends whom the Norsemen called Skraelingers.

Truly there was something grand in the look and bearing of the tall man with the flat face, as he led his band to attack the warlike Norsemen, and there was something almost sublime in the savage, resolute aspect of the men who followed him — each being armed with a large walrus spear, and each being, moreover, an adept in the use of it.

Flatface (in default of a better, let that name stick to him) had ascertained beyond a doubt that the entire available force of Norsemen in Ericsfiord had, in consequence of fishing and other expeditions, been reduced to barely thirty fighting men. He himself could muster a band of at least one hundred and fifty good men and true — not to mention hairy, a hundred and fifty seals having unwillingly contributed their coats to cover these bloodthirsty Skraelingers. The Norsemen, Flatface knew, were strong men and bold, besides being large, but he resolved to take them by surprise, and surely (he argued with himself) a hundred and fifty brave men with spears will be more than a match for thirty sleepy men unarmed and in bed!

Flatface had screwed himself up with such considerations; made a few more inflammatory speeches to his men, by way of screwing them up also, and then, a little before midnight, set forth on his expedition.

Now it chanced that there was a man among the Norsemen who was a great hunter and trapper. His name was Tyrker — the same Tyrker mentioned by Leif as being the man who had found grapes in Vinland. Leif said he was a German, but he said so on no better authority than the fact that he had originally come to Norway from the south of Europe. It is much more probable that he was a Turk, for, whereas the Germans are known to be a well-sized handsome race of fair men, this Tyrker was an ugly little dark wiry fellow, with a high forehead, sharp eyes, and a small face; but he was extremely active, and, although an elderly man, few of the youths in Ericsfiord could beat him at feats requiring dexterity.

But, whether German or Turk, Tyrker was an enthusiastic trapper of white, or arctic foxes. These creatures being very numerous in that part of Greenland, he was wont to go out at all hours, late and early, to visit his traps. Hence it happened that, on the night in question, Tyrker found himself in company with two captured arctic foxes at, the extremity of the mountain spur before referred to.

He could see round the corner of the spur into the country beyond, but as the country there was not attractive, even at its best, he paid no attention to it. He chanced, however, to cast upon it one glance after setting his traps, just as he was about to return home. That glance called forth a steady look, which was followed by a stare of surprise, and the deep guttural utterance of the word "zz-grandimaghowl!" which, no doubt, was Turkish, at that ancient date, for "hallo!"

It was the band of hairy creatures that had met his astonished sight. Tyrker shrank behind the spur and peeped round it for a few seconds to make quite sure. Then, turning and creeping fairly out of sight, he rose and bounded back to the hamlet, as though he had been a youth of twenty. As we have seen, he arrived, gasping, in time to warn his friends.

Between the hamlet and the spur where Tyrker's traps were set there were several promontories, or projections from the cliffs, all of which had to be passed before the spur came in view. Leif led his men past the first and second of these at a run. Then, believing that he had gone far enough, he ordered his band to draw close up under the cliffs, where the shadow was deepest, saying that he would go alone in advance to reconnoitre.

"And mark me, lads," he said, "when I give a loud sneeze, do you give vent to a roar that will only stop short of splitting your lungs; then give chase, and yell to your hearts' content as you run; but see to it that ye keep together and that no man runs past *me*. There is plenty of moonlight to let you see what you're about. If any man tries to overshoot me in the race I'll hew off his head."

This last remark was no figure of speech. In those days men were but too well accustomed to hewing off heads. Leif meant to have his orders attended to, and the men understood him.

On reaching the second projection of cliff after leaving his men, Leif peeped round cautiously and beheld the advancing Skraelingers several hundred yards off. He returned at once to his men and took up a position at their head in the deep shadow of the cliffs.

Although absolutely invisible themselves, the Norsemen could see the Skraelingers quite plainly in the moonlight, as they came slowly and with great caution round each turn of the footpath that led to the hamlet. There was something quite awe-inspiring in the manner of their approach. Evidently Flatface dreaded a surprise, for he put each leg very slowly in advance of the other, and went on tiptoe, glancing quickly on either side between each step. His followers — in a compact body, in deep silence and with bated breath — followed his steps and his example.

When they came to the place where the men crouched in ambush, Leif took up a large stone and cast it high over their heads. So quietly was this done that none even of his own party heard him move or saw the stone, though they heard it fall with a *thud* on the sand beyond.

The Skraelingers heard it too, and stopped abruptly — each man on one leg, with the other leg and his arms more or less extended, just as if he had been suddenly petrified. So in truth he had been — with horror!

To meet an open enemy, however powerful, would have been a pleasure compared with that slow nervous advance in the midst of such dead silence! As nothing followed the sound, however, the suspended legs began to descend slowly again towards the ground, when Leif sneezed!

If Greenland's icy mountains had become one monstrous polar bear, whose powers of voice, frozen for prolonged ages, had at last found vent that night in one concentrated roar, the noise could scarcely have excelled that which instantly exploded from the Norsemen.

The effect on the Skraelingers was almost miraculous. A bomb-shell bursting in the midst of a hundred and fifty Kilkenny cats could not have been more effective, and the result would certainly have borne some marks of resemblance. Each hairy creature sprang nearly his own height into the air, and wriggled while there, as if impatient to turn and fly before reaching the ground.

Earth regained, the more active among them overshot and overturned the clumsy, whereby fifty or sixty were instantly cast down, but these rose again like spring-jacks and fled, followed by a roar of laughter from their foes, which, mingled as it was with howls and yells, did infinitely more to appal the Skraelingers than the most savage war-cry could have done.

But they were followed by more than laughter. The Norsemen immediately gave chase – still yelling and roaring as they ran, for Leif set the example, and his followers remembered his threat.

Karlsefin and Biarne kept one on each side of Leif, about a pace behind him.

"If they fight as well as they run," observed the former, "they must be troublesome neighbours."

"They are not bad fighters," replied Leif; "but sometimes they deem it wise to run."

"Not unlike to other people in that respect," said Biarne; "but it seems to me that we might overhaul them if we were to push on."

He shot up to Leif as he spoke, but the latter checked him.

"Hold back, Biarne; I mean them no harm, and wish no bloodshed – only they must have a good fright. The lads, no doubt, would like to run in and make short work of them; but I intend to breathe the lads, which will in the end do just as well as fighting to relieve their feelings. Enough. It is ill talking and running."

They were silent after that, and ran thus for fully an hour, at nearly the top of their speed. But Leif sometimes checked his men, and sometimes urged them on, so that they fancied he was chasing with full intent to run the Skraelingers down. When the fugitives showed signs of flagging, he uttered a tremendous roar, and his men echoed it, sending such a thrill to the hearts of the Skraelingers that they seemed to recover fresh wind and strength; then he pushed after them harder than ever, and so managed that, without catching or killing one, he terrified them almost out of their wits, and ran them nearly to death.

At last they came to a place where there was an abrupt bend in the mountains. Here Leif resolved to let them go. When they were pretty near the cliff round which the path turned, he put on what, in modern sporting phraseology, is termed a spurt, and came up so close with the flying band that those in rear began to glance despairingly over their shoulders. Suddenly Leif gave vent to a roar, into which he threw all his remaining strength. It was taken up and prolonged by his men. The horror-struck Skraelingers shrieked in reply, swept like a torrent round the projecting cliff, and disappeared!

Leif stopped at once, and held up his hand. All his men stopped short also, and though they heard the Skraelingers still howling as they fled, no one followed them any farther. Indeed, most of the Norsemen were panting vehemently, and rather glad than otherwise to be allowed to halt.

There were, however, two young men among them – tall, strong-boned, and thin, but with broad shoulders, and grave, earnest, though not exactly handsome countenances – who appeared to be perfectly cool and in good wind after their long run. Leif noticed them at once.

"Yonder youths seem to think little of this sort of thing," he said to Karlsefin.

"You are right, Leif; it is mere child's play to them. These are the two Scots — the famous runners — whom I was charged by King Olaf to present to you. Why, these men, I'll engage to say, could overtake the Skraelingers even yet, if they chose."

"Say you so?" cried Leif. "Do they speak Norse?"

"Yes; excellently well."

"Their names?"

"The one is Heika, the other Hake."

"Ho! Hake and Heika, come hither," cried Leif, beckoning to the men, and hastening round the point, where the Skraelingers could be seen nearly a mile off, and still running as if all the evil spirits of the North were after them.

"See there, carls; think you that ye could overtake these rascals?"

The Scots looked at each other, nodded, smiled, and said they thought they could.

"Do it, then. Let them see how you can use your legs, and give them a shout as you draw near; but have a care: do them no hurt, and see that they do no injury to you. Take no arms; your legs must suffice on this occasion."

The Scots looked again at each other, and laughed, as if they enjoyed the joke; then they started off like a couple of deer at a pace which no Norseman legs had ever before equalled, or even approached.

Leif, Biarne, and the men gazed in speechless wonder, much to the amusement of Karlsefin and Thorward, while Hake and Heika made straight for the flying band and came up with them. They shouted wildly as they drew near. The Skraelingers looked back, and seeing only two unarmed men, stopped to receive them.

"As the saying goes," remarked Biarne, "a stern chase is a long one; but tonight proves the truth of that other saying, that there is no rule without an exception."

"What are they doing now?" cried Leif, laughing. "See — they are mad!"

Truly it seemed as if they were; for, after separating and coursing twice completely round the astonished natives, the two Scots performed a species of war-dance before them, which had a sort of fling about it, more easily conceived than described. In the middle of this they made a dart at the group so sudden and swift that Hake managed to overturn Flatface with a tremendous buffet, and Heika did the same to his second in command with an energetic cuff. The Skraelingers were taken so thoroughly by surprise that the Scots had sheered off and got out of reach before a spear could be thrown.

Of course a furious rush was made at them, but the hairy men might as well have chased the wind. After tormenting and tantalising them a little longer, the Scots returned at full speed to their friends, and the Skraelingers, glad to be rid of them, hastened to seek the shelter of the gloomy gorge from which they had originally issued, "like a wolf on the fold."

CHAPTER IV.

Important Events Transpire,
Which End in a Voyage of Discovery.

Some weeks afterwards, Karlsefin and Gudrid went down to walk together on the sea-beach. It would appear that lovers were as fond of rambling together in those olden times as they are in these modern days. It was evening when they went to ramble thus – another evidence of similarity in taste between the moderns and ancients.

"Karlsefin," said Gudrid, stopping at the margin of the fiord, and looking pensively towards the horizon, where golden clouds and air and sea appeared to mingle harmoniously, "I wonder that you, with good ships and many stout men and plenty of means, should choose to remain in this barren spot, instead of searching out the famous Vinland and making a settlement there."

"This barren spot is very bright to me, Gudrid; I have no desire to leave it yet a while. Since you and I were betrothed the ocean has lost its attractions. Besides, would you have me set out on a voyage of discovery at the beginning of winter."

"Nay; but you do not even talk about going when spring comes round."

"Because I have other things to talk of, Gudrid."

"I fear me that you are a lazy man," returned the widow, with a smile, "and will prove but a sorry husband. Just think," she added, with sudden animation, "what a splendid country it must be; and what a desirable change for all of us. Thick and leafy woods like those of old Norway, instead of these rugged cliffs and snowclad hills. Fields of waving grass and rye, instead of moss-covered rocks and sandy soil. Trees large enough to build houses and merchant-ships, instead of willow bushes that are fit for nothing except to save our poor cattle from starvation when the hay crop runs out; besides, longer sunshine in winter and more genial warmth all the year round, instead of howling winds and ice and snow. Truly I think our adopted home here has been woefully misnamed."

"And yet I love it, Gudrid, for I find the atmosphere genial and the sunshine very bright."

"Foolish man!" said Gudrid, with a little laugh. "And then," she added, recurring to her theme, "there are grapes – though, to be sure, I know not what these are, never having tasted them. Biarne says they are very good – do you think so too?"

"They are magnificent," answered Karlsefin. "In southern lands, where Tyrker comes from, they have a process whereby they can make a drink from grapes, which maddens youth and quickens the pulse of age – something like our own beer."

"It does not please me to hear that," replied Gudrid gravely; "some of our carls are too fond of beer. When old Heriulf was sick, a little of it did him good, and when Eric the Red was in his last days he seemed to gather a little strength and comfort from beer; but I never could perceive that it ever did anything to young men except make them boast, and talk nonsense, and look foolish — or, what is worse, quarrel and fight."

"Right, Gudrid, right," said Karlsefin; "my opinion at least is the same as yours, whether it be right or wrong. There is some reason in applying heat to cold, but it seems to me unnecessary to add heat to warmth, artificial strength to natural vigour, and it is dangerous sometimes to add fuel to fire. I am glad you think as I think on this point, for it is well that man and wife should be agreed in matters of importance. But to return to Vinland: I have been thinking much about it since I came here, though saying little — for it becomes a man to be silent and circumspect in regard to unformed plans. My mind is to go thither next spring, but only on one condition."

"And what may that be?" asked Gudrid, looking up with a little surprise, and some interest.

"That you shall go with me, Gudrid; for which end it will be needful that you and I should wed this winter."

Gudrid could not help blushing a little and looking down, for Karlsefin, despite his suavity, had a way with him, when thoroughly in earnest, that was very impressive. She did not hesitate, however, but answered with straightforward candour, "I will not say nay to that if my brother Leif is willing."

"It is settled then," replied Karlsefin decisively, "for Leif has already told me that he is willing if you are, and so —"

At this interesting point in the conversation they were interrupted by a loud merry laugh not very far from them, and next moment little Olaf, starting out from behind a bush, ran shouting into Gudrid's extended arms. "Oh, what do you think?" he exclaimed, "aunt Freydissa has come over from Heriulfness, and is in *such* a rage because Biarne has told her that Thorward has been making love to his cousin Astrid, and —"

"Hush, boy," said Gudrid, covering his mouth with her hand, "you should not talk so of your aunt. Besides, you know that it is an evil thing to get the name of a tale-bearer."

"I did not think it was tale-bearing," replied the lad, somewhat abashed, "for it is no secret. Leif was there, and Astrid herself, and all the house-carls in the hall must have heard her, for she spoke very loud. And oh! you should have seen her give Thorward the cold shoulder when he came in!"

"Well, well, Olaf, hold your noisy tongue," said Gudrid, laughing, "and come, tell me how would you like to go to Vinland?"

"Like to go to Vinland!" echoed the boy, turning an ardent gaze full on Karlsefin, "are you going there, sir? Will you take *me*?"

Karlsefin laughed, and said, "You are too quick in jumping to conclusions, child. Perhaps I may go there; but you have not yet answered Gudrid's question — would you like to go?"

"I would like it well," replied Olaf, with a bright look of hopeful expectation that said far more than words could have expressed.

Just then Thorward was seen approaching along the beach. His brows were knit, his lips pursed, and his eyes fixed on the ground. He was so engrossed with his thoughts that he did not perceive his friends.

"Here he comes," said Karlsefin — "in the blues evidently, for he does not see us."

"We had better leave you to his company," said Gudrid, laughing; "a man i' the blues is no pleasure to a woman. Come, Olaf, you and I shall to the dairy and see how the cattle fare."

Olaf's capacity for imbibing milk and cream being unlimited, he gladly accepted this invitation, and followed his aunt, while Karlsefin advanced to meet his friend.

"How now, Thorward, methinks an evil spirit doth possess thee!"

"An evil spirit!" echoed Thorward, with a wrathful look; "nay, a legion of evil spirits possess me! A plague on that fellow Biarne: he has poisoned the ears of Freydissa with lies about that girl Astrid, to whom I have never whispered a sweet word since we landed."

"I trust you have not whispered sour words to her," said Karlsefin, smiling.

"And Freydissa, forsooth, gives me the cold shoulder," continued the exasperated Norseman, not noticing the interruption, "as if I were proved guilty by the mere assertion."

"It is my advice to you, Thorward, that you return the compliment, and give the cold shoulder to Freydissa. The woman has a shrewish temper; she is a very vixen, and will lead you the life of a dog if you marry her."

"I had rather," said Thorward between his teeth, and stamping, "live a dog's life with Freydissa than live the life of a king without her!"

Karlsefin laughed at this, and Thorward, taking offence, said fierily, and with some scorn — "Thinkest thou that because thy Gudrid is so smooth-tongued she is an angel?"

"That is what I am inclined to think," answered Karlsefin, with a smile that still further exasperated his friend.

"Perchance you may find yourself mistaken," said Thorward. "Since you are so free with your warnings, let me remind you that although the course of your courtship runs smooth, there is an old proverb — descended from Odin himself, I believe — which assures us that *true* love never did so run."

"Then I recall my words, Thorward, and congratulate you on your true love — for assuredly your courtship runs in an uncommonly rugged course."

At this Thorward turned on his heel and walked away in a towering passion.

It so happened that, on drawing near to Brattalid, he met Biarne coming in the opposite direction. Nothing could have pleased him better — for in the state of his mind at the time he would have turned savagely on himself, had that been possible, in order to relieve his feelings.

"So!" he cried, confronting Biarne, "well met! Tell me, Biarne, didst thou poison the ears of Freydissa by telling her that I had been courting thy cousin Astrid?"

Biarne, who was not aware of the consequences of what he had said in jest, felt inclined to laugh, but he checked himself and flushed somewhat, not being accustomed to be addressed in such haughty tones. Instead of explaining the matter, as he might otherwise have done, he merely said, "I did."

"Liar!" exclaimed Thorward fiercely, for he was a very resolute man when roused; "go, tell her that the assertion was a falsehood. Go *now*, and come back to tell me thou hast done it, else will I chop thy carcase into mince-meat. Go; I will await thee here."

He laid his hand upon his sword, but Biarne said quietly, "I go, sir;" and, turning round, hastened up to the hamlet.

Thorward could scarcely believe his eyes, for Biarne was fully as stout as himself, and somewhat taller, besides having the look of a courageous man. He had issued his imperative mandate more as a defiance and challenge than anything else, so that he gazed after the retreating Biarne with mingled feelings of surprise, contempt, and pity; but surprise predominated. He had not long to wait, however, for in about ten minutes Biarne returned.

"Well, have you told her?"

"I have," replied Biarne.

"Hah!" exclaimed Thorward, very much perplexed, and not knowing what to say next.

"But, Thorward," said Biarne, after a momentary pause, "methinks that you and I must fight now."

"With all my heart," answered Thorward, much relieved, and again grasping his sword.

"Nay, not with such weapons," said Biarne, stepping up to him, "but with the weapons of friendship."

With that he bestowed such a hearty buffet on Thorward's left ear that it turned the irascible man head over heels, and laid him at full length on the sand.

Thorward rose slowly, being somewhat stunned, with a confused impression that there was something wrong with his head. Before he had quite recovered, Biarne burst into a laugh and seized him by the hand.

"Freydissa bids me tell you —" he said, and paused.

The pause was intentional. He saw that Thorward was on the point of snatching away his hand and returning the blow or drawing his sword; but he restrained himself in order to hear Freydissa's message.

"She bids me tell you," repeated Biarne, "that you are a goose."

This was not calculated to soothe an angry man, but Thorward reflected that the epithet was figurative, and bore a peculiar signification when uttered by a woman; he therefore continued his self-restraint and waited for more.

"She also said," added Biarne, "that she never for a moment believed my statement (which, by the way, was only made in jest), and that she thinks you deserve a good buffet on the ear for taking the thing up so hotly. Agreeing with her entirely in this, I have fulfilled her wish and given you your deserts. Moreover, she expects you to accompany her to Heriulfness tonight. So now," said Biarne, releasing Thorward's hand and touching his sword-hilt, "if you are still inclined — ."

"Well, well," said Thorward, whose visage, while his friend was speaking, had undergone a series of contortions indicative of a wild conflict of feelings in his breast, "well, well, I am a goose, and deserved the buffet. After all, I did call you a liar, so we are quits, Biarne — tit for tat. Come, let us shake hands and go up to Leif's cottage. You said Freydissa was there, I think."

During that winter Karlsefin married Gudrid and Thorward Freydissa, and, in the following spring, they embarked in Karlsefin's ship — with a large party of men, women, children, and cattle — and set sail for Vinland.

CHAPTER V.

Freydissa Shows Her Temper and a Whale Checks it —
Poetical and Other Touches.

The expedition which now set out for Vinland was on a much larger scale than any of the expeditions which had preceded it. Biarne and Leif had acted the part of discoverers only — not colonisers — and although previous parties had passed several winters in Vinland, they had not intended to take up a permanent abode there — as was plain from the fact that they brought neither women nor flocks nor herds with them. Karlsefin, on the contrary, went forth fully equipped for colonisation.

His ship, as we have said, was a large one, with a decked poop and fore-castle, fitted to brave the most tempestuous weather — at least as well fitted to do so as were the ships of Columbus — and capable of accommodating more than a hundred people. He took sixty men with him and five women, besides his own wife and Thorward's. Thorward himself, and Biarne, accompanied the expedi-tion, and also Olaf — to his inexpressible joy, but Leif preferred to remain at home, and promised to take good care of Thorward's ship, which was left behind. Astrid was one of the five women who went with this expedition; the other four were Gunhild, Thora, Sigrid, and Bertha. Gunhild and Sigrid were wives to two of Biarne's men. Thora was handmaiden to Gudrid; Bertha hand-maid to Freydissa. Of all the women Bertha was the sweetest and most beautiful, and she was also very modest and good-tempered, which was a fortunate circum-stance, because her mistress Freydissa had temper enough, as Biarne used to remark, for a dozen women. Biarne was fond of teasing Freydissa; but she liked Biarne, and sometimes took his pleasantries well — sometimes ill.

It was intended that, when the colony was fairly established, the ship should be sent back to Greenland to fetch more of the men's wives and children.

A number of cattle, horses, and sheep were also carried on this occasion to Vinland. These were stowed in the waist or middle of the vessel, between the benches where the rowers sat when at work. The rowers did not labour much at sea, as the vessel was at most times able to advance under sail. During calms, however, and when going into creeks, or on landing — also in doubling capes when the wind was not suitable — the oars were of the greatest value. Karlsefin and the principal people slept under the high poop. A number of the men slept under the forecastle, and the rest lay in the waist near the cattle — sheltered from the weather by tents or awnings which were called tilts.

It may perhaps surprise some readers to learn that men could venture in such vessels to cross the northern seas from Norway to Iceland, and thence to Greenland; but it is not so surprising when we consider the small size of the ves-sels in which Columbus afterwards crossed the Atlantic in safety, and when we reflect that those Norsemen had been long accustomed, in such vessels, to tra-verse the ocean around the coasts of Europe in all directions — round the shores of Britain, up the Baltic, away to the Faroe Islands, and up the Mediterranean even as far as the Black Sea. In short, the Norsemen of old were magnificent seamen, and there can be no question that much of the ultimate success of Britain on the sea is due, not only to our insular position, but also to the insufficiently appreciated fact that the blood of the hardy and adventurous vikings of Norway still flows in our veins.

It was a splendid spring morning when Karlsefin hoisted his white-and-blue sail, and dropped down Ericsfiord with a favouring breeze, while Leif and his people stood on the stone jetty at Brattalid, and waved hats and shawls to their departing friends.

For Olaf, Thora, and Bertha it was a first voyage, and as the vessel gradually left the land behind, the latter stood at the stern gazing wistfully towards the shore, while tears flowed from her pretty blue eyes and chased each other over her fair round face — for Bertha left an old father behind her in Greenland.

"Don't cry, Bertha," said Olaf, putting his fat little hand softly into that of the young girl.

"Oh! I shall perhaps *never* see him again," cried Bertha, with another burst of tears.

"Yes, you will," said Olaf, cheerily. "You know that when we get comfortably settled in Vinland we shall send the ship back for your father, and mine too, and for everybody in Ericsfiord and Heriulfness. Why, we're going to forsake Greenland altogether and never go back to it any more. Oh! I am *so* glad."

"I wish, I *wish* I had never come," said Bertha, with a renewed flow of tears, for Olaf's consolations were thrown away on her.

It chanced that Freydissa came at that moment upon the poop, where Karlsefin stood at the helm, and Gudrid with some others were still gazing at the distant shore.

Freydissa was one of those women who appear to have been born women by mistake — who are always chafing at their unfortunate fate, and endeavouring to emulate — even to overwhelm — men; in which latter effort they are too frequently successful. She was a tall elegant woman of about thirty years of age, with a decidedly handsome face, though somewhat sharp of feature. She possessed a powerful will, a shrill voice and a vigorous frame, and was afflicted with a short, violent temper. She was decidedly a masculine woman. We know not which is the more disagreeable of the two — a masculine woman or an effeminate man.

But perhaps the most prominent feature in her character was her volubility when enraged — the copiousness of her vocabulary and the tremendous force with which she shot forth her ideas and abuse in short abrupt sentences.

Now, if there was one thing more than another that roused the ire of Freydissa, it was the exhibition of feminine weakness in the shape of tears. She appeared to think that the credit of her sex in reference to firmness and self-command was compromised by such weakness. She herself never wept by any chance, and she was always enraged when she saw any other woman relieve her feelings in that way. When, therefore, she came on deck and found her own handmaid with her pretty little face swelled, or, as she expressed it, "begrutten," and heard her express a wish that she had never left home, she lost command of herself – a loss that she always found it easy to come by – and, seizing Bertha by the shoulder, ordered her down into the cabin instantly.

Bertha sobbingly obeyed, and Freydissa followed. "Don't be hard on her, poor soul," murmured Thorward.

Foolish fellow! How difficult it is for man – ancient or modern – to learn when to hold his tongue! That suggestion would have fixed Freydissa's determination if it had not been fixed before, and poor Bertha would certainly have received "a hearing," or a "blowing-up," or a "setting down," such as she had not enjoyed since the date of Freydissa's marriage, had it not been for the fortunate circumstance that a whale took it into its great thick head to come up, just then, and spout magnificently quite close to the vessel.

The sight was received with a shout by the men, a shriller shout by the women, and a screech of surprise and delight by little Olaf, who would certainly have gone over the side in his eagerness, had not Biarne caught him by the skirts of his tunic.

This incident happily diverted the course of Freydissa's thoughts. Curiosity overcame indignation, and Bertha was reprieved for the time being. Both mistress and maid hastened to the side of the ship; the anger of the one evaporated and the tears of the other dried up when they saw the whale rise not more than a hundred yards from the ship. It continued to do this for a considerable time, sometimes appearing on one side, sometimes on the other; now at the stern, anon at the bow. In short it seemed as if the whale had taken the ship for a companion, and were anxious to make its acquaintance. At last it went down and remained under water so long that the voyagers began to think it had left them, when Olaf suddenly gave a shriek of delight and surprise: – "Oh! Oh! OH!" he exclaimed, looking and pointing straight down into the water, "here is the whale – right under the ship!"

And sure enough there it was, swimming slowly under the vessel, not two fathoms below the keel – its immense bulk being impressively visible, owing to the position of the observers, and its round eyes staring as if in astonishment at the strange creature above.[4] It expressed this astonishment, or whatever feeling it might be, by coming up suddenly to the surface, thrusting its big blunt head, like the bow of a boat, out of the sea, and spouting forth a column of water and spray with a deep snort or snore – to the great admiration of the whole ship's crew, for, although most of the men were familiar enough with whales, alive and dead, they had never, in all probability, seen one in such circumstances before.

Four or five times did the whale dive under the vessel in this fashion, and then it sheered off with a contemptuous flourish of its tail, as if disgusted with

---

4   The author has seen a whale in precisely similar circumstances in a Norwegian fiord.

the stolid unsociable character of the ship, which seen from a submarine point of view must have looked uncommonly like a whale, and quite as big!

This episode, occurring so early in the voyage, and trifling though it was, tended to create in the minds of all — especially of the women and the younger people — a feeling of interest in the ocean, and an expectation of coming adventure, which, though not well defined, was slightly exciting and agreeable. Bertha, in particular, was very grateful to that whale, for it had not only diverted her thoughts a little from home-leaving and given her something new to think and talk about, but it had saved her from Freydissa and a severe scold.

The first night at sea was fine, with bright moonlight, and a soft wind on the quarter that carried them pleasantly over the rippling sea, and everything was so tranquil and captivating that no one felt inclined to go to rest. Karlsefin sat beside the helm, guiding the ship and telling sagas to the group of friends who stood, sat, or reclined on the deck and against the bulwarks of the high poop. He repeated long pieces of poetry, descriptive of the battles and adventures of their viking forefathers, and also gave them occasional pieces of his own composing, in reference to surrounding circumstances and the enterprise in which they were then embarked — for Karlsefin was himself a skald or poet, although he pretended not to great attainments in that way.

From where they sat the party on the poop could see that the men on the high forecastle were similarly engaged, for they had gathered together in a group, and their heads were laid together as if listening intently to one of their number who sat in the centre of the circle. Below, in the waist of the ship, some humorous character appeared to be holding his mates enchained, for long periods of comparative silence — in which could be heard the monotonous tones of a single voice mingled with occasional soft lowing from the cattle — were suddenly broken by bursts of uproarious laughter, which, however, quickly subsided again, leaving prominent the occasional lowing and the prolonged monotone. Everything in and around the ship, that night, breathed of harmony and peace — though there was little knowledge among them of Him who is the Prince of Peace. We say "little" knowledge, because Christianity had only just begun to dawn among the Norsemen at that time, and there were some on board of that discovery-ship who were tinged with the first rays of that sweet light which, in the person of the Son of God, was sent to lighten the world and to shine more and more unto the perfect day.

"Now," said Karlsefin, at the conclusion of one of his stories, "that is the saga of Halfdan the Black — at least it is part of his saga; but, friends, it seems to me that we must begin a saga of our own, for it is evident that if we are successful in this venture we shall have something to relate when we return to Greenland, and we must all learn to tell our saga in the same words, for that is the only way in which *truth* can be handed down to future generations, seeing that when men are careless in learning the truth they are apt to distort it so that honest men are led into telling lies unwittingly. They say that the nations of the south have invented a process whereby with a sharp-pointed tool they fashion marks on skins to represent words, so that once put down in this way a saga never changes.

Would that we Norsemen understood that process!" said Karlsefin meditatively.

"It seems to me," said Biarne, who reclined on the deck, leaning against the weather-bulwarks and running his fingers playfully through Olaf's fair curls, "It seems to me that it were better to bestow the craft of the skald on the record of our voyage, for then the measure and the rhyme would chain men to the words, and so to the truth — that is, supposing they get truth to start with! Come, Karlsefin, begin our voyage for us."

All present seemed to agree to that proposal, and urged Karlsefin to begin at once.

The skipper — for such indeed was his position in the ship — though a modest man, was by no means bashful, therefore, after looking round upon the moonlit sea for a few minutes, he began as follows:

"When western waves were all unknown,
And western fields were all unsown,
When Iceland was the outmost bound
That roving viking-keels had found —
Gunbiorn then — Ulf Kraka's son —
Still farther west was forced to run
By furious gales, and there saw land
Stretching abroad on either hand.
Eric of Iceland, called the Red,
Heard of the news and straightway said —
'This western land I'll go and see;
Three summers hence look out for me.'
He went; he landed; stayed awhile,
And wintered first on 'Eric's Isle;'
Then searched the coast both far and wide,
Then back to Iceland o'er the tide.
'A wondrous land is this,' said he,
And called it Greenland of the sea.
Twenty and five great ships sailed west
To claim this gem on Ocean's breast.
With man and woman, horn and hoof,
And bigging for the homestead roof.
Some turnèd back — in heart but mice —
Some sank amid the Northern ice.
Half reached the land, in much distress,
At Ericsfiord and Heriulfness.
Next, Biarne — Heriulf's doughty son —
Sought to trace out the aged one.[5]
From Norway sailed, but missed his mark;

5   His father.

Passed snow-topped Greenland in the dark;
And came then to a new-found land –
But did not touch the tempting strand;
For winter winds oppressed him sore
And kept him from his father's shore.
Then Leif, the son of Eric, rose
And straightway off to Biarne goes,
Buys up his ship, takes all his men,
Fares forth to seek that land again.
Leif found the land; discovered more,
And spent a winter on the shore;
Cut trees and grain to load the ship,
And pay them for the lengthened trip.
Named 'Hella-land' and 'Markland' too,
And saw an island sweet with dew!
And grapes in great abundance found,
So named it Vinland all around.
But after that forsook the shore,
And north again for Greenland bore.
And now – we cross the moonlit seas
To search this land of grapes and trees
Biarne, Thorward, Karlsefin –
Go forth this better land to win,
With men and cattle not a few,
And household gear and weapons too;
And, best of all, with women dear,
To comfort, counsel, check, and cheer.
Thus far we've made a prosp'rous way,
God speed us onward every day!"

They all agreed that this was a true account of the discovery of Vinland and of their own expedition as far as it had gone, though Gudrid said it was short, and Freydissa was of opinion that there was very little in it.

"But hold!" exclaimed Biarne, suddenly raising himself on his elbows; "Karlsefin, you are but a sorry skald after all."

"How so?" asked the skipper.

"Why, because you have made no mention of the chief part of our voyage."

"And pray what may that be?"

"Stay, I too am a skald; I will tell you."

Biarne, whose poetical powers were not of the highest type, here stretched forth his hand and said:

"When Biarne, Thorward, Karlsefin,
This famous voyage did begin,
They stood upon the deck one night,
And there beheld a moving sight.
It made the very men grow pale,

Their shudder almost rent the sail!
For lo! they saw a mighty whale!
It drew a shriek from Olaf brave,
Then plunged beneath the briny wave,
And, while the women loudly shouted,
Up came its blundering nose and spouted.
Then underneath our keel it went,
And glared with savage fury pent,
And round about the ship it swum,
Striking each man and woman dumb.
Stay – one there was who found a tongue
And still retained her strength of lung.
Freydissa, beauteous matron bold,
Resolved to give that whale a scold!
But little cared that monster fish
To gratify Freydissa's wish;
He shook his tail, that naughty whale,
And flourished it like any flail,
And, ho! for Vinland he made sail!"

"Now, friends, was not that a great omission on the part of Karlsefin?"

"If the whale had brought his flail down on your pate it would have served you right, Biarne," said Freydissa, flushing, yet smiling in spite of herself.

"I think it is capital," cried Olaf, clapping his hands — "quite as good as the other poem."

Some agreed with Olaf, and some thought that it was not quite in keeping with Karlsefin's composition, but, after much debate, it was finally ruled that it should be added thereto as part and parcel of the great Vinland poem. Hence it appears in this chronicle, and forms an interesting instance of the way in which men, for the sake of humorous effect, mingle little pieces of fiction with veritable history.

By the time this important matter was settled it was getting so late that even the most enthusiastic admirer among them of moonlight on a calm sea became irresistibly desirous of going to sleep. They therefore broke up for the night; the women retired to their cabin, and none were left on deck except the steersman and the watch. Long before this the saga-tellers on the forecastle had retired; the monotone and the soft lowing of the cattle had ceased; man and beast had sought and found repose, and nothing was heard save the ripple of the water on the ship's sides as she glided slowly but steadily over the sleeping sea.

CHAPTER VI.

Changes in Wind and Weather Produce Changes in Temper and Feeling — Land Discovered, and Freydissa Becomes Inquisitive.

There are few things that impress one more at sea than the rapidity of the transitions which frequently take place in the aspect and the condition of vessel, sea, and sky. At one time all may be profoundly tranquil on board; then, perhaps, the necessity for going "about ship" arises, and all is bustle; ropes rattle, blocks clatter and chirp, yards creak, and seamen's feet stamp on the deck, while their voices aid their hands in the hauling of ropes; and soon all is quiet as before. Or, perhaps, the transition is effected by a squall, and it becomes more thorough and lasting. One moment everything in nature is hushed under the influence of what is appropriately enough termed a "dead calm." In a few seconds a cloudbank appears on the horizon and one or two cats-paws are seen shooting over the water. A few minutes more and the sky is clouded, the glassy sea is ruffled, the pleasant light sinks into a dull leaden grey, the wind whistles over the ocean, and we are — as far as feeling is concerned — transported into another, but by no means a better, world.

Thus it was with our adventurers. The beautiful night merged into a "dirty" morning, the calm into a breeze so stiff as to be almost a gale, and when Olaf came out of the cabin, holding tight to the weather-bulwarks to prevent himself from being thrown into the lee-scuppers, his inexperienced heart sank within him at the dreary prospect of the grey sky and the black heaving sea.

But young Olaf came of a hardy seafaring race. He kept his feelings to himself, and staggered toward Karlsefin, who still stood at his post. Olaf thought he had been there all night, but the truth was that he had been relieved by Biarne, had taken a short nap, and returned to the helm.

Karlsefin was now clad in a rough-weather suit. He wore a pair of untanned sealskin boots and a cap of the same material, that bore a strong resemblance in shape and colour to the sou'-westers of the present day, and his rough heavy coat, closed up to the chin, was in texture and form not unlike to the pilot-cloth jackets of modern seamen — only it had tags and loops instead of buttons and buttonholes. With his legs wide apart, he stood at the tiller, round which there was a single turn of a rope from the weather-bulwarks to steady it and himself. The boy was clad in miniature costume of much the same cut and kind, and proud was he to stagger about the deck with his little legs ridiculously wide apart, in imitation of Thorward and Biarne, both of whom were there, and had, he observed, a tendency to straddle.

"Come hither, Olaf, and learn a little seamanship," said Karlsefin, with a good-humoured smile.

Olaf said he would be glad to do that, and made a run towards the tiller, but a heavy plunge of the ship caused him to sheer off in quite a different direction, and another lurch would have sent him head-foremost against the lee-bulwarks had not Biarne, with a laugh, caught him by the nape of the neck and set him against Karlsefin's left leg, to which he clung with remarkable tenacity.

"Ay, hold on tight to that, boy," said the leg's owner, "and you'll be safe. A few days will put you on your sea-legs, lad, and then you won't want to hold on."

"Always hold your head up, Olaf, when you move about aboard ship in rough weather," said Biarne, pausing a minute in his perambulation of the deck to give the advice, "and look overboard, or up, or away at the horizon – anywhere except at your feet. You can't see how the ship's going to roll, you know, if you keep looking down at the deck."

Olaf acted on this advice at once, and then began to question Karlsefin in regard to many nautical matters which it is not necessary to set down here, while Biarne and Thorward leaned on the bulwarks and looked somewhat anxiously to windward.

Already two reefs of the huge sail had been taken in, and Biarne now suggested that it would be wise to take in another.

"Let it be done," said Karlsefin.

Thorward ordered the men to reef; and the head of the ship was brought up to the wind so as to empty the sail while this was being done.

Before it was quite accomplished some of the women had assembled on the poop.

"This is not pleasant weather," observed Gudrid, as she stood holding on to her husband.

"We must not expect to have it all plain sailing in these seas," replied Karlsefin; "but the dark days will make the bright ones seem all the brighter."

Gudrid smiled languidly at this, but made no reply.

Freydissa, who scorned to receive help from man, had vigorously laid hold of the bulwarks and gradually worked her way aft. She appeared to be very much out of sorts – as indeed all the women were. There was a greenish colour about the parts of their cheeks that ought to have been rosy, and a whitey blue or frosted appearance at the points of their noses, which damaged the beauty of the prettiest among them. Freydissa became positively plain – and she knew it, which did not improve her temper. Astrid, though fair and exceedingly pretty by nature, had become alarmingly white; and Thora, who was dark, had become painfully yellow. Poor Bertha, too, had a washed-out appearance, though nothing in the way of lost colour or otherwise could in the least detract from the innocent sweetness of her countenance. She did not absolutely weep, but, being cold, sick, and in a state of utter wretchedness, she had fallen into a condition of chronic whimpering, which exceedingly exasperated Freydissa. Bertha was one of those girls who are regarded by *some* of their own sex with a species of mild contempt, but who are nevertheless looked upon with much tenderness by men, which perhaps makes up to them for this to some extent. Gudrid was the least affected among them all by that dire malady, which appears to have been as virulent in the tenth as it is in the nineteenth century, and must have come in with the Flood, if not before it.

"Why don't you go below," said Freydissa testily, "instead of shivering up here?"

"I get so sick below," answered Bertha, endeavouring to brighten up, "that I thought it better to try what fresh air would do for me."

"H'm! it doesn't appear to do much for you," retorted Freydissa.

As she spoke a little spray broke over the side of the ship and fell on the deck near them. Karlsefin had great difficulty in preventing this, for a short cross-sea was running, and it was only by dint of extremely good and careful steering that he kept the poop-deck dry. In a few minutes a little more spray flew inboard, and some of it striking Bertha on the head ran down her shoulders. Karlsefin was much grieved at this, but Freydissa laughed heartily.

Instead of making Bertha worse, however, the shock had the effect of doing her a little good, and she laughed in a half pitiful way as she ran down below to dry herself.

"It serves you right," cried Freydissa as she passed; "I wish you had got more of it."

Now Karlsefin was a man whose temper was not easily affected, and he seldom or never took offence at anything done or said to himself; but the unkindness of Freydissa's speech to poor Bertha nettled him greatly.

"Get behind me, Gudrid," he said quickly.

Gudrid obeyed, wondering at the stern order, and Karlsefin gave a push to the tiller with his leg. Next moment a heavy sea struck the side of the ship, burst over the bulwarks, completely overwhelmed Freydissa, and swept the deck fore and aft — wetting every one more or less except Gudrid, who had been almost completely sheltered behind her husband. A sail which had been spread over the waist of the ship prevented much damage being done to the men, and of course all the water that fell on the forecastle and poop ran out at the scupper-holes.

This unexpected shower-bath at once cleared the poop of the women. Fortunately Thora and Astrid had been standing to leeward of Biarne and Thorward, and had received comparatively little of the shower, but Freydissa went below with streaming hair and garments — as Biarne remarked — like an elderly mermaid!

"You must have been asleep when that happened," said Thorward to Karlsefin in surprise.

"He must have been sleeping, then, with his eyes open," said Biarne, with an amused look.

Karlsefin gazed sternly towards the ship's head, and appeared to be attending with great care to the helm, but there was a slight twinkle in his eye as he said — "Well, it *was* my intention to wash the decks a little, but more spray came inboard than I counted on. 'Tis as dangerous to play with water, sometimes, as with fire."

"There is truth in that," said Biarne, laughing; "and I fear that this time water will be found to have kindled fire, for when Freydissa went below she looked like the smoking mountain of Iceland — as if there was something hot inside and about to boil up."

Karlsefin smiled, but made no reply, for the gale was increasing every moment, and the management of the ship soon required the earnest attention of all the seamen on board.

Fortunately it was a short-lived gale. When it had passed away and the sea had returned to something like its former quiescent state, and the sun had burst through and dissipated the grey clouds, our female voyagers returned to the deck and to their wonted condition of health.

Soon after that they came in sight of land.

"Now, Biarne," said Karlsefin, after the lookout on the forecastle had shouted "Land ho!" "come, give me your opinion of this new land that we have made. Do you mind the helm, Thorward, while we go to the ship's head."

The two went forward, and on the forecastle they found Olaf, flushed with excitement, and looking as if something had annoyed him.

"Ho, Olaf! you're not sorry to see land, are you?" said Biarne.

"Sorry! no, not I; but I'm sorry to be cheated of my due."

"How so, boy?"

"Why, *I* discovered the land first, and that fellow there," pointing to the man on lookout, "shouted before me."

"But why did you not shout before *him*?" asked Karlsefin, as he and Biarne surveyed the distant land with keen interest.

"Just because he took me unawares," replied the boy indignantly. "When I saw it I did not wish to be hasty. It might have turned out to be a cloud, or a fog-bank, and I might have given a false alarm; so I pointed it out to him, and asked what he thought; but instead of answering me he gaped with his ugly mouth and shouted 'Land ho!' I could have kicked him."

"Nay, Olaf; that is not well said," observed Karlsefin, very gravely; "if you *could* have kicked him you *would* have kicked him. Why did you not do it?"

"Because he is too big for me," answered the boy promptly.

"So, then, thy courage is only sufficient to make thee kick those who are small enough," returned Karlsefin, with a frown. "Perhaps if you were as big as he you would be afraid to kick him."

"That would not I," retorted Olaf.

"It is easy for you to say that, boy, when you know that he *would* not strike you now, and that there is small chance of your meeting again after you have grown up to prove the truth of what you say. It is mere boasting, Olaf; and, mark me, you will never be a brave man if you begin by being a boastful boy. A truly brave and modest man — for modesty and bravery are wont to consort together — never says he will strike until he sees it to be right to do so. Sometimes he does not even go the length of speaking at all, but, in any case, having made up his mind to strike, he strikes at once, without more ado, let the consequences be what they will. But in my opinion it is best not to strike at all. Do you know, Olaf, my boy, some of the bravest men I ever knew have never struck a blow since they came to manhood, excepting, of course, when compelled to do so in battle; and *then* they struck such blows as made shields and helmets fly, and strewed the plain with their foes."

"Did these men never boast when they were boys?" asked Olaf, with a troubled air.

Karlsefin relaxed into a smile as he said, "Only when they were very little boys, and very foolish; but they soon came to see how contemptible it is to threaten and not perform; so they gave up threatening, and when performance came to be necessary they found that threats were needless. Now, Olaf, I want you to be a bold, brave man, and I must lull you through the foolish boasting period as quickly as possible, therefore I tell you these things. Think on them, my boy."

Olaf was evidently much relieved by the concluding remarks. While Karlsefin was speaking he had felt ashamed of himself; because he was filled with admiration of the magnificent skipper, and wanted to stand well in his opinion. It was therefore no small comfort to find that his boasting had been set down to his foolishness, and that there was good reason to hope he might ultimately grow out of it.

But Olaf had much more of the true metal in him than he himself was aware of. Without saying a word about it, he resolved not to wait for the result of this slow process of growth, but to jump, vault, or fly out of the boastful period of life, by hook or by crook, and that without delay. And he succeeded! Not all at once, of course. He had many a slip; but he persevered, and finally got out of it much sooner than would have been the case if he had not taken any trouble to think about the matter, or to *try*.

Meanwhile, however, he looked somewhat crestfallen. This being observed by the lookout, that worthy was prompted to say — "I'm sure, Olaf, you are welcome to kick me if that will comfort you, but there is no occasion to do so, because I claim not the honour of first *seeing* the land — and if I had known the state of your mind I would willingly have let you give the hail."

"You may have been first to discover it at this time, Olaf," said Biarne, turning round after he had made up his mind about it, "and no doubt you were, since the lookout admits it; nevertheless this is the land that I discovered twenty years ago. But we shall make it out more certainly in an hour or two if this breeze holds."

The breeze did hold, and soon they were close under the land.

"Now am I quite certain of it," said Biarne, as he stood on the poop, surrounded by all his friends, who gazed eagerly at the shore, to which they had approached so close that the rocks and bushes were distinctly visible; "that is the very same land which I saw before."

"What, Vinland?" asked Freydissa.

"Nay, not Vinland. Are you so eager to get at the grapes that ye think the first land we meet is Vinland?"

"A truce to your jesting, Biarne; what land is it?"

"It is the land I saw *last* when leaving this coast in search of Greenland, so that it seems not unnatural to find it *first* on coming back to it. Leif, on his voyage, went on shore here. He named it Helloland, which, methinks, was a fitting name, for it is, as you see, a naked land of rocks."

"Now, then," said Karlsefin, "lower the sail, heave out the anchor, and let two men cast loose the little boat. Some of us will land and see what we shall see; for it must not be said of us, Biarne, as it was unfairly said of you, that we took no interest in these new regions."

The little boat was got ready. The Scottish brothers, Hake and Heika, were appointed to row. Karlsefin, Biarne, Thorward, Gudrid, Freydissa, and Olaf embarked and proceeded to the shore.

This land, on which the party soon stood, was not of an inviting aspect. It was sterile, naked, and very rocky, as Biarne had described it, and not a blade of grass was to be seen. There was a range of high snow-capped mountains in the interior, and all the way from the coast up to these mountains the land was covered with snow. In truth, a more forbidding spot could not easily have been found, even in Greenland.

"It seems to me," said Freydissa, "that your new land is but a sorry place — worse than that we have left. I wonder at your landing here. It is plain that men see with flushed eyes when they look upon their own discoveries. Cold comfort is all we shall get in this place. I counsel that we return on board immediately."

"You are too hasty, sister," said Gudrid.

"Oh! of course, always too hasty," retorted Freydissa sharply.

"And somewhat too bitter," growled Thorward, with a frown.

Thorward was not an ill-natured man, but his wife's sharp temper tried him a good deal.

"Your interrupting me before you heard all I had to say *proves* you to be too hasty, sister," said Gudrid, with a playful laugh. "I was about to add that it seems we have come here rather early in the spring. Who knows but the land may wear a prettier dress when the mantle of winter is gone? Even Greenland looks green and bright in summer."

"Not in those places where the snow lies *all* the summer," objected Olaf.

"That's right, Olaf," said Biarne; "stick up for your sweet aunt. She often takes a stick up for you, lad, and deserves your gratitude. But come, let's scatter and survey the land, for, be it good or bad, we must know what it is, and carry with us some report such as Karlsefin may weave into his rhymes."

"This land would be more suitable for your rhymes, Biarne, than for mine," said Karlsefin, as they started off together, "because it is most dismal."

After that the whole party scattered. The three leaders ascended the nearest heights in different directions, and Gudrid with Olaf went searching among the rocks and pools to ascertain what sort of creatures were to be found there, while Freydissa sat down and sulked upon a rock. She soon grew tired of sulking, however, and, looking about her, observed the brothers, who had been left in charge of the boat, standing as if engaged in earnest conversation.

She had not before this paid much attention to these brothers, and was somewhat struck with their appearance, for, as we have said before, they were good specimens of men. Hake, the younger of the two, had close-curling auburn hair, and bright blue eyes. His features were not exactly handsome, but the expression of his countenance was so winning that people were irresistibly attracted by it. The elder brother, Heika, was very like him, but not so attractive in his appearance. Both were fully six feet high, and though thin, as has been said, their limbs were beautifully moulded, and they possessed much greater strength than most people gave them credit for. In aspect, thought, and conversation, they were naturally grave, and very earnest; nevertheless, they could be easily roused to mirth.

Going up to them, Freydissa said — "Ye seem to have earnest talk together."

"We have," answered Heika. "Our talk is about home."

"I am told that your home is in the Scottish land," said Freydissa.

"It is," answered Hake, with a kindling eye.

"How come you to be so far from home?" asked Freydissa.

"We were taken prisoners two years ago by vikings from Norway, when visiting our father in a village near the Forth fiord."

"How did that happen? Come, tell me the story; but, first, who is your father?"

"He is an earl of Scotland," said Heika.

"Ha! and I suppose ye think a Scottish earl is better than a Norse king?"

Heika smiled as he replied, "I have never thought of making a comparison between them."

"Well — how were you taken?"

"We were, as I have said, on a visit to our father, who dwelt sometimes in a small village on the shores of the Forth, for the sake of bathing in the sea — for he is sickly. One night, while we slept, a Norse long-ship came to land. Those who should have been watching slumbered. The Norsemen surrounded my father's house without awaking anyone, and, entering by a window which had not been securely fastened, overpowered Hake and me before we knew where we were. We struggled hard, but what could two unarmed men do among fifty? The noise we made, however, roused the village and prevented the vikings from discovering our father's room, which was on the upper floor. They had to fight their way back to the ship, and lost many men on the road, but they succeeded in carrying us two on board, bound with cords. They took us over the sea to Norway. There we became slaves to King Olaf Tryggvisson, by whom, as you know, we were sent to Leif Ericsson."

"No doubt ye think," said Freydissa, "that if you had not been caught sleeping ye would have given the Norsemen some trouble to secure you."

They both laughed at this.

"We have had some thoughts of that kind," said Hake brightly, "but truly we did give them some trouble even as it was."

"I knew it," cried the dame rather sharply; "the conceit of you men goes beyond all bounds! Ye always boast of what valiant deeds you *would* have done *if* something or other had been in your favour."

"We made no boast," replied Heika gravely.

"If you did not speak it, ye thought it, I doubt not. But, tell me, is your land as good a land as Norway?"

"We love it better," replied Heika.

"But *is* it better?" asked Freydissa.

"We would rather dwell in it than in Norway," said Hake.

"We hope not. But we would prefer to be in our own land," replied the elder brother, sadly, "for there is no place like home."

At this point Karlsefin and the rest of the party came back to the shore and put an end to the conversation. Returning on board they drew up the anchor, hoisted sail, and again put out to sea.

CHAPTER VII.

Songs and Sagas — Vinland at Last!

In days of old, just as in modern times, tars, when at sea, were wont to assemble on the "fo'c'sle," or forecastle, and spin yarns — as we have seen — when the weather was fine and their work was done.

One sunny afternoon, on the forecastle of Karlsefin's ship — which, by the way, was called "*The Snake*," and had a snake's head and neck for a figurehead — there was assembled a group of seamen, among whom were Tyrker the Turk, one of Thorward's men named Swend, who was very stout and heavy, and one of Karlsefin's men called Krake, who was a wild jocular man with a peculiar twang in his speech, the result of having been long a prisoner in Ireland. We mention these men particularly, because it was they who took the chief part in conversations and in storytelling. The two Scots were also there, but they were very quiet, and talked little; nevertheless, they were interested and attentive listeners. Olaf was there also, all eyes and ears — for Olaf drank in stories, and songs, and jests, as the sea-sand drinks water — so said Tyrker; but Krake immediately contradicted him, saying that when the sea-sand was full of water it drank no more, as was plain from the fact that it did not drink up the sea, whereas Olaf went on drinking and was *never* satisfied.

"Come, sing us a song, Krake," cried Tyrker, giving the former a slap on the shoulder; "let us hear how the Danish kings were served by the Irish boys."

"Not I," said Krake, firmly. "I've told ye two stories already. It's Hake's turn now to give us a song, or what else he pleases."

"But you'll sing it after Hake has sung, won't you, Krake?" pleaded several of the men.

"I'll not say 'No' to that."

Hake, who possessed a soft and deep bass voice of very fine quality, at once acceded to the request for a song. Crossing his arms on his chest, and looking, as if in meditation, towards the eastern horizon, he sang, to one of his national airs, "The Land across the Sea."

The deep pathos of Hake's voice, more than the words, melted these hardy Norsemen almost to tears, and for a few minutes effectually put to flight the spirit of fun that had prevailed.

"That's your own composin', I'll be bound," said Krake, "an' sure it's not bad. It's Scotland you mean, no doubt, by the land across the sea. Ah! I've heard much of that land. The natives are very fond of it, they say. It must be a fine country. I've heard Irishmen, who have been there, say that if it wasn't for Ireland they'd think it the finest country in the world."

"No doubt," answered Hake with a laugh, "and I dare say Swend, there, would think it the finest country in the world after Norway."

"Ha! Gamle Norge[6]," said Swend with enthusiasm, "there is no country like *that* under the sun."

"Except Greenland," said Olaf, stoutly.

"Or Iceland," observed Biarne, who had joined the group. "Where can you show such mountains — spouting fire, and smoke, and melted stones — or such boiling fountains, ten feet thick and a hundred feet high, as we have in Iceland?"

"That's true," observed Krake, who was an Icelander.

"Oh!" exclaimed Tyrker, with a peculiar twist of his ugly countenance, "Turkey is the land that beats all others completely."

At this there was a general laugh.

"Why, how can that be?" cried Swend, who was inclined to take up the question rather hotly. "What have you to boast of in Turkey?"

"Eh! What have we *not*, is the question. What shall I say? Ha! we have *grapes* there; and we do make *such* a drink of them — Oh! —"

Here Tyrker screwed his face and figure into what was meant for a condition of ecstasy.

"'Twere well that they had no grapes there, Tyrker," said Biarne, "for if all be true that Karlsefin tells us of that drink, they would be better without it."

"I wish I had it!" remarked Tyrker, pathetically.

"Well, it is said that we shall find grapes in Vinland," observed Swend, "and as we are told there is everything else there that man can desire, our new country will beat all the others put together — so hurrah for Vinland!"

The cheer was given with right good-will, and then Tyrker reminded Krake of his promise to sing a song. Krake, whose jovial spirits made him always ready for anything, at once struck up to a rattling ditty:

The Danish Kings.

> *One night when one o' the Irish Kings*
> *Was sleeping in his bed,*
> *Six Danish Kings — so Sigvat sings —*
> *Came an' cut off his head.*
> *The Irish boys they heard the noise,*
> *And flocked unto the shore;*
> *They caught the kings, and put out their eyes,*
> *And left them in their gore.*
>
> *Chorus — Oh! this is the way we served the kings,*
> *An' spoiled their pleasure, the dirty things,*
> *When they came to harry and flap their wings*

6   Old Norway.

Upon the Irish shore-ore,
Upon the Irish shore.

Next year the Danes took terrible pains
To wipe that stain away;
They came with a fleet, their foes to meet,
Across the stormy say.
Each Irish carl great stones did hurl
In such a mighty rain,
The Danes went down, with a horrible stoun,
An' never came up again!

Oh! this is the way, etc.

The men were still laughing and applauding Krake's song when Olaf, who chanced to look over the bow of the vessel, started up and shouted "Land, ho!" in a shrill voice, that rang through the whole ship.

Instantly, the poop and forecastle were crowded, and there, on the starboard bow, they saw a faint blue line of hills far away on the horizon. Olaf got full credit for having discovered the land first on this occasion; and for some time everything else was forgotten in speculations as to what this new land would turn out to be; but the wind, which had been getting lighter every hour that day, died away almost to a calm, so that, as there was no prospect of reaching the land for some hours, the men gradually fell back to their old places and occupation.

"Now, then, Krake," said Tyrker, "tell us the story about that king you were talking of the other day; which was it? Harald —"

"Ay, King Harald," said Krake, "and how he came to get the name of Greyskin. Well, you must know that it's not many years ago since my father, Sigurd, was a trader between Iceland and Norway. He went to other places too, sometimes — and once to Ireland, on which occasion it was that I was taken prisoner and kept so long in the country, that I became an Irishman. But after escaping and getting home I managed to change back into an Icelander, as ye may see! Well, in my father's younger days, before I was born — which was a pity! for he needed help sorely at that time, and I would have been just the man to turn myself handy to any sort of work; however, it wasn't *my* fault — in his younger days, my father one summer went over from Iceland to Norway — his ship loaded till she could hardly float, with skins and peltry, chiefly grey wolves. It's my opinion that the reason she didn't go down was that they had packed her so tight there was no room for the water to get in and sink her. Anyway, over the sea she went and got safe to Norway.

"At that time King Harald, one of the sons of Eric, reigned in Norway, after the death of King Hakon the Good. He and my father were great friends, but they had not met for some time; and not since Harald had come to his dignity. My father sailed to Hardanger, intending to dispose of his pelts there if he could. Now, King Harald generally had his seat in Hordaland and Bogaland,

and some of his brothers were usually with him; but it chanced that year that they went to Hardanger, so my father and the king met, and had great doings, drinking beer and talking about old times when they were boys together.

"My father then went to the place where the greatest number of people were met in the fiord, but nobody would buy any of his skins. He couldn't understand this at all, and was very much annoyed at it, and at night when he was at supper with the king he tells him about it. The king was in a funny humour that night. He had dashed his beard with beer to a great extent, and laughed heartily sometimes without my father being able to see what was the joke. But my father was a knowing man. He knew well enough that people are sometimes given to hearty laughter without troubling themselves much about the joke — especially when they are beery — so he laughed too, out of friendliness, and was very sociable.

"When my father went away the king promised to pay him a visit on board of his ship next day, which he did, sure enough; and my father took care to let it be known that he was coming, so there was no lack of the principal people thereabouts. They had all come down together, by the merest chance, to the place where the ship lay, just to enjoy the fresh air — being fresher there that day than at most other places on the fiord, no doubt!

"King Harald came with a fully-manned boat, and a number of followers. He was very condescending and full of fun, as he had been the night before. When he was going away he looked at the skins, and said to my father, 'Wilt thou give me a present of one of these wolf-skins?'

"'Willingly,' says my father, 'and as many more as you please.'

"On this, the king wrapped himself up in a wolf-skin and went back to his boat and rowed away. Immediately after, all the boats in his suite came alongside and looked at the wolf-skins with great admiration, and every man bought just such another wolf-skin as the king had got. In a few days so many people came to buy skins, that not half of them could be served with what they wanted, and the upshot was that my father's vessel was cleared out down to the keel, and thereafter the king went, as you know, by the name of Harald Greyskin.

"But here we are, comrades," continued Krake, rising, "drawing near to the land — I'll have a look at it."

The country off which they soon cast anchor was flat and overgrown with wood; and the strand far around consisted of white sand, and was very low towards the sea. Biarne said that it was the country to which Leif had given the name of Markland,[7] because it was well-wooded; they therefore went ashore in the small boat, but finding nothing in particular to attract their interest, they soon returned on board and again put to sea with an onshore wind from the north-east.

7   Some antiquaries appear to be of opinion that Helloland must have been Newfoundland, and Markland some part of Nova Scotia.

For two days they continued their voyage with the same wind, and then made land for the third time and found it to be an island. It was blowing hard at the time, and Biarne advised that they should take shelter there and wait for good weather. This they did, and, as before, a few of them landed to explore the country, but there was not much to take note of. Little Olaf, who was one of the explorers, observed dew on the grass, and, remembering that Leif had said that the dew on one of the islands which he met with was *sweet*, he shook some into the hollow of his hand and tasted it, but looked disappointed.

"Are you thirsty, Olaf?" asked Karlsefin, who, with Biarne, walked beside him.

"No, but I wondered if the dew would be sweet. My father said it was, on one of the islands he came to."

"Foolish boy," said Biarne, laughing; "Leif did but speak in a figure. He was very hot and tired at the time, and found the dew sweet to his thirsty spirit as well as refreshing to his tongue."

"Thus you see, Olaf," observed Karlsefin, with a sly look at Biarne, "whenever you chance to observe your father getting angry, and hear him say that his beer is sour, you are not to suppose that it is really sour, but must understand that it is only sour to his cross spirit as well as disagreeable to his tongue."

Olaf received this with a loud laugh, for, though he was puzzled for a moment by Biarne's explanation, he saw through the jest at once.

"Well, Biarne," returned Olaf; "whether the dew was sweet to my father's tongue or to his spirit I cannot tell, but I remember that when he told us about the sweet dew, he said it was near to the island where he found it that the country he called Vinland lay. So, if this be the sweet-dew island, Vinland cannot be far off."

"The boy is sharp beyond his years," said Karlsefin, stopping abruptly and looking at Biarne; "what thinkest thou of that?"

"I think," replied the other, "that Olaf will be a great discoverer some day, for it seems to me not unlikely that he may be right."

"Come, we shall soon see," said Karlsefin, turning round and hastening back to the boat.

Biarne either had not seen this particular spot on his former visit to these shores, which is quite probable, or he may have forgotten it, for he did not recognise it as he had done the first land they made; but before they left Ericsfiord, Leif had given them a very minute and careful description of the appearance of the coast of Vinland, especially of that part of it where he had made good his landing and set up his booths, so that the explorers might be in a position to judge correctly when they should approach it. Nevertheless, as every one knows, regions, even when well defined, may wear very different aspects when seen by different people, for the first time, from different points of view. So it was on this occasion. The voyagers had hit the island a short distance further south than the spot where Leif came upon it, and did not recognise it in the least. Indeed they had begun to doubt whether it really was an island at all. But now that Olaf had awakened their suspicions, they hastened eagerly on board the

"*Snake*," and sailed round the coast until they came into a sound which lay between the Island and a cape that jutted out northward from the land.

"'Tis Vinland!" cried Biarne in an excited tone.

"Don't be too sure of that," said Thorward, as a sudden burst of sunshine lit up land and sea.

"I cannot be too sure," cried Biarne, pointing to the land. "See, there is the ness that Leif spoke of going out northwards from the land; there is the island; here, between it and the ness, is the sound, and yonder, doubtless, is the mouth of the river which comes out of the lake where the son of Eric built his booths. Ho! Vinland! hurrah!" he shouted, enthusiastically waving his cap above his head.

The men were not slow to echo his cheer, and they gave it forth not a whit less heartily.

"'Tis a noble land to look upon," said Gudrid, who with the other females of the party had been for some time gazing silently and wistfully towards it.

"Perchance it may be a *great* land some day," observed Karlsefin.

"Who knows?" murmured Thorward in a contemplative tone.

"Ay, who knows?" echoed Biarne; "time and luck can work wonders."

"God's blessing can work wonders," said Karlsefin, impressively; "may He grant it to us while we sojourn here!"

With that he gave orders to prepare to let go the anchor, but the sound, over which they were gliding slowly before a light wind, was very shallow, and he had scarcely ceased speaking when the ship struck with considerable violence, and remained fast upon the sand.

CHAPTER VIII.

A Chapter of Incidents and Exploration,
in which a Bear and a Whale Play Prominent Parts.

Although arrested thus suddenly and unexpectedly in their progress toward the shore, these resolute Norsemen were not to be balked in their intention of reaching the land that forenoon — for it was morning when the vessel stuck fast on the shallows.

The tide was ebbing at the time, so that Karlsefin knew it would be impossible to get the ship off again until the next flood-tide. He therefore waited till the water was low enough, and then waded to the land accompanied by a large band of men. We need scarcely say that they were well-armed. In those days men never went abroad either by land or sea without their armour, which consisted of swords, axes, spears and bows for offence, with helmets and shields for defence. Some of the men of wealth and position also wore defensive armour on their breasts, thighs, and shins, but most of the fighting men were content to trust to the partial protection afforded by tunics of thick skin.

They were not long of reaching the mouth of the river which Biarne had pointed out, and, after proceeding up its banks for a short distance, were convinced that this must be the very spot they were in search of.

"Now, Biarne," said Karlsefin, stopping and sitting down on a large stone, "I have no doubt that this is Leif's river, for it is broad and deep as he told us, therefore we will take our ship up here. Nevertheless, before doing so, it would be a satisfaction to make positively certain that we are in the right way, and this we may do by sending one or two of our men up into the land, who, by following the river, will come to the lake where Leif built his booths, and so bring us back the news of them. Meanwhile we can explore the country here till they return."

Biarne and Thorward thought this advice good, and both offered to lead the party to be sent there.

"For," said Thorward, "they may meet with natives, and if the natives here bear any resemblance to the Skraelingers, methinks they won't receive us with much civility."

"I have thought of that," returned Karlsefin with a smile, "but I like not your proposal. What good would it do that either you or Biarne should lead so small a party if ye were assaulted by a hundred or more savages, as might well be the case?"

"Why, we could at all events retreat fighting," retorted Thorward in a slightly offended tone.

"With fifty, perhaps, in front, to keep you in play, and fifty detached to tickle you in rear."

Thorward laughed at this, and so did Biarne. "Well, if the worst came to the worst," said the latter, "we could at any rate sell our lives dearly."

"And, pray, what good would that do to *us*?" demanded Karlsefin.

"Well, well, have it your own way, skipper," said Biarne; "it seems to me, nevertheless, that if we were to advance with the whole of the men we have brought on shore with us, we should be in the same predicament, for twenty men could not easily save themselves from a hundred — or, as it might be, a thousand — if surrounded in the way you speak of."

"Besides that," added Thorward, "it seems to me a mean thing to send out only one or two of our men without a leader to cope with such possible dangers, unless indeed they were possessed of more than mortal powers."

"Why, what has become of your memories, my friends?" exclaimed Karlsefin. "Are there none of our men possessed of powers that are, at all events, more than those of *ordinary* mortals?"

"O-ho! Hake and Heika! I forgot them," cried Biarne; "the very men for the work, to be sure!"

"No doubt of it," said Karlsefin. "If they meet with natives who are friendly, well and good; if they meet with no natives at all — better. If they meet with unfriendly natives, they can show them their heels; and I warrant you that, unless the natives here be different from most other men, the best pair of savage legs in Vinland will fail to overtake the Scottish brothers."

Thorward agreed that this was a good plan, but cautioned Karlsefin to give the brothers strict injunctions to fly, and not upon any account to fight; "for," said he, "these doughty Scots are fiery and fierce when roused, and from what I have seen of them will, I think, be much more disposed to use their legs in running after their foes than in running away from them."

This having been settled, the brothers were called, and instructed to proceed into the woods and up the bank of the river as quickly as possible, until they should come to a lake on the margin of which they would probably see a few small huts. On discovering these they were to turn immediately and hasten back. They were also particularly cautioned as to their behaviour in the event of meeting with natives, and strictly forbidden to fight, if these should be evil disposed, but to run back at full speed to warn their friends, so that they might be prepared for any emergency.

"Nevertheless," said Karlsefin, in conclusion, "ye may carry weapons with you if ye will."

"Thanks," replied Heika. "As, however, you appear to doubt our powers of self-restraint, we will relieve your mind by going without them."

Thus instructed and warned, the brothers tightened their belts, and, leaping nimbly into the neighbouring brake, disappeared from view.

"A pair of proper men," said Karlsefin. "And now, comrades, we will explore the neighbourhood together, for it is advisable to ascertain all we can of the nature of our new country, and that as quickly as may be. It is needful, also, to do so without scattering, lest we be set upon unexpectedly by any lurking foe. This land is not easily surveyed like Iceland or Greenland, being, as you see, covered with shrubs and trees, which somewhat curtail our vision, and render caution the more necessary."

While the Norsemen were engaged in examining the woods near the coast, the two Scots held on their way into the interior. There was something absolutely exhilarating, as Krake once remarked, in the mere beholding of these brothers' movements. They had been famed for agility and endurance even in their own country. They did not run, but trotted lightly, and appeared to be going at a moderate pace, when in reality it would have compelled an ordinary runner to do his best to keep up with them. Yet they did not pant or show any other symptom of distress. On the contrary, they conversed occasionally in quiet tones, as men do when walking. They ran abreast as often as the nature of the ground would allow them to do so, taking their leaps together when they came to small obstructions, such as fallen trees or brooks of a few feet wide; but when they came to creeks of considerable width, the one usually paused to see the other spring over, and then followed him.

Just after having taken a leap of this kind, and while they were running silently side by side along the margin of the river, they heard a crash among the bushes, and next instant a fine deer sprang into an open space in front of them. The brothers bent forward, and, flying like the wind, or like arrows from a bow, followed for a hundred yards or so — then stopped abruptly and burst into a hearty fit of laughter.

"Ah! Heika," exclaimed the younger, "that fellow would be more than a match for us if we could double our speed. We have no chance with four-legged runners."

While he was speaking they resumed the jog-trot pace, and soon afterwards came to a rocky ridge, that seemed to traverse the country for some distance. Here they were compelled to walk, and in some places even to clamber, the ground being very rugged.

Here also they came to a small branch or fork of the river that appeared to find its way to the sea through another channel. It was deep, and although narrow in comparison with the parent stream, was much too broad to be leaped over. The pioneers were therefore obliged to swim. Being almost as much at home in the water as otters, they plunged in, clothes and all, without halting, and in a few seconds had gained the other side.

When they reached the top of the ridge they stopped and gazed in silent admiration, for there lay stretched out before them a vast woodland scene of most exquisite beauty. Just at their feet was the lake of which they were in search; some parts of it bright as the blue sky which its unruffled breast reflected; other parts dark almost to blackness with the images of rocks and trees. Everywhere around lay a primeval wilderness of wood and water which it is beyond the power of mortal pen adequately to describe; and while all was suffused with the golden light of an early summer sun, and steeped in the repose of an absolutely calm day, the soft and plaintive cries of innumerable wild-fowl enlivened, without disturbing, the profound tranquillity of the scene.

"Does it not remind you of our own dear land?" said Heika in a low soft voice.

"Ay, like the lowlands on the shores of the Forth fiord," replied Hake, in the same low tone, as if he feared to break the pleasing stillness; "and there, surely, are the booths we were to search for — see, in the hollow, at the head of yonder bay, with the gravelly beach and the birch-trees hanging from the rocks as if they wished to view themselves in the watery mirror."

"True — there are three of them visible. Let us descend and examine."

"Hist! Some one appears to have got there before us," said Hake, laying his hand on his brother's shoulder and pointing in the direction of the huts.

"It is not a human visitor, methinks," observed Heika.

"More like a bear," returned Hake.

In order to set the question at rest the brothers hastened round by the woods to a spot immediately behind the huts. There was a hill there so steep as to be almost a precipice. It overlooked the shores of the lake immediately below where the huts were, and when the pioneers came to the crest of it and peeped cautiously over, they beheld a large brown bear not far from the hut that stood nearest to the hill, busily engaged in devouring something.

"Now it is a pity," whispered Heika, "that we brought no arms with us. Truly, little cause have we men to be proud of our strength, for yonder beast could match fifty of us if we had nothing to depend on save our fists and feet and fingers."

"Why not include the teeth in your list, brother?" asked Hake, with a quiet laugh; "but it is a pity, as you say. What shall —"

He stopped abruptly, for a large boulder, or mass of rock, against which he leaned, gave way under him, made a sudden lurch forward and then stuck fast.

"Ha! a dangerous support," said Hake, starting back; "but, hist! suppose we shove it down on the bear?"

"A good thought," replied Heika, "if we can move the mass, which seems doubtful; but let us try. Something may be gained by trying — nothing lost."

The boulder, which had been so balanced on the edge of the steep hill that a gentle pressure moved it, was a mass of rock weighing several tons, the moving of which would have been a hopeless task for twenty men to attempt, but it stood balanced on the extreme edge of the turn of the hill, and the little slip it had just made rendered its position still more critical; so that, when the young men lay down with their backs against a rock, placed their feet upon it and pushed with all their might, it slowly yielded, toppled over, and rolled with a tremendous surge through a copse which lay immediately below it.

The brothers leaped up and gazed in breathless eagerness to observe the result. The bear, hearing the crash, looked up with as much surprise as the visage of that stupid creature is capable of expressing. The thing was so suddenly done that the bear seemed to have no time to form an opinion or get alarmed, for it stood perfectly still, while the boulder, bounding from the copse, went crashing down the hill, cutting a clear path wherever it touched, attaining terrific velocity, and drawing an immense amount of débris after it. The direction it took happened to be not quite straight for the animal, whose snout it passed within six or eight feet — causing him to shrink back and growl — as it rushed smoking onward over the level bit of sward beneath, through the mass of willows beyond, across the gravelly strand and out to the lake, into which it plunged and disappeared amid a magnificent spout of foam. But the avalanche of earth and stones which its mad descent had created did not let Bruin off so easily. One after another these latter, small and large, went pattering and dashing against him, – some on his flank, some on his ribs, and others on his head. He growled of course, yet stood the fire nobly for a few seconds, but when, at last, a large boulder hit him fairly on the nose, he gave vent to a squeal which terminated in a passionate roar as he turned about and made for the open shore, along which for some distance he ran with the agility of a monstrous wild-cat, and finally leaped out of sight into his forest home!

The brothers looked at each other with sparkling eyes, and next moment the woods resounded with their merriment, as they held their sides and leaned for support against a neighbouring cliff.

Heika was first to recover himself.

"Hold, brother," he exclaimed, "we laugh loud enough to let Bruin know who it was that injured him, or to bring all the savages in these woods down upon us. Peace, man, peace, and let us return to our friends."

"As soon as ye please, brother," said Hake, still laughing as he tightened his belt, "but was it not rare fun to see Bruin stand that stony rain so manfully until his tender point was touched? And then how he ran! 'Twas worth coming here to see a bear leave off his rolling gait so and run like a very wildcat. Now I'm ready."

Without staying to make further examination of Leif's old huts – for from the place where they stood all the six of them could be clearly seen – the young pioneers started on their return to the coast. They ran back with much greater speed than they had pushed forward – fearing that their companions might be getting impatient or alarmed about them. They did not even converse, but with heads up, chests forward, and elbows bent, addressed themselves to a quick steady run, which soon brought them to the branch of the river previously mentioned. Here they stopped for a moment before plunging in.

"Suppose that we run down its bank," suggested Hake, "and see whether there be not a shallow crossing."

"Surely ye have not grown afraid of water, Hake?"

"No, not I, but I should like to see whither this branch trends, and what it is like; besides, the divergence will not cost us much time, as we can cross at any point we have a mind to, and come at the main river again through the woods."

"Well, I will not balk you – come on."

They accordingly descended the smaller streams and found it to be broken by various little cascades and rapids, with here and there a longish reach of pebbly ground where the stream widened into a shallow rippling river with one or two small islands in it. At one of these places they crossed where it was only knee-deep in the centre, and finally stopped at the end of a reach, where a sudden narrowing of the banks produced a brawling rapid. Below this there was a deep pool caused by a great eddy.

"Now, we go no further," said Heika. "Here we shall cross through the woods to the main branch."

"'Tis a pretty stream," observed Hake when they were about to leave it.

As he spoke a large salmon leaped high out of the pool below, flashed for one moment in the sunshine like a bar of living silver, and fell back into the water with a sounding splash. Hake caught his breath and opened wide his eyes!

"Truly that is a good sight to the eyes of a Scotsman," said Heika, gazing with interest at the place where the fish had disappeared; "it reminds me of my native land."

"Ay, and me of my dinner," observed Hake, smacking his lips.

"Out upon thee, man!" cried Heika, "how can ye couple our native land with such a matter-o'-fact thought as dinner?"

"Why, it would be hard to uncouple the thought of dinner from our native land," returned Hake, with a laugh, as they entered the forest; "for every man — not to mention woman — within its circling coastline is a diner, and so by hook or crook must daily have his dinner. But say, brother, is it not matter of satisfaction, as well as matter of fact, that the waters of this Vinland shall provide us with abundance of food not less surely than the land? If things go on as they have begun I shall be well content to stay here."

"Ye do not deserve the name of Scot, Hake," said the other gravely. "My heart is in Scotland; it is not here."

"True, I know it," replied Hake, with a touch of feeling; "in a double sense, too, for your betrothed is there. Nevertheless, as *I* did not leave my heart behind me; surely there is no sin in taking some pleasure in this new land. But heed not my idle talk, brother. You and I shall yet live to see the bonny hills of —. Ha! here we are on the big stream once more, sooner than I had expected, and, if I mistake not, within hail of our comrades."

Hake was right. The moment they emerged from the woods upon the open bank of the large river they saw a party of men in the distance approaching them, and, an instant later, a loud halloo assured them that these were their friends.

When the pioneers had related all that they had seen and done, the whole party returned to the shore and hailed the ship, for, the tide having risen, they could not now reach it by wading. A boat was immediately sent for them, and great was the interest manifested by all on board to learn the news of Vinland. They had time to give an account of all that had been done and seen, because it still wanted an hour of flood-tide, and the ship still lay immoveable.

While they were thus engaged, Gudrid happened to cast her eyes over the stern of the ship, and thought she saw an object moving in the water.

"What is that I see?" she said, pointing towards it.

"The great sea-serpent!" exclaimed Biarne, shading his eyes with his hand.

"Or his ghost," remarked Krake.

From which observations, coupled together, it would appear that the famous monster referred to was known by repute to the Norsemen of the eleventh century, though he was to some extent regarded as a myth!

Be this as it may, the object which now attracted the attention and raised the eyebrows of all on board the "*Snake*" evidently possessed life, for it was very active — wildly so — besides being large. It darted hither and thither, apparently without aim, sending the water in curling foam before it. Suddenly it made straight for the ship, then it turned at a tangent and made for the island; anon it wheeled round, and rushed, like a mad creature, to the shore.

Then arose a deafening shout from the men —

"A whale! an embayed whale!"

And so in fact it was; a large whale, which, as whales will sometimes do — blind ones, perhaps — had lost its way, got entangled among the sandbanks lying between the island and the shore, and was now making frantic efforts to escape.

Need we say that a scene of the wildest excitement ensued among the men! The two boats — one of which was, as we have said, a large one — were got ready, barbed spears and lances and ropes were thrown into them, as many men as they could hold with safety jumped in, and pulled away, might and main, after the terrified whale.

You may be sure, reader, that little Olaf was there, fast by the side of his friend and hero Karlsefin, who took charge of the large boat, with Thorward in the bow to direct him how to steer. Biarne was there too as a matter of course, in charge of the little boat, with Krake as his bowman and Tyrker pulling the stroke-oar. For Tyrker was strong, though little, ugly, and old, and had a peculiar talent for getting involved in any fighting, fun, or mischief that chanced to be in hand. Men said that he was afraid of dying in his bed, and had made up his mind to rush continually into the jaws of danger until they should close upon and crush him; but we are of opinion that this was a calumny. Those of the men who were necessarily left in the ship could scarce be prevented from swimming after the boats as they shot away, and nothing but the certainty of being drowned restrained them from making the mad attempt. As it was, they clambered upon the figurehead and up the rigging, where, with gaping mouths and staring eyes, they watched the movements of their more fortunate companions.

Meanwhile the whale had made what appeared to be a grand and final neck-or-nothing rush in the direction of the shore. Of course he was high, although not dry, in a few seconds. That is to say, he got into water so shallow that he stuck fast, with his great head and shoulders raised considerably out of the sea, in which position he began to roll, heave, spout, and lash his mighty tail with a degree of violence that almost approached sublimity.

He was in these circumstances when the Norsemen came up; for though too shallow for the whale, the water was quite deep enough for the boats.

Being light, the small boat reached the scene of action first. Krake stood up in the bow to be ready. He held in his hand a curious wooden spear with a loose barb tipped with the tusk of a walrus. It had been procured from one of the Greenland Skraelingers. A rope was attached to it.

As they drew near, the whale stopped for an instant, probably to recover breath. Krake raised his spear — the fish raised his tail. Whizz! went the spear. Down came the tail with a thunderclap, and next moment mud, sand, water, stones, foam, and blood, were flying in cataracts everywhere as the monster renewed its struggles.

"Back! back oars!" shouted Biarne, as they were almost swamped by the flood.

The men obeyed with such good-will that Krake was thrown head-foremost over the bow.

"Hold fast!" yelled Krake on coming to the surface.

"If ye had held fast ye wouldn't have been there," said Biarne; "where are ye?"

He rose again out of the foam, yelled, and tossed up his arms.

"Can the man not swim?" cried Biarne, in alarm; "pull, boys, pull!"

The men were already pulling with such force that they almost went over the man. As they rubbed past him Hake dropped his oar and caught him by the hair, Biarne leaned over the side and got him by the breeches, and with a vigorous heave they had him inboard.

"Why, Krake, I thought you could swim!" said Biarne.

"Ay, so I can, but who could swim with a coil of rope round his neck and legs?"

The poor man had indeed been entangled in the rope of the spear, so that he could not use his limbs freely.

No more was said, however, for they were still in dangerous proximity to the tail of the struggling fish, and had to pull out of its way.

Meanwhile the large boat, profiting by the experience of the small one, had kept more towards the whale's head, and, before Krake had been rescued, Thorward sent a Skraelinger spear deep into its shoulder. But this only acted as a spur to the huge creature, and made it heave about with such violence that it managed to slew right round with its head offshore.

At this the men could not restrain a shout of alarm, for they knew that if the whale were to succeed in struggling again into water where it could swim, it would carry away spears and ropes; or, in the event of these holding on, would infallibly capsize and sink the boats.

"Come, drive in your spears!" shouted Karlsefin in a voice of thunder, for his usually quiet spirit was now deeply stirred.

Thorward and one of the men threw their spears, but the latter missed and the former struck his weapon into a part that was too thick to do much injury, though it was delivered with great force and went deep.

"This will never do!" cried Karlsefin, leaping up; "here, Swend, take the helm. Ho! hand me that spear, quick! Now, lads, pull, pull, with heart and limb!"

As he spoke he sprang like a roused giant into the bow of the boat and caught up a spear. The men obeyed his orders. The boat rushed against the whale's side, and, with its impetus added to his own Herculean strength, Karlsefin thrust the spear deep down into the monster's body just behind the shoulder fin.

The crimson stream that immediately gushed forth besprinkled all in the boat and dyed the sea around.

"That is his life-blood," said Karlsefin, with a grim smile; "you may back off now, lads."

This was done at once. The small boat was also ordered to back off, and those in it obeyed not a moment too soon, for immediately after receiving the deadly wound the whale went into a violent dying struggle. It soon subsided. There were one or two mighty heavings of the shoulder; then a shudder ran through the huge carcase, and it rolled slowly over in a relaxed manner which told significantly that the great mysterious life had fled.

CHAPTER IX.

The First Night in Vinland.

The prize which had thus fallen into the hands of the Norsemen was of great importance, because it furnished a large supply of food, which thus enabled them to go leisurely to work in establishing themselves, instead of, as would otherwise have been the case, spending much of their time and energy in procuring that necessity of life by hunting and fishing.

It was also exceedingly fortunate that the whale had been killed a little before the time of high water, because that enabled them to fasten ropes through its nose and row with it still farther in to the shore. This accomplished, the boats made several trips back to the ship and landed all the men, and these, with a number of ropes, hauled up the carcase foot by foot as the tide rose. After reaching a certain point at high water they could get it up no farther, and when the tide turned all the men twice doubled could not have budged it an inch. The ropes were therefore tied together and lengthened until they reached a strong tree near the beach, to which they were fastened.

Leaving their prize thus secured they hastened back to the ship, hauled up the anchor, and made for the mouth of the river, but they had lost so much of the flood-tide, in consequence of their battle with the whale, and the evening was so far advanced, that they resolved to delay further proceedings until the following day.

The ship was therefore hauled close in to the land at the river's mouth and allowed to take the ground on a spit of sand. Here the men landed and soon built up a pile of stones, between which and the ship a gangway was made. The women were thus enabled to walk comfortably ashore. And here, on a grassy spot, they pitched their tents for the first time in Vinland.

Provisions were now brought on shore and large fires were kindled which blazed up and glared magnificently as the night drew on, rendering the spit of sand with the grassy knoll in the centre of it quite a cheerful and ruddy spot. A few trees were cut down and stretched across the spit at its neck on the land side, and there several sentinels were placed as a precaution — for which there seemed little occasion.

Karlsefin then set up a pole with a flag on it and took formal possession of this new land, after which the whole colony sat down on the grass — some under the tents, others under the starry sky — to supper. The cattle, it may here be noted, were not landed at this place, as they were to be taken up the river next day, but their spirits were refreshed with a good supply of new-mown grass, so that it is to be hoped, and presumed, they rejoiced not less than their human companions in the satisfactory state of things.

In the largest tent, Karlsefin, Biarne, Thorward, Gudrid, Freydissa, Astrid, and Olaf, sat down to a sumptuous repast of dried Greenland-fish and fresh Vinland-whale, besides which they had soup and beer. Being healthy and hungry, they did full justice to the good things. Bertha and Thora served and then joined in the repast.

"This is pleasant, isn't it, Freydissa?" asked Biarne, with his mouth full.

Freydissa, with her mouth not quite so full, admitted that it was, for she happened to be in an amiable humour — as well she might!

"Come, let us pledge the new land in a can of beer," cried Biarne, pouring the beverage out of an earthenware jar into a squat old Norse flagon of embossed silver. "Thorward, fill up!"

"I will join you heartily in that," cried Thorward, suiting the action to the word.

"And I," said Karlsefin, raising an empty flagon to his lips, "will pledge it in a wish. I wish — prosperity to Vinland!"

"Come, Karlsefin," remonstrated Biarne, "forego austerity for once, and drink."

"Not I," returned the skipper, with a laugh.

"Wherefore not?"

"First, because a wish is quite as potent as a drink in that respect; second, because our beer is nearly finished, and we have not yet the means to concoct more, so that it were ill-advised to rob *you*, Biarne, by helping to consume that which I do not like; and, last of all, I think it a happy occasion this in which to forswear beer altogether!"

"Have thy way," said Biarne, helping himself to another whale-steak of large dimensions. "You are too good a fellow to quarrel with on such trifling ground. Here, pass the jar, Thorward; I will drink his portion as well as my own."

"And I will join you both," cried little Olaf with a comical turn of his eyebrows. "Here, I wish prosperity to Vinland, and drink it, too, in water."

"We can all join thee in that, Olaf," said Gudrid I with an approving nod and laugh. "Come, girls, fill up your cups and pledge to Vinland."

"Stop!" shouted Biarne in sudden anxiety.

They all paused with the cups halfway to their lips.

"*You* must not drink, Freydissa," he continued seriously. "Gudrid did call upon the *girls* to join her: surely ye don't —"

He was cut short by Freydissa throwing her cup of water in his face.

With a burst of laughter Biarne fell backwards, and, partly to avoid the deluge, partly for fun, rolled out of the tent, when he got up and dried his dripping beard.

"No more of that, fair girl, I beseech thee," he said, resuming his place and occupation. "I will not again offend — if thou wilt not again misunderstand!"

Freydissa made no reply to this, silence being her usual method of showing that she condescended to be in good humour — and they were all very merry over their evening meal. From the noise and laughter and songs around them, it was evident that the rest of the company were enjoying their first night on shore to the full, insomuch that Olaf was led, in the height of his glee, to express a wish that they could live in that free-and-easy fashion for ever.

"'Tis of no use wishing it," observed Karlsefin; "if you would insure success you must, according to Biarne, drink it in beer."

"I cry you mercy, skipper," said Biarne; "if you persecute me thus I shall not be able to drink any more tonight. Hand me the jar, Thorward, and let me drink again before I come to that pass."

"Hark!" exclaimed Gudrid, "there must be something going to happen, for all the men have become suddenly quiet."

They listened intently for a moment or two, when Krake's voice broke the deep silence: — "Come, now, don't think so long about it, as if ye were composing something new. Every one knows, sure, that it's about sweet Scotland you're going to sing."

"Right, Krake, right," replied a rich deep voice, which it required no sight to tell belonged to Hake, the young Scot; "but there are many songs about sweet Scotland, and I am uncertain which to choose."

"Let it be lively," said Krake.

"No, no, no," chorussed some of the men; "let it be slow and sad."

"Well well," laughed the half-Irishman — as he was fond of styling himself — "have it your own way. If ye won't be glad, by all means be sad."

A moment after, Hake's manly tones rose on the still air like the sound of an organ, while he sang one of the ancient airs of his native land, wherein, like the same airs of modern days, were sounded the praises of Scotland's heather hills and brawling burns — her bonny daughters and her stalwart sons.

To those in the large tent who had listened, with breathless attention and heads half averted, it was evident that song, sentiments, and singer were highly appreciated, from the burst of hearty applause at the conclusion, and the eager demand for another ditty. But Hake protested that his ruling motto was "fair play," and that the songs must circle round.

"So let it be," cried Swend. "Krake, it is your turn next."

"I won't keep ye waiting," said that worthy, "though I might do it, too, if I was to put off time selecting from the songs of old Ireland, for it's endless they are — and in great variety. Sure, I could give ye songs about hills and streams that are superior to Scotland's burns and braes any day — almost up to those of Gamle Norge if they were a bit higher — the hills I mean, not the songs, which are too high already for a man with a low voice — and I could sing ye a lament that would make ye shed tears enough to wash us all off the spit of land here into the sea; but that's not in my way. I'm fond of a lively ditty, so here you are."

With that Krake struck up an air in which it was roundly asserted that Ireland was the finest country in the world (except Iceland, as he stopped in his song to remark); that Irish boys and girls lived in a state of perpetual hilarity and good-will, and that the boys displayed this amiable and pleasant condition chiefly in the way of kissing the girls and cracking each other's crowns.

After that, Swend was called on to sing, which he did of Norway with tremendous enthusiasm and noise but little melody. Then another man sang a love-ditty in a very gruff voice and much out of tune, which, nevertheless, to the man's evident satisfaction, was laughingly applauded. After him a sentimental youth sang, in a sweet tenor voice, an Icelandic air, and then Tyrker was called on to do his part, but flatly refused to sing. He offered to tell a saga instead, how-ever, which he did in such a manner that he made the sides of the Norsemen ache with laughter — though, to say truth, they laughed more at the teller than the tale.

Thus with song and saga they passed the first hours of the night, while the campfires blazed ruddily on their weather-beaten faces, and the heavenly con-stellations shone, not only on the surrounding landscape, but appeared to light up another world of cloudland beneath the surface of the sleeping sea.

At last Karlsefin went out to them.

"Now, lads," said he, "it is high time that you laid your heads on your pil-lows. Men who do not sleep well cannot labour well. Tomorrow we have hard work before us in taking possession and settling our new home. God has pros-pered us thus far. We have made a good beginning in Vinland. May it be the fore-taste of a happy ending. Away, then, and get you to rest before the night is older, and let your sleep be sound, for I will see to it that the sentinels posted round the camp are vigilant."

The men received this brief speech with a murmur of willing acquiescence, and at once obeyed the order; though Krake observed that he fell in with the custom merely out of respect to the opinions of his comrades, having himself long ago learned to do without sleep in Ireland, where the lads were in the habit of working — or fighting — all day, dancing all night, and going home with the girls in the morning! Each Norseman then sought a spot upon the grassy knoll suited to his taste; used his arm, or a hillock, or stone, for a pillow, or anything else that came conveniently to hand, and with his sword or axe beside him, and his shield above him as a coverlet, courted repose, while the bright stars twinkled him to sleep, and the rippling wavelets on the shore discoursed his lullaby.

CHAPTER X.

Taking Possession of the New Home, an Event which is Celebrated by an Explosion and a Reconciliation.

Every one knows — at least a well-known proverb assures us — that "early to bed and early to rise" conduces to health, wealth, and wisdom. The Norsemen of old would appear to have been acquainted with the proverb and the cheering prospect it holds out; perhaps they originated it; at all events, that they acted on it, and probably experienced the happy results, is evident from the fact that Karlsefin and his men not only went to bed in good time at night — as related in the last chapter — but were up and doing by daybreak on the following morning.

Having roused the women, relieved the sentinels, struck the tents, and carried everything safely on board the *Snake*, they manned the oars, or large sweeps, with the stoutest of the crew, and prepared to row their vessel up the river into the lake on the shores of which they designed to fix their future home. Previous to this, however, a party of men were told off to remain behind and cut up the whale, slice the lean portions into thin layers, and dry them in the sun for winter use.

"See that you make a good job of it," said Karlsefin to Swend, who was left behind as the leader of the whale-party — because he was fat, as Krake said, and, therefore, admirably suited for such work — "and be careful not to let sand get amongst the meat. Cut out the whalebone too, it will be of use to us; and don't forget that there may be enemies lurking in the woods near you. Keep your windward eye uncovered, and have your weapons always handy."

Swend promised to attend to these orders, and, with twenty men, armed with axes, scythes, and large knives, besides their swords, shields, bows and arrows, stood on the ness and cheered their comrades as they rowed away.

The force of the current was not great, so that the *Snake* made rapid progress, and in a few hours reached the place where the small stream forked off from the main river. This they named Little River. Above that point the current was more rapid, and it became necessary to send a large party of men on shore with a tracking-rope, by means of which and the oars they at last overcame all obstacles, and finally swept out upon the bosom of the beautiful sheet of water which had afforded such delight to the eyes of the two Scots.

"Here, then, we have got *home* at last," said Karlsefin, as they rowed over the still water to a spit, or natural landing-place, near Leif's old booths.

"It is very beautiful," said Gudrid, "but I find it difficult to call it home. It seems so strange, though so pleasant."

"You were always difficult to please, Gudrid," said Freydissa; "surely you don't think Greenland — cold, windy, bleak, nasty Greenland — a better home than this?"

"Nay, sister, I made no comparison. I did but say that it seemed strange, and I'm sure that Bertha agrees with me in that — don't you, Bertha?"

"Indeed I do," replied the maiden; "strange the land is, but beautiful exceedingly."

"Of course she'll agree with what *you* say," cried Freydissa, testily. "I would that she agreed as readily with me. It is a wonder that she is not weeping, as she is always so ready to do on the smallest provocation, or without any provocation at all."

"I only wept on leaving my father," remonstrated Bertha with a winning smile. "I'm sure you have not seen me shed a tear since then. Besides, I do agree with you in this case, for I think Vinland will be a pleasant home. Don't you too?" she added, turning round to Thora, who had been standing at her side, but Thora had moved away, and her place had been taken by Hake, the Scot.

Bertha blushed on meeting the youth's gaze, and the blush deepened when Hake said in a quiet undertone, that Vinland could not but be a pleasant home to him, and added that Greenland, Iceland, Norway — anywhere — would be equally pleasant, if only *she* were there!

Poor Bertha was so taken aback by the cool and sudden boldness of this unexpected reply, that she looked hastily round in alarm lest it had been overheard; but Hake, not intending that it should be overheard, had addressed it to her ear, and fortunately at the moment the grating of the keel upon the pebbly shore drew the attention of all to the land.

"Now, then, jump ashore, lads," cried Biarne, "and get out the gangway. Make it broad, for our cattle must not be allowed to risk their limbs by tumbling off."

While Biarne superintended the gangway, Thorward prepared the live stock for their agreeable change, and Karlsefin went up to examine the state of the huts. They were found to be in excellent condition, having been well built originally, and the doors and windows having been secured against the weather by those who had used them last.

"No natives can have been here," observed the leader of the party to those who accompanied him, "because every fastening is secured, apparently, as it was left."

"Nevertheless, Sigrid and I have seen footprints in the sand," remarked the woman Gunhild, coming up at that moment.

"Show them to me," said Karlsefin, with much interest.

"Yonder they are," replied the woman, pointing towards a sandy spot on her left, "and he who made them must have been a giant, they are so large."

"Truly, a dangerous giant to meet with," observed Karlsefin, laughing, when he reached the place, "these are none other, Gunhild, than the footprints of the bear that the two Scots sent away with the toothache. But come, we will open these huts and have them put in order and made comfortable against supper-time. So, get to work all of you and see how active you can be."

While some of the party were busily engaged in sweeping out and arranging the huts, others shouldered their axes and went into the woods to cut down a few dead trees for firewood, and when the gangway between the ship and the shore was completed the live stock was driven on shore.

There was something quite impressive in this part of the landing. There was a deliberate slowness in the movements of most of the animals that gave to it quite the air of a solemn procession, and must have been a good illustration, on a small scale, of the issuing of the beasts from Noah's Ark on the top of Ararat!

The first creature which, appropriately enough, led the van, was a lordly black bull. Little Olaf, whose tastes were somewhat peculiar, had made a pet of this bull during the voyage, and by feeding it, scratching it behind the ears, patting its nose, giving it water, and talking to it, had almost, if not altogether, won its affections. He was therefore permitted to superintend the landing of it.

"Come, get on, Blackie," cried Olaf, giving the bull a push on the flank as it stood on the gangway with its head high, tail slightly raised, nostrils expanded, and eyes flashing. It glanced from side to side as if to take a general survey of its new domains.

Olaf advised it to "get on" again, but Blackie deigned to take no further notice than by a deep-toned internal rumbling.

"Not unlike Mount Hecla when it is going to explode," said Biarne, laughing.

"Come back, boy, he will do you a mischief," cried Gudrid in some alarm.

"Why, Olaf," said Karlsefin, "your pet is going to be disobedient. Speak louder to him."

Instead of speaking louder Olaf quietly grasped the brute's tail and gave it a twist.

The effect was wonderful and instantaneous. The huge animal rushed wildly along the gangway, leaped across the beach, making the pebbles fly as he went, scampered over the green turf and plunged into the forest, kicking up his heels, flourishing his tail and bellowing in frantic delight!

Most of the cows went slowly and placidly along the gangway, and landed with easy-going satisfaction expressed in their patient faces, to the supreme contempt of Freydissa, who said she wished that they had all been bulls. There was one young heifer amongst them, however, which proved an exception to the rule. It glared savagely round, as if in imitation of the bull, refused point-blank to land, swerved from side to side of the gangway, backed right into the ship at the risk of its neck and limbs, attempted to charge the men, created dire confusion and alarm among the poultry, and finally fell off the gangway into the water, and scrambled on shore in a way that must have thrilled Freydissa's heart with admiration — although she did not say so, but maintained a grim silence all the time.

Next came the sheep, which, owing perhaps to seasickness, or home-sickness, or some other cause, looked remarkably sheepish, and walked on shore with as much solemnity as if each had been attending the funeral of the rest. There were about twenty of these, and after them came a dozen or so of Icelandic ponies, which, although somewhat more active than the sheep, were evidently suffering in their spirits from the effects of the recent voyage. One of them, however, on feeling the soft turf under his feet, attempted to neigh, without much success, and another said something that sounded more like a horse-laugh than anything else.

Then followed the fowls, some of which walked, some flew, and others fluttered, according to their varying moods, with an immense deal of fuss and cackling, which was appropriately capped by the senior cock mounting on one of the huts and taking possession of the land with an ecstatic crow.

The procession was brought up by the ducks, which waddled out of the ship, some with an expression of grave surprise, some with "quacks" of an inquiring nature, others with dubious steps and slow, while a few, with an eye to the "main chance" made ineffectual dabs at little roughnesses in their pathway, in the hope that these might turn out to be edible.

At last all were landed and driven up into the woods, where they were left without any fear being entertained as to their going astray, seeing that they were guarded by several fine dogs, which were too much associated with the men as companions to be included in the foregoing list of the lower animals.

"Shall we set the nets?" said Hake, going up to Karlsefin, who was busy arranging the principal hut, while the men were bringing their goods and chattels on shore. "You know we saw a salmon leap from a pool on Little River. Doubtless they are in the lake also."

"Try it, Hake, by all means. Go with your brother in the little boat and set them where you think best. Fresh salmon for supper would be a rare treat just now. Are you sure it *was* a salmon you saw, and not a large trout?"

"Sure? Ay, as sure as I am that a horse is not a cow," replied Hake, smiling.

"Go then, and luck go with you."

The nets were soon set in the bay, near the point of the ness on which the huts were built, and near to which a small mountain-stream entered the lake.

Suddenly a shrill angry voice was heard issuing from one of the smaller huts near the lake. It was Freydissa storming at poor Bertha. There was an occasional bass growl intermingled with it. That was Thorward remonstrating.

"Poor Bertha," said Karlsefin to Biarne, who was standing beside him at the time, "she has a hard mistress."

"Poor Thorward," said Biarne, "he has a tough wife."

"Thorward will cure or kill her," rejoined Karlsefin, with a laugh. "He is a long-suffering man, and very tender to women withal, but he is not made of butter."

Biarne shook his head. He evidently had not much opinion of Thorward's resolution when opposed by the will and passion of such a termagant as Freydissa.

"How much better 'twould have been," said he, "if Thorward had married her maid — the sweet little fair-haired blue-eyed Bertha."

"Why, Biarne, methinks that *thou* art somewhat like to try that plan," said his friend, looking at him in surprise, for he had spoken with much enthusiasm.

"Not I, man," returned Biarne, with a smile and a shake of the head. "It is long since my heart was buried in Iceland. I am doomed to be an old bachelor now."

They both listened at this point, for the domestic brawl in the small hut seemed to be waxing furious. Thorward's voice was not heard so often, but when it did sound there was an unusually stern tone in it, and Freydissa's became so loud that her words were audible.

"It has been killed, I tell you, Bertha, by sheer carelessness. If you had fed it properly it would have been as well as the others. *Don't* say you did your best for it. You didn't. You *know* you didn't. You're a smooth-faced vixen. You are. Don't speak. Don't speak back, I say. Hold your tongue. You killed that kitten by carelessness."

"If you don't hold your tongue, wife," said Thorward, in a loud stern voice, "I'll kill the cat too."

There was a pause here, as if the threat had taken away Freydissa's breath.

"Oho! that's the poor little kitten," whispered Karlsefin to Biarne, referring to one of a litter that had been born at sea, "that was nigh eaten by one of the dogs. Bertha had no hand in its death. I wonder it lived so long."

"Kill the cat?" shrieked Freydissa, stamping her foot.

This was instantly followed by an unearthly caterwaul and the sudden appearance of a dark object in the air, which, issuing from the door of the hut, flew upwards like a sky-rocket, described a wide curve, and fell heavily about fifty yards out into the lake. Next moment Freydissa sprang from the hut and stood with clasped hands on the shore in speechless horror. Thorward immediately after came forth with a dark frown on his face, and walked away into the forest. Freydissa stood like a statue for some minutes, and then, seeing that the cat lay quite motionless, she turned, and, with a face that was deadly pale, reentered the hut.

"It was cruel," observed Karlsefin sadly.

"But salutary, perhaps," said Biarne.

"It may be so," rejoined the other; "but even if Thorward's end be a good one, a right end does not justify a wrong action. Ah! here comes sunshine. How goes it, Gudrid?"

Gudrid, who came forward at the moment, and knew nothing of what had occurred, said that she wanted Karlsefin's help, if he could spare time, in order to arrange some of the fixtures in their new home.

Assuring her that she herself was the most valuable "fixture" in the house, Karlsefin left his work and the two walked off together, while Biarne went down to the ship.

Meanwhile Thorward returned to his hut, where he found Freydissa alone, sitting on a box with her face buried in her hands. She did not move, so he sat down beside her with a subdued look.

"Freydissa," he said, "I'm sorry I did that. 'Twas cruel, 'twas hard; but it is done now, and can't be undone. Forgive me, lass, if you can."

She raised her head suddenly, and gazed at him with a flushed countenance.

"Thorward," she said with energy, "if you had come with any other tone or word I would have hated you with all the power of my heart —"

"And that's a strong power, Freydissa."

"It is. But now —"

She threw her arms round her husband's neck and kissed him. Thorward returned the kiss with the vigour of a man who is wont to give back more than he gets.

"Thanks, my girl," said he, rising, "thanks. That puts my heart at ease. As for the poor cat, she's beyond the influence of anger or repentance now; but trust me, Freydissa, I shall fetch you the handsomest cat that can be had for love or money in all Greenland, or Iceland; ay, even if I should have to make a special voyage to get hold of it."

Thus did Thorward and Freydissa fall out, and thus were they reconciled, on the first day in their new home in Vinland.

Talking this matter over with Thorward next day, Karlsefin took occasion to give his friend some sage advice.

"Depend upon it, Thorward," said he, "no good ever comes of quarrelling or violence, but, on the contrary, much evil. 'Tis well that you confessed your fault to her, else had she ever after held you in light esteem; because, although *she* deserved reproof, the cat did not deserve to be killed."

"Beshrew me!"

"Nay," interrupted Karlsefin, with a laugh, "*that* is the last thing you ought to say, seeing that you have had so much beshrewing already."

"Well, well," said Thorward, "thou art wonderfully smart at giving good advice."

"Would that I could say thou wert equally smart at taking it! However, I have hope of thee, Thorward. Come, let us go see what the nets have produced. I observe Hake and Heika rowing to land."

It was found that the fishermen had loaded their boat with magnificent trout of all sizes — some above five or six pounds' weight — besides a large quantity of excellent fish of other kinds, but not a single salmon had been taken. Nevertheless they had good reason to be content with their success, for the supply was sufficient to provide a hearty supper for the whole party, so that the first night in the new home — like the first night in the new land — was a merry one.

CHAPTER XI.

Settling Down — Hake Proves that his Arms, as well as his Legs, are Good — A Wonderful Fishing Incident, which Ends in a Scene Between Freydissa and Krake.

The little hamlet on the Vinland lake, which had been so long silent and deserted, resounded from that time forth with the voices and activities of energetic labourers, for these adventurous Norsemen had much to do before their new home could be made comfortable.

The forest and undergrowth around had to be cleared; the huts, of which there were six, had to be cleaned out, fitted up with new parchment in the windows — for there was no glass in those days — and new thatch on the roofs, besides being generally repaired; additional huts had to be built for the people, pens for the sheep, and stabling for the cattle, all of which implied felling and squaring timber, while the smaller articles of household furniture and fittings kept the people generally in full occupation. Of course a party had to be told off as hunters for the community, while another party were set to attend to the nets in the lake, and a third, under the special charge of Karlsefin, went out at intervals to scour the woods, with the double purpose of procuring food and investigating the character and resources of the new land.

In regard to this last these settlers had every reason to be satisfied. The country appeared to be boundless in extent, and was pleasantly diversified in form; the waters teemed with fish, the land was rich with verdure, and the forests swarmed with game, large and small.

One day Karlsefin and Biarne, attended by Hake and several men, went out for a ramble of exploration in the direction of the small river, or branch of the large river, mentioned in a previous chapter. Some of the party were armed with bows and arrows, others had spears, the leader and his friend carried short spears or javelins. All wore their swords and iron headpieces, and carried shields. Indeed, no party was ever allowed to go beyond the neighbourhood of the settlement without being fully armed, for although no natives had yet been seen, it was quite possible, nay, highly probable, that when they did appear, their arrival would be sudden and unexpected.

As they advanced, they heard a rustle of leaves behind a knoll, and next instant a large deer bounded across their path. Karlsefin hurled his spear with sudden violence, and grazed its back. Biarne flung his weapon and missed it. There was an exclamation of disappointment among the men, which, however, was turned into a cheer of satisfaction when Hake let fly an arrow and shot it through the heart. So forcibly was the shaft sent that it passed quite through the animal, and stood, bloodstained and quivering, in the stem of a tree beyond, while the deer leaped its own height into the air, and fell stone-dead upon the sward.

"A brave shot — excellently done!" exclaimed Karlsefin, turning to the young Scot with a look of admiration; "and not the first or second time I have seen thee do something of the same sort, from which I conclude that it is not chance, but that your hand is always quick, and your eye generally true. Is it not so?"

"I never miss my mark," said Hake.

"How now? you *never* miss your mark? It seems to me, young man, that though your air is modest, your heart and words are boastful."

"I never boast," replied Hake gravely.

"Say you so?" cried Karlsefin energetically, glancing round among the trees. "Come, clear yourself in this matter. See you yonder little bird on the topmost branch of that birch-tree that overhangs the stream? It is a plain object, well defined against the sky. Touch it if you can."

"That little bird," said Hake, without moving, "is not *my mark*. I never make a mark of the moon, nor yet of an object utterly beyond the compass of my shafts."

"Well, it *is* considerably out of range," returned Karlsefin, laughing; "but come, I will test you. See you the round knot on the stem of yonder pine? It is small truly, so small that I can barely see it, nevertheless it is not more than half a bow-shot off. Do you object to make *that* your mark?"

The words had scarcely left his lips when an arrow stood quivering in the knot referred to.

With an exclamation and look of surprise Karlsefin said it must have been a chance, and Biarne seemed inclined to hold the same opinion; but while they were yet speaking, Hake planted another arrow close by the side of the first.

"Once more, Hake," said Krake, who stood close behind the archer; "there's a saying in Ireland that there's good fortune in odd numbers: try it again."

The Scot readily complied, and sent a third shaft into the knot, with its head touching the heads of the other two arrows.

"Enough, enough, your arms are as good as your legs," said Karlsefin. "Ye are a valuable thrall, Hake, and Leif Ericsson has reason to be grateful to King Olaf of Norway for his gift. Here, two of you, sling that deer on a pole and bear it to Gudrid. Tell her how deftly it was brought down, and relate what you have seen just now. And hark 'ee," he added, with a peculiar smile, "there is no occasion to say anything about what occurred before the successful shot. It always adds to the value of a good story that it be briefly as well as pithily told, and disencumbered from unnecessary details. A wise tongue is that which knows when to wag and when to lie still. Come, Biarne, we will proceed in our examination of this stream."

Leaving behind them the two men who were to return to the huts with the deer, they proceeded down the banks of Little River, until they came to the pool where Hake and his brother had seen the salmon leap. On the way down, however, the leader had been convinced of the fact that many salmon were there, having seen several rise, and observed others passing over some of the pebbly shallows.

"It was here, was it not," asked Biarne, "that you and your brother saw the salmon leaping on the occasion of your first visit?"

"It was," replied Hake.

"At what part of the pool?"

"Just below the tail of the island, where the water is deep, and rolls with numberless oily ripples."

"Ha! a likely spot," said Karlsefin.

At that moment a salmon leaped out of the pool, as if to assure him that Hake's statement was true, and immediately afterwards another fish rose and flourished its fanlike tail, as if to make assurance doubly sure.

For some time they went about examining that part of the river, which, the reader will remember, has been described as being divided for some distance by a long island into two streams, which again united after spreading out into a broad rippling shallow. Here Biarne was very silent and very close in his inspection of the bed of the river, particularly at the top and lower end of the island.

"It appears to me as if some plan were rolling in your head, Biarne," said Karlsefin; "what may it be?"

"Truly a plan is forming in my brain. Simple enough too, only the details require consideration."

"Well, we must now return home, so we can discuss it on the way."

"You know of our custom in Iceland," said Biarne, as they retraced their steps, "in regard to a river which is similar to this in the matter of having two channels – they shut off the water from one channel and catch the fish when the bed is dry."

"Know it? Ay, I know it well; why, man, how comes it that this did not occur to me before? We will have it tried, and that without delay. What is worth doing at all is worth doing at once, unless it can be clearly shown that there shall be distinct gain by delay. As this cannot be shown on the present occasion we will begin tomorrow."

Accordingly, in pursuance of this resolve, Karlsefin went down to the island on Little River with a large party of men, and set to work. Biarne undertook to superintend what may be termed the engineering operations, and Thorward, who was a handy fellow, directed the mechanical details.

First of all, Biarne fixed on the spot at the top of the island where a dam was to be thrown across the right branch of the stream – that being the channel which was to be run dry – and planned the direction in which it was to be placed and the form it was to take. Then strong stakes were driven into the bed of the river all across the head of that branch. While this was being done Thorward marked off some tall straight trees in the forest, and set men to cut them down, while Karlsefin directed, and with his own hands aided, a party appointed to collect large piles of earth, sand, stones, mud, and branches, on the river's bank.

Although the men were numerous and active, the work was so extensive that it was sunset before all the stakes were driven, the first of the heavy logs laid down in the bed of the stream, and the rest of the material collected in readiness on the banks. Having completed these preparations they returned to the huts and made arrangements for a grand effort on the following day.

Early in the morning nearly the whole body of the people set off to Little River, leaving the settlement in charge of one or two men who chanced at that time to be sick. Of course Olaf was with them, armed with a huge iron hook fastened to the end of a stout pole. All the women also went, being quite as anxious as the men to witness the sport.

The island reached, Karlsefin divided his party into two bands. The smaller body, numbering about twenty-five, were stationed in the water at the lower end of the channel, at equal distances from each other, so as to extend from the tail of the island to the right bank of the stream. These carried strong poles about seven feet long, and were placed there to frighten back any fish that might attempt to rush down the river. The rest of the men went in a body to the dam, and there awaited orders.

When all was ready Karlsefin said to them — "My lads, if we would act well we must act together. Here is the plan on which you are to proceed. On getting the word from Biarne to begin, you will all set to work to dam up the water, right across from this bank to the head of the island. You see that we have already done the work in part, so that it only requires to be completed, and to have the centre gap stopped up. That will be the difficult point, for the great rush of water will be there, and you will have to do it quickly — to heave in the logs and stones and rubbish, not forgetting the branches and the turf, which will keep all together — as if your very lives depended on your speed. A certain number of you, who shall be told off presently, will do your best at the same time to deepen the channel of the other branch of the stream. When this is done you will have a little breathing space, for doubtless the water will take a little time to run off. You will take advantage of this time to get your hooks and poles and landing-nets in readiness. For the rest your own sense will guide you. Now, Biarne, tell off the men and go to work."

Reader, you should have seen the countenance of little Olaf Ericsson when all this was being said and done! Many a time had he seen nets hauled and fish taken, and often had he dreamt of netting whales and other sea-monsters, but never before had he imagined such a thing as laying the bed of a river dry; and his exuberant fancy depicted to him scenes which it is not possible to describe. His visage glowed, and his large blue eyes glared with excitement, while his little bosom heaved and his heart beat high with expectation.

This condition of course increased tenfold when he saw the men cast off more or less of their upper garments and spring to the work with the energy of lunatics. In his own small way he carried logs and branches and mud and stones till he was as dirty and dishevelled as the best of them; and when Gudrid looked horrified at him, and said that it would be next to impossible to clean him, he burst into such a fit of laughter that he lost his balance, fell head over heels into the river, which was only knee-deep at the place, and came out more than half washed in a moment!

"You see it won't be so difficult as you think," he cried, laughing and gasping when he emerged; "another plunge like that would make me quite clean, aunty."

"Ho! Olaf, were you after a salmon?" cried Swend, as he passed with a large log on his shoulder.

"Not I, Swend; it was a whale I was after."

"You don't say that, boy?" cried Krake, in a tone of admiration. "Was he a big one?"

"Oh! frightful — so big that — that — I couldn't see him all."

"Couldn't see him *at all?* Ah, then, he *was* a big one, sure. The things we can't see at all are always the most wonderful."

"Foolish boy," said Gudrid; "come, I will wring the water out of your clothes."

"'Tis hardly worth while, aunty," said Olaf, coming on shore; "I'll be as wet, as ever in a few minutes."

The careful Gudrid nevertheless wrung as much water out of his dripping garments as was possible without taking them off. By the time this was done the dam had been completed, and the men stood on the banks of the river wiping off and wringing out the superabundant mud and water from their clothes, besides getting ready hooks, nets, and staves. Some of the nets were several fathoms in length. Others were small bags fastened to wooden rings at the end of long poles.

Presently a shout was heard from the men at the lower end of the pool, and they were seen to use their staves smartly several times, as some of the fish, alarmed no doubt at the strange doings above, endeavoured to shoot down the river. Ere long the stony ground on which these men stood became a rippling shallow, and, soon afterwards, a neck of land connecting the lower end of the island with the shore. They therefore abandoned it and rejoined their comrades higher up. The fish were now imprisoned in a pool, retreat having been effectually cut off above and below, and the whole river diverted into the bed of its left branch.

As the water lowered it became obvious that the pool thus isolated was absolutely swarming with salmon, for they could be seen darting hither and thither in shoals, making for the deeper parts of the pool, and jostling one another under stones. Gradually little islets began to appear as the water continued to sink, and then the fish seemed to be seized with a panic. They shot like silver arrows from bank to bank — up the pool and down again, as if enjoying a piscatorial country dance, or, in blind flight, rushed clear out upon the pebbly islets, in half dozens at a time, where they leaped, slid, twirled, and bounded frantically, in what bore some resemblance to a piscatorial reel. Then, slipping into the water again, and recovering their fins and tails, they shot away to encounter similar misfortune elsewhere, or to thrust their noses under stones, and — entertaining the same delusive notions that are said to characterise the ostrich — imagine that they were not seen!

By degrees the islets enlarged until they joined here and there, and, finally, the state of things being inverted, the bed of the stream became a series of little ponds, which were absolutely boiling with fish — not unlike, as Krake remarked, to the boiling springs of Iceland, only that those boiled with heat instead of with living fish.

And now commenced a scene such as, unquestionably, had not been witnessed there since Vinland was created. The Norsemen were half mad with excitement. The women ran up and down the banks clapping their hands and shouting with delight, while Freydissa, unable to contain herself, cast appearances to the dogs, leaped among the men, and joined in the fray.

"The big pool first; this way, lads!" shouted Karlsefin, as he seized the end of a long net and dragged it towards the pool in question.

Twenty willing hands assisted. The net encircled the pool and was thrust in; men with poles forced one side of it down to the bottom, and the two ends were hauled upon might and main. At the same moment, other men went with hand nets to smaller pools, and, scooping up the fish, sent them writhing and struggling through the air towards the bank, where Gudrid, Thora, Astrid, Gunhild, Sigrid, and even timid Bertha, sought in vain to restrain their struggles and prevent them from wriggling back into the almost dry bed of the stream.

"Haul away with heart, men!" shouted Biarne, who was at one end of the large net.

Already the stout ropes were strained to the uttermost — at last the net came out bursting with salmon; more hands were hailed; it was run over the pebbles, up the bank, and onwards to a flat open spot, where, with a shout, it was emptied on the greensward.

Talk of silver bars! The simile is wretched. No simile is of any avail here. The brightest and freshest silver bars ever cast might shine as much as these salmon did, but they could not glitter so, for they could not wriggle and spring and tumble. They could not show that delicate pink which enhanced the silvery sheen so wondrously. They could not exhibit that vigorous life which told of firm flakes — suggestive of glorious meals for many a day to come. Pooh! even their intrinsic value could not suggest anything in this case — for all the silver bars that ever were coined on earth could not have purchased the appetites which made the mouths of these Norsemen to water, as they gazed in admiration on that vast hecatomb of splendid salmon! They absolutely danced round the fish — it might almost be said they danced *with* them — in triumphant glee!

"Come, come," cried Karlsefin loudly; "to work! to work! Ye may dance after that is done. Here, sweep this pool also."

With a cheer the men ran down the bank, and little Olaf followed, having already used his hook with such effect that he had pulled six large fish out of various holes and added them to the general pile.

"Take care, Olaf, that you don't fall in and get drowned," cried Biarne as he ran past.

"Hurrah!" shouted Olaf, with a flourish of his weapon, which made the narrowest possible miss of *cleeking* Tyrker by the nose.

"Have a care!" roared the Turk.

"You've much need to say that," replied Olaf, with a laugh, for Tyrker at that moment set his heel upon a salmon, fell, and rolled heavily down the bank.

But Tyrker was tough. He rose with a growl and a grin and ran on to join his comrades.

A second pool was netted, and with the like result. As the net was being dragged forth, Olaf saw that several fish had escaped. He struck in his hook at random, for the pools, being by that time a thick compound of mud and water, could not be seen into.

"Oh! I've got him!" he shouted, struggling with the handle of his hook, which jerked so violently that the sturdy little fellow was almost thrown to the ground.

"Hold on!" cried Thorward, running to his aid.

"Why, Olaf, what's this? Have a care. Not too fast. There. Hallo! — an eel."

And so it was — an enormous eel, that went twirling round the pole in wondrous fashion until it freed itself, and, after twisting round the limbs of Olaf and Thorward, who in vain sought to hold it fast, made off over the wet stones as if they were its native element, and slid into another large pool, where it disappeared.

"Never mind, Olaf," cried Thorward, with a laugh, "you'll catch hold of it again. Hook away at it, lad. Don't give."

A tremendous shriek arose from the women on the bank at this juncture.

"Oh! look! look at Freydissa!" cried Gunhild, pointing wildly to the river bed.

And there Freydissa stood — up to the armpits in mud and salmon!

Whether she had fallen in or been pushed in no one could tell, but unquestionably she *was* in, having gone in, too, head-foremost, so that, although she had struggled right-end up she reappeared coated with mud to an extent that might have suggested a sculptor's clay model — had sculptors been known to the Norsemen of those days.

There was an irresistible roar of laughter at first, and then loud expressions of condolence and sympathy, while a dozen strong, but wet and dirty, hands were stretched forth to the rescue.

"Here, lay hold of my hand, poor thing," cried Krake; "there, now, don't cry; it would only be wasting tears, with so much water on your face already."

If anything could have made Freydissa cry it would have been that remark, for it implied that she was inclined to weep, while nothing was further from her thoughts at that time.

She did, however, grasp Krake's hand, but instead of aiding herself by it to get out of the hole, she gave it such a vigorous and hearty pull that Krake went souse into the mud beside her. Before he could recover himself Freydissa had put her knee on his body, and, using him as a footrest, thrust him deeper down as she stepped out.

The delight with which this was hailed is beyond description, and many a year passed after that before men grew tired of twitting Krake about the pleasant mud-bath that had been given him by Freydissa on the occasion of the celebrated take of salmon at Little River in Vinland.

CHAPTER XII.

*Sage Converse Between Hake And Bertha —
Biarne Is Outwitted — A Monster is Slain, and Savages
Appear on the Scene.*

Not long after this an event occurred which produced great excitement in the new settlement; namely, the appearance of natives in the woods. It occurred under the following circumstances.

One morning Karlsefin gave orders for one of the exploring parties to be got ready to go out immediately. Karlsefin's plan from the beginning had been to class his men in two divisions. One half stayed at home to work, the other half searched the land — always taking care, however, not to travel so far but that they could return home in the evening. They were careful also not to wander far from each other. Sometimes Karlsefin went with the exploring party, at other times stayed at home to superintend the work there, while Biarne or Thorward filled his place. On the occasion in question Biarne was in charge.

Soon after the party had started, Hake, who was one of them, observed a female figure disappear round a copse near the shores of the lake. At that part they were about to strike off into the thick woods, so Hake went up to Biarne and asked leave to go along by the borders of the lake, saying that he could over-take the party again before they had reached the Willow Glen, a well-known rendezvous of the hunters and explorers of the colony.

"Go as thou wilt, Hake," replied Biarne; "only see to it that ye overtake us before noon, as I intend to go on a totally new path today."

The youth left with a light step, and, on overtaking the female, found, as he had expected, that it was Bertha.

"You wander far from home today," he said, with a deferential salutation, for Hake's bondage had not robbed him of his breeding.

"I love to wander," answered Bertha, blushing.

Poor Bertha, she could not help blushing. It was her unfortunate nature to do so. When her feelings were touched — ever so little — she blushed, and then she blushed *because* she had blushed, and blushed again to think herself so silly!

"I fear it may be somewhat dangerous to wander far," said Hake, stopping, for Bertha had stopped and seated herself on the stump of a fallen tree.

"Dangerous! Why so?"

"Why, because Skraelingers may find us out any day, and if they should come upon you unawares so far from home they might carry you off, and no one would be aware that you were gone until too late to pursue."

"I never thought of that," returned Bertha, with a slightly troubled look. "Well, I shall be more careful in future. But how come you to be wandering here alone, Hake? did I not hear your name called this morning among those appointed to go forth and search out what is good and beautiful and useful in the land?"

"Most true, Bertha, and I have gone forth, and not gone far, and yet have found something both good and beautiful and useful in the land."

"And pray what may that be?" asked the maiden, with a look of surprise.

Hake did not answer, but the expression of his eyes was more eloquent than speech.

"Nay, then," said Bertha, looking hastily away, and again blushing — as a matter of course! "I am no reader of riddles; and I hate riddles — they perplex me so. Besides, I never could find them out. But, Hake, has your party gone yet?"

"Yes, some time ago."

"And are you left behind?"

"No, I have leave to go by the margin of the lake."

"Then if you put off time talking with me you will not find it easy to overtake them; but I forgot: I suppose you count it an easy matter to overtake ordinary men?"

"I shall not find it difficult," replied the youth briefly; and then, perceiving that Bertha felt uneasy — apparently at the tenor of the conversation — he quietly changed it by remarking that he preferred to walk by the lake for several reasons, one of which was that it reminded him of Scotland.

"Ah, you profess to love Scotland very much," said Bertha archly, "but your brother evidently loves it more than you do."

"With good reason, too," replied Hake, "for it has given him a bride, and it had no such favours for me."

"Indeed! what is her name?" asked the maiden, with much interest.

"Emma."

"Poor Emma," sighed Bertha; "but I hope that Heika will be freed one day and return to his native land to wed Emma. Perchance by that time Scotland may smile upon you too, and give you cause to love it better."

"I love it well already," said Hake, with enthusiasm, "yet am I content to stay here."

"For shame, Hake! you do not deserve to be a Scot if you mean what you say."

"I mean what I say, yet do I deserve to be a Scot."

"Come, tell me, then, what this Scotland of yours is like. I suppose you deem it more beautiful than Iceland?"

The youth smiled. "It is not more *wonderful* than Iceland. I can say that with truth — but it is passing fair to look upon. It is a land of mountain and flood, of heath-clad braes and grassy knowes. Its mountain peaks rise bare and rugged to the skies, where lordly eagles soar. Its brawling burns in their infancy dash down these rugged steeps, but as they grow older flow on through many a hazel dell, where thrush and blackbird fill the woods with melody — through many flowering pastures, where cattle browse and lambkins skip on the sunny braes. Wild-fowl breed on its reedy lochs, and moor-fowl dwell on its heather hills. Its waters teem with the spotted trout and the royal salmon. Temperate breezes fan its cheeks, and beauty, in form and colour, revels everywhere. Its sons are lovers of their native land, and its daughters are wondrous fair."

"And yet it would seem," said Bertha, "that not one is fair enough for you?"

"Nay, Bertha, thy speech is hardly fair. The heart cannot command its affection," said Hake, with a smile, "but I regret it not."

"And where does Emma dwell?" asked Bertha.

"Beside my father, near the shores of Forth, not far from a noted town and castle that stand on the summit of a rocky ridge. It is named after Edwin, a Northumbrian king. A sweet romantic spot — my own dear native town. Beside it stands a mountain, which, those who have travelled in far southern lands tell us, bears some resemblance to a couching lion. But I never saw a lion, and know not what truth there is in that."

"You almost make me wish to see that land," said Bertha, with a sigh.

"I would you might see it and that it were my fortune to show it to you."

"That is not likely," said Bertha, with a little laugh.

"I know not. The most unlikely things happen, and often those that seem most likely do not come to pass. What more unlikely than that Karlsefin should forsake the religion of his fathers? Yet Karlsefin is now a Christian."

"Do you know, Hake, much about the nature of this new religion that has come amongst us, and made so many people change?" asked Bertha, with sudden earnestness.

"To say truth I don't know much about it. Only this do I know, that Karlsefin says the foundation of it is God and man united in Jesus Christ, and that the guiding principle of it is *love*. If so, it must be a sweet religion, and, as far as Karlsefin is concerned, it seems both good and true; but there are some of its professors whom I know whose guiding star is self — not love — which goes rather against it, methinks."

"You do not reason well, Hake; that is against the professors, not against the religion."

"True; but this religion is said to change those who profess it — what if they are not changed?"

"Why, then, they are *false* professors," said Bertha, with a smile.

"It may be so; I know not. But if you would have further light on the point, Karlsefin will gladly give it you."

"Well, I will go find him and inquire," said Bertha, rising; "I have kept you too long already from your comrades. Farewell."

"Farewell, Bertha," replied the youth, gazing after her as she tripped lightly away and disappeared behind a thicket. Then, turning into the woods, he went off at his utmost speed in the direction of the Willow Glen.

"Just in time, Hake," said Biarne, as the Scot approached; "we are about to start off westward today, and go as far inland as we can before dark. I have long had a desire to search out the land in that direction. From the distance of these blue ridges, the size of our lake and river, and other signs, I am of opinion that this is a great land — not an island."

"It may be so," replied Hake, looking round on the vast and beautiful landscape; "I should like well to traverse it. If a thrall may be permitted to remark, I would say that a spirited chief would explore somewhat farther than a day's march from home."

"Perchance a spirited chief might see fit to have his homestead put well in order before undertaking explorations for his amusement," replied Biarne, who was not much pleased with Hake's speech.

The Scot made no answer, and after that the party advanced to the westward, sometimes clearing their way through dense thickets, sometimes walking under the branching canopy of large trees, and frequently coming to more open places, in many of which there were little ponds swarming with wild-fowl.

Towards the afternoon they came to a rocky ridge which was crowned with trees. On the other side of it was a deep gorge, near the end of which some large animal was observed sitting on its haunches.

"Hist! a brown bear!" whispered Biarne.

The bear looked up and growled, for it had heard the approach of the party. Nevertheless it appeared to be in a sluggish as well as a sulky humour, for it gave no indication of any intention either to attack or run away, but sat still on its haunches swaying its huge head and shoulders to and fro, and glowering — as Krake said — horribly.

"A fierce monster truly!" observed Hake, fitting an arrow to his bow.

Biarne laid his hand on Hake's arm.

"Hast seen such a brute before?" he inquired.

"Not I," replied Hake.

"Wouldst like to see how the Skraelingers of Greenland treat the white bears of their land, when so few as only two men chance to meet one in this fashion?"

"I should like it well."

"Good — I will show you; but first I must explain the manner of it. When two Skraelingers see a bear they go up to him with spears. On approaching him they separate. One settles that he is to kill him, the other agrees to distract his attention. He who is to kill approaches on the side next the *heart*. His comrade goes up and pricks the bear on the *other* side. The bear turns full on him who wounds, exposes his heart-side, and is instantly thrust through by him who is to kill. Dost understand?"

"Perfectly," replied Hake.

"Perhaps you would like to join me in such an adventure, though of course there is some danger," said Biarne, who was very anxious to punish Hake for his late advice by giving him a good fright.

Hake smiled in a grim fashion, and taking a short spear from one of his comrades, looked at Biarne, pointed to the bear, and said:

"Come!"

They advanced together, Biarne also carrying a short spear, while their comrades stood on the ridge and looked on with much interest.

When Bruin saw the two men approach, he got up and showed himself to be an uncommonly large bear indeed, insomuch that Biarne glanced at Hake with some anxiety, and asked if he felt sure of himself, and wasn't frightened.

Hake laughed lightly, but made no other reply.

"Well, then, have a care, and see that ye be prompt in action. I will go to the left side and kill, being used to such work. Do you separate from me here and give him the prick on the right side. Don't get flurried. We must approach and act together. He seems inclined to meet us halfway, and must not be trifled with; and, harkee, prick him well, for methinks his hide will prove a tough one."

Hake nodded, and separated from his companion. Seeing this the bear stopped. It had been advancing with a rapidly increasing step, growling all the way, and with an extremely savage aspect, but this movement of the enemy perplexed it. Looking first on one side, and then on the other, it remained in a state of uncertainty as to which of the two it should attack. The enemy took advantage of this — both men ran in upon it. As they did so the bear rose on its hind legs, still glancing savagely from one side to the other, and in this position appearing a larger monster than it had seemed before.

"Give it him sharply!" cried Biarne, delaying his death-thrust till the proper time.

Hake stepped close up to the bear, and plunged his spear into its side with such vigorous good-will that it went straight through its heart, and came out at the other side just under the shoulder.

With a tremendous roar it fell and writhed on the ground in a dying state, while a loud cheer burst from the men on the ridge.

"Why did ye that?" cried Biarne fiercely, stepping up to Hake as though he would strike him. "Was it not arranged that *I* should kill him?"

"The Fates arranged it otherwise," answered the Scot. "I felt afraid that my fears might weaken my arm. To make sure, I gave him a good thrust. Besides, did you not tell me that his hide was tough, and advise me to prick him well?"

Hake looked so innocent, and spoke so gently, that Biarne, who was a good-natured fellow, laughed in spite of himself as he said —

"Truly thou didst prick him to some purpose. Well, I do not grudge thee the honour, and unquestionably it was deftly done. Here, two of you, stay behind and skin this fellow. Cut off the best parts of the meat also. Bears of this kind are not bad for food, I dare say. We will go on a little farther, and return to you in a short time."

Saying this Biarne resumed his march, followed by the rest of the men.

They had not gone far, however, when one of the party uttered a sudden exclamation, and pointed to footprints on a soft part of the ground.

"Perhaps the bear's footprints," said one.

"Too small and narrow for that," remarked another.

"We shall trace them till we come to soft ground and make certain," said Biarne.

They did so, and after walking a hundred yards or so came to a sandy piece, where the footprints were so clearly defined that there remained no doubt they were those of a man. That the marks had not been made by any wandering member of their own band, was evident also from the form of the sole of the shoe, as indicated by the prints.

"Now must we be ready to meet with men who may be foes, although I hope they shall turn out to be friends," said Biarne. "Come, Hake, there may be need for haste, therefore do you hie back before us and inform Karlsefin what we have seen. We will follow as swiftly as may be, and fetch your bear along with us."

Hake started off at a smart run without a word of reply, and never paused a moment until he reached the hamlet, which he found in a considerable state of confusion and excitement.

"What now?" demanded Karlsefin as Hake came forward.

"Strange footprints have been seen, and —"

"Strange footprints!" exclaimed Karlsefin. "Why, man, strange *men* have been seen by us, so I have stranger news to tell than thou. Biarne is returning, of course?"

"He is, with all the men, as fast as he can."

"That's well. Now, Hake, get your weapons ready and help the men to make preparations for the reception of the strangers. I go to set the ship in order."

Hake found, on inquiry, that one of a wood-cutting party having strayed a little way beyond his fellows, but not far from the hamlet, had come suddenly on a native who was crouching behind a rock and gazing intently at the wood-cutters. He was at the moment fitting an arrow to the string of a short bow which he carried, and was so absorbed that he did not at first observe the Norseman. The instant he saw him, however, he sprang up and discharged an arrow, which the other avoided. The savage immediately turned to fly, but the Norseman sprang after him and struck him to the ground. At the same instant a dozen or more savages rushed from the woods to the rescue, and the Norseman immediately ran back to his comrades. More savages appeared, and the Norsemen, seeing that they were greatly outnumbered, retreated to the hamlet. They were not followed by the savages, but there could be no doubt that now the colony had been discovered they were certain to receive a visit from them. Whether that visit was likely to be amicable or otherwise remained to be seen.

Meanwhile Karlsefin and his men did their best to put the place in a state of defence. A breastwork of large trees, which had been long ago thrown all round the hamlet, was repaired and strengthened before dark, and sentinels were posted around in all directions, so that when Biarne arrived, somewhat late at night, he was amused as well as gratified to find that unseen though well-known voices challenged him several times as he drew near home, and that, finally, a rude but effectual barrier stopped him altogether, until a friend from within conducted him to the proper entrance.

Thus the night passed away without anything transpiring, and at last the longed-for dawn appeared.

CHAPTER XIII.

A Great but Comparatively Bloodless Fight, Which Ends Peculiarly, and with Singular Results.

When the sun rose above the trees next day, Karlsefin began to think that the natives had left the place, for there was no sign of them anywhere, and he was about to issue from behind his defences and go out to reconnoitre, when a man came running from the ship shouting "Skraelingers!"

It is probable that by that term he meant savages generally, because the men who had been seen bore very little resemblance to the hairy savages of Greenland. They were taller, though not stouter, and clothed in well-dressed skins of animals, with many bright colours about them. But whatever they were, the sensation they created among the Norsemen was considerable, for it was found, on going to the margin of the lake, that they were now approaching in canoes by water. This at once accounted for the delay in their appearance.

That their intentions were hostile was plain from the fact that the canoes came on abreast of each other in regular order, while the men shouted fiercely and brandished their weapons. There could not have been fewer than three or four hundred of them.

Karlsefin saw at once that his only chance of saving the ship was to go on board of it and fight on the water.

"Get on board all of you," he cried to those who stood beside him. "Away, Biarne, Thorward, call in the outposts and have them on board without delay. Here, Swend, Heika, Tyrker, station the men as they arrive. Get up the war-screens round the sides of the ship; and, harkee, give orders that the men use their weapons as little as possible, and spare life. I shall want you on the poop, Hake. See that no one throws down the gangway or loosens the ropes till the order is given. I will see to the women. Away!"

Each man ran with speed to obey, for the case was urgent.

Karlsefin found the women, with Olaf, assembled in the large house waiting for orders.

"Come," he cried; "not a moment to be lost. Give me your hand, Gudrid."

He seized it as he spoke, and hurried down to the ship, where the men were already trooping on board as fast as they could. The women were soon put under cover out of the reach of missiles, and in a few minutes more all were on board. Of course the cattle, and live stock generally, being scattered about the hamlet, were left to their fate. Then the ropes were cast loose, the gangway was thrown down, the ship was pushed out into the bay, and the anchor let go.

All this had barely been accomplished when the canoes came sweeping round the nearest point of land and made straight for the ship, with the foam curling at their bows.

Then Karlsefin's voice rose loud and clear as he issued his final commands.

"My lads," he cried, "remember my orders about using your weapons as little as possible. Be careful to throw only the smaller stones. Kill no one if you can avoid it, but give as many of them the toothache as you can. We must be friends with these people if we are to live in peace here, and that won't be possible if we kill many of them."

The men answered with a great shout, mingled with some laughter, which latter was such a strange sound to hear on the eve of an engagement, that the savages stopped short for a moment. But soon they came on again with redoubled impetuosity.

No sooner were they within range than the Norsemen rose up in a body and hurled a shower of stones at them. They were evidently not prepared for such artillery, for they again stepped short, but after a brief pause once more advanced. Three times did they receive a shower of stones before getting alongside. These hurt many, but disabled none, for, according to orders, no heavy stones were used. When within a few yards of the ship the canoes surrounded her and lay still while the savages began to discharge arrows in abundance. The Norsemen kept well behind the shields, which formed a screen round the ship, and replied with stones, only a few of the best marksmen using arrows, when they saw a chance to wound without killing any of the foe.

Karlsefin stood exposed on the high poop with Hake and Heika beside him. All three wore iron helmets, and the leader protected himself with his shield. Heika devoted his attention to warding off missiles from his brother, who, having to use his bow, could not manage a shield.

Presently the savages made a grand assault. But the moment they came to close quarters they found that they had to cope with a formidable foe, for the Norsemen, using only bludgeons, knocked them down whenever they came within reach, and one or two of the boldest among them who succeeded in clambering up the sides were seized by the legs and arms and hurled back into the lake as if they had been mere puppets.

Thus beaten off they continued the arrow shower, and some of the Norsemen were wounded.

All this time Karlsefin stood close to the helm, looking sharply about him, and whenever he saw a savage who was bolder and stouter than his fellows, he made Hake send an arrow through his right hand. In this way most of the best men among them were sent off howling with pain, and for the time disabled. Suddenly a very tall active savage succeeded in clambering up by the rudder unobserved, and leaping on the poop, stood behind Karlsefin with uplifted club. Karlsefin, without turning quite round, gave him a back-handed slap under the left ear and sent him flying overboard. He fell into a canoe in his descent and sank it.

At this juncture a number of the canoes were detached from the fight, and Karlsefin observed, with much anxiety, that the savages were going to ransack the houses.

"Would that I were on shore with twenty of my best men!" he said bitterly. "Send a shaft, Hake, at yonder fellow who leads. It is out of range, I fear, but — ha! well hit!" he exclaimed, on seeing an arrow from Hake's prompt hand strike the man full in the back. The savage fell, and his comrades crowded round him.

By that time others of the canoes had put ashore, and their owners ran up to the crowd who surrounded the fallen leader.

At this moment an incident occurred which put a most unexpected termination to the fight.

For a considerable time Olaf's huge pet, Blackie, had viewed the fight with calm indifference from the heart of a thicket close by, in which he chanced to be cooling himself at the time. Now, it happened that one of the many arrows which were discharged by the savages on the offshore side of the ship glanced from a neighbouring tree and hit the bull on the flank. Associating the pain resulting therefrom with the group of savages before him, Blackie at once elevated his tail, lowered his head, and, with a bellow that would have shamed a thousand trumpets, charged furiously down upon the foe.

Horror-struck is but a feeble word to indicate the feelings of that foe! Although, no doubt, some of them might have heard of, perhaps seen, the ponderous and comparatively quiet bison of the Western prairies, none of them had ever imagined anything so awful as a little black bull with tremendous horns, blood-red nostrils, flashing eyes, and catlike activity. One awe-struck look they gave it, and then fled howling into the woods. The sounds were so startling that those of the enemy still round the ship were panic-stricken and made off by water as fast as their fellows had escaped by land, leaving the Norsemen victorious!

"Hurrah for Blackie!" shouted Olaf, who was wild with excitement and delight.

The cheer thus claimed was given with intense enthusiasm, and then the ship was rowed back to the shore.

Here a great prize was found, in the shape of twenty canoes, which had been left by the party that had fled to the woods. These were carried carefully up to the hamlet and placed in security. On the way up another prize was found, which afterwards turned out to be of the utmost importance. This was the wounded savage, who had been forsaken by his friends when the bull charged, and who only escaped from the horns of that infuriated animal by lying quite motionless beside a log which fortunately chanced to be near him.

"Take care, Krake; lift him gently," said Biarne, as he came up and found that worthy turning the poor savage over as if he had been already a dead carcase. "Let me see; the arrow does not seem to have gone far in. He'll recover, perhaps. Come, Hake and Swend, lift his shoulders, and run, Olaf, tell Astrid or one of the other women to — ha! Bertha, well met. Here is a subject for your care. You are a good nurse, I'm told."

"I try to be," replied Bertha.

"She who tries to be is sure to be," returned Biarne; "nursing, like fighting, is an art, and must be acquired; though, to say truth, some folk seem born to learn more rapidly than others, whether as regards nursing or fighting. Have the poor fellow into the house, and do your best for him, Bertha."

While this was being said the native was lying on his back, looking very stern, but pale. It is probable that the poor wretch expected to be taken off summarily to have his eyes punched out, or to be roasted alive – for the natives of Vinland, no doubt, expected from their foes, in those days, the same treatment that they accorded to them – although the Saga says nothing to that effect. When, therefore, he was put into a comfortable bed, had his wound dressed, and an agreeable though strange drink given to him by the fair hands of Bertha, the expression of his countenance seemed to imply that he believed himself to have passed from earth and got into the happy hunting-grounds of his fathers. If so, the increasing pain of his wound must have perplexed him not a little. However, it is due to him to say that he bore his surprises and pains with the uncomplaining resignation of a Stoic.

Karlsefin employed the remainder of that day in strengthening his defences and connecting them in such a way with that part of the shore where his vessel lay, that there would be no possibility of surrounding him in the event of future hostilities.

This accomplished, he organised his men into three bands, which were to be commanded respectively by Biarne, Thorward, and himself. These were appointed to particular localities and duties in the little fortress – for it was now almost entitled to such an appellation. When night drew on, sentinels were posted as before. But there was no alarm during the night. The savages appeared to have had enough of fighting for that time, and next morning's sun arose, as it was wont to do, on a peaceful scene.

"Do you think they will attack us again?" asked Gudrid as she sat at breakfast.

"I think not," replied her husband. "They cannot but know that we are troublesome fellows to deal with, even when taken unawares."

"I hope they won't go off without giving us a chance to show that we desire to be friendly," observed Thorward.

"No fear of that," said Biarne; "we have got one of their chiefs – at least I think he is so, for he looks like one – and that is as good as a string tied to their great toe."

"By the way, how *is* the chief, Bertha?" asked Karlsefin.

"Much better this morning. He slept well, and is even now sitting up on his bed. He looked so well, indeed, that I took the precaution to fasten the door on the outside when I left him just now."

"Ha! Didst fasten the window, wench?" cried Thorward, starting up and hastening from the room.

"Truly, no," remarked the girl, with a somewhat confused look; "I never thought of the window."

Thorward returned a minute later with a peculiar smile.

"He's all safe," said he; "I peeped through a small shot-hole in the parchment, and saw him sitting there meditating as deeply as if he hoped to meditate himself out of his prison."

"Not a difficult thing to do that," said Karlsefin. "I suspect that most prisoners manage to free themselves in that way pretty often! But who comes here in such hot haste? Why, Swend, what's i' the wind now?"

"The Skraelingers are coming," said he. "They come unarmed, and only ten of them."

"Oho! good," exclaimed Karlsefin, rising. "Come, methinks I see my way out of this difficulty. Fetch me nine of our smartest men, Biarne. I will go forth with them unarmed, to meet those messengers of peace. You and Thorward will keep the defences, to be ready for any emergency. Let the Scottish brothers be among the nine."

When the selected men had assembled, their leader took them aside and conferred with them for a few minutes, after which he led them towards that part of the defences nearest the woods, when they saw the ten natives approaching holding up their empty hands and making other demonstrations of a peaceful nature. Far away on the heights in the background the whole army of savages could be seen watching the proceedings of their messengers.

When these latter had come within about a hundred yards of the hamlet, they selected a low grassy knoll in an open spot, in full view of both parties. Here they sat down in a row and made signs to the Norsemen to approach.

"Now, lads, we will accept their invitation," said Karlsefin; "follow me."

With that he passed through the opening in the defences, holding up his hands as he went to show that he was unarmed, his followers doing the same. Karlsefin went up to the native who appeared to be the chief of the band, and, with a bland smile, took his hand gently and shook it.

If the savage did not understand the shake of the hand, he evidently understood the smile, for he returned it and sat down again. Karlsefin and his men did the same, and for a few moments the two rows of men sat looking benignantly at one another in silence. The savage chief then spoke. Of course Karlsefin shook his head and touched his ear, brow, and lips, by way of intimating that he heard, but could neither understand nor reply. He then spoke Norse, with similar results. After that the savage leader rose up, touched his back, and fell down as if badly wounded. Upon this one of his comrades rose, pointed to the hamlet, lifted the wounded man in his arms, carried him behind his companions, and laid him down exclaiming "Utway!" whereupon another savage took a small bundle of beautiful furs from the ground, and laid them at the feet of Karlsefin with much humility.

"Sure he wants to buy back the wounded chief with these furs," said Krake, who found it difficult to conceal his amusement at all this dumb show.

"No doubt of it, and I suppose Utway is his name," replied Karlsefin; "but my object is to get them inside the defences, in order to show them that when we have them in our power we will treat them well. If I let their chief go for these furs nothing will have been gained."

Karlsefin now did his best, by means of signs and encouraging looks, to induce the ten natives to enter the hamlet, but no persuasion would induce them to do this. They held stoutly to their original proposition, and kept constantly pointing to the bundle of furs and going through the pantomime with the wounded man. At last Karlsefin appeared to agree to their proposal.

"Now, Heika and Hake," said he, "nothing remains to be done but to try the plan I have described to you. Up, and bring the wounded chief hither without delay."

The two men obeyed, and in a few minutes were seen reissuing from the fortress bearing a litter between them, on which lay the wounded chief with a blanket thrown over him, only his head being visible. Carrying him towards the row of natives, the brothers laid the burden at their feet as they sat still on the ground looking on with great interest. Karlsefin removed the blanket, and revealed the chief bound hand and foot. Something covered by another blanket lay at his side. Karlsefin took hold of this. As he did so the Norsemen rose. The blanket was cast off, and ten naked swords were revealed, which were instantly grasped by ten stalwart arms, and flashed with the speed of light over the ten native heads!

Taken thus by surprise they remained seated, and, supposing that to move would be the signal for instant death, they were perfectly motionless, though the colour of their countenances revealed to some extent the state of their feelings.

A terrific yell from the distant heights told that the deed had been noticed and understood. It was answered by a shout from the Norsemen as they issued from their fortress, secured their prisoners, and carried them within the defences. In a few minutes thereafter not a man was to be seen on the heights, and the region became as silent and apparently as deserted as it had been before the advent of the savages.

"Now then, Biarne, get the things ready. Is the kettle boiling?" said Karlsefin.

"All is prepared," answered Biarne.

"'Tis well. We must carry out our plan as quickly as may be," rejoined Karlsefin. "We may be sure that these fellows have only retired behind the heights to hold a council of war, and, in their present humour, it won't be long before they come on to make an effort to retaliate upon us for our supposed treachery."

The ten men were conveyed to the largest house in the hamlet, and there ranged in a row against the wall. They looked very grave, but were firm and stern. Evidently they imagined that death by torture was to be their doom, and had braced themselves up to die like brave men in the presence of their foes.

Karlsefin hastened to relieve them from this state of mind as quickly as possible. He placed before them ten plates of splendid boiled salmon. They regarded this proceeding with some surprise, but shook their heads and refused to eat. Doubtless their appetites were not good at the time!

"Fetch the wounded chief hither," said Karlsefin, "and tell Bertha that she is wanted."

When the wounded man was carried in and seated opposite to his comrades, a box being placed for him to lean against, Karlsefin said to Bertha — "Now, lass, do thy best to induce the chief to show his friends how to eat. He has had some experience of you, and will doubtless understand."

With a winning smile that would have compelled any susceptible man to eat or drink, or do anything else that he was bid whether inclined or not, Bertha put a plate of salmon before the chief and made signs to him to eat. He smiled in return, and began at once. Then Bertha patted him on the shoulder, pointed to the ten prisoners, and made signs again. The chief smiled intelligently, and spoke to his companions. He evidently said more than was necessary to order them to eat, for their faces brightened perceptibly, and they commenced dinner in these peculiar circumstances without delay.

It was clear that their appetites had not been much impaired by alarm, for the salmon disappeared in a twinkling. Then Karlsefin ordered ten plates of fried venison to be placed before them, which was done, and they applied themselves to the consumption of this with equal relish. Having concluded the repast, each man received a can of warm water and milk, highly sweetened with sugar. At first they took a doubtful sip of this, and looked at each other in surprise. It was a new sensation! One of them smacked his lips; the rest said "Waugh!" nodded their heads, and drained their cans to the bottom at a single draught; after which, observing that there was some sediment left, they scraped it out with their fingers and sucked them.

"So far that is satisfactory," said Karlsefin, with a smile. "Now, Biarne — the gifts."

A wooden tray was now brought, on which lay a variety of silver brooches, rings, and other baubles. These were distributed to the prisoners. Last of all, each received a yard of bright-coloured cloth, and then they were ordered by signs to rise.

They obeyed with alacrity, and were led out of the house, at the door of which they found a litter similar to the one which they had seen before. It was simply a blanket fastened to two long poles, and rolled round them so as to form a couch of about a yard in width. On this the wounded chief was laid, and two of the natives were ordered to grasp the ends of the poles and raise him. They did so, and were conducted by the Norsemen in single file out into the forest. Here, to their intense surprise, Karlsefin shook hands with them all very kindly, and then, going back with his men to the fortress, left them to return to their kindred!

Karlsefin remarked quietly to Biarne, as he went along, that one of the precepts of the new religion, which he had remembered well, because it seemed to him so very wise, was, that men should always try to "overcome evil with good."

Thus was established a warm friendship between the natives of Vinland and the Norsemen; a friendship which might have lasted for ever — to the great modification, no doubt, of American history — had not unfortunate circumstances intervened to break it up. As it was, it lasted for a considerable time.

CHAPTER XIV.

The First American Fur Traders — Strange Devices — Anxious Times and Pleasant Discoveries.

The business of the colony progressed admirably after this. A large house was erected, with a central hall and numerous sleeping-rooms or closets off it, where all the chief people dwelt together, and a number of the men messed daily. Grass was found in abundance, and a large quantity of this was cut and stacked for winter use, although there was good reason to believe that the winter would be so mild that the cattle might be left out to forage for themselves. Salmon were also caught in great numbers, not only in Little River but in the main stream, and in the lake at their very doors. What they did not consume was dried, smoked, and stored. Besides this, a large quantity of fine timber was felled, squared, cut into lengths, and made suitable for exportation. Eggs were found on the islands offshore, and feathers collected, so that early in the summer they had more than enough wherewith to load the ship. Among other discoveries they found grain growing wild. The Saga-writers have called it wheat, but it is open to question whether it was not wild rice, of which large quantities grow in the uninhabited parts of America at the present time. They also found a beautiful kind of wood, called massurwood, of which samples were sent to Greenland and Norway; but what this wood really was we cannot tell.

Meanwhile an extensive traffic in valuable furs was commenced with the natives, who were more than satisfied with the scraps of bright cloth, beads, and other trifling ornaments they received in exchange for them. Some of the natives wanted to purchase weapons with their furs, but Karlsefin would not allow this. At first the Norsemen gave their cloth and other wares in exchange with liberal hand, cutting the bright cloth into stripes of three or four inches in breadth; but they soon found that at this rate their supplies would become exhausted too early in the year. They therefore reduced their prices, and began to give stripes of cloth only two inches in width, and at last reduced the measure to one inch, for furs that had previously fetched four. But the unsophisticated natives were quite content with the change, and appeared to enjoy nothing so much as to twist these stripes of cloth into their long black hair.

One day Karlsefin said to Gudrid that he had a new plan in his head.

"What is that?" said she.

"I think that our goods are going away too fast, so I mean to try if these Skraelingers will give their furs for dairy produce. We have a good deal of that, and can spare some."

"I don't know how Astrid will like that," she said, laughing. "You know she has charge of the dairy, and is very proud of it."

"That is well, Gudrid, for Astrid will be all the more pleased to have her produce turned to such good account. Milk is pleasant to the throat, and cream delights the tongue. Methinks these fellows will be tempted by it."

"Would they not like beer better?"

"Beer!" cried Karlsefin, with a shout of laughter. "You should have seen the faces they made, and the way they spat it out, the only time they were asked to taste it. Biarne was very keen to let them try it, and I did not object, for I partly expected some such result. No, no, a man must *learn* to like beer. Nature teaches him to like milk. But go, tell Astrid to fill twenty cans with milk, and twenty small cups with good cream. Let her also set out twenty cakes, with a pat of fresh butter and a lump of cheese on each. Let her spread all on the table in the great hall, and see that she does it speedily. I will go and fetch the company to this feast."

He left the room as he spoke, and in less than an hour his orders had been executed. When he entered the hall a short time afterwards, followed by twenty natives, he found everything prepared according to his directions.

That he was correct in his expectation was clearly proved ere many minutes had passed, for the twenty natives raised their forty eyes, and looked on each other with rapturous delight when they tasted the good things. They finished them in a twinkling, and then wished for more; but it is only justice to their good-breeding and self-restraint to add that they did not *ask* for more! From that day nothing would please them but that they should have dairy produce for their furs.

Some time after this Karlsefin was walking, one afternoon, on the shores of the lake with Thorward. He suddenly asked him how he should like to take a trip to Greenland.

"I should like it well," replied Thorward.

"Then if you will go in charge of the *Snake* I should be pleased," said the other, "for we have collected more than enough of merchandise to fill her, and if you set sail at once you will have time to bring back a cargo of such things as we need before autumn comes to an end."

"I will go," said Thorward, "tomorrow, if you choose."

"Nay, not quite so fast. The ship is only half loaded yet; but in a day or two she will be ready. There are two things I am anxious you should manage. One is to persuade Leif Ericsson to come and visit us — if he will not come to stay with us. The other is to tempt as many married men as you can to come over and join us — especially those men who chance to have a good many daughters, for we would be the better of a few more busy little hands, fair faces, and silvery tones in this beautiful Vinland of ours."

"I will do what I can," replied Thorward, "and I would advise that Olaf should go with me, that his glowing descriptions may tempt his father to come."

"Nay; that would spoil all," objected Karlsefin, "for, having had a sight of his son he would be content to let him come back alone. No, no; we will keep Olaf here as a bait to tempt him. But go now and make your arrangements, for you set sail as soon as the ship is ready."

Not long after that the *Snake* left her anchorage with a full cargo, rowed down the river, hoisted sail, and bore away for Greenland.

While she was gone an event of deep and absorbing interest occurred in

Vinland.

One fine morning in autumn the heart of the entire hamlet was moved by the sound of a new voice! It was not a musical voice — rather squawky, indeed, than otherwise — and it was a feeble voice, that told of utter helplessness. In short, a son had been born to Karlsefin and Gudrid, and they called him Snorro. We record it with regret — for it went a long way to prove that, in regard to sweet sounds, Karlsefin and his wife were destitute of taste. It is our business, however, to record facts rather than to carp at them, therefore we let Snorro pass without further comment.

The little body that was attached to the little voice, although far from beautiful at first, was an object of intense affection to the parents, and of regard, almost amounting to veneration, to the rugged men by whom it was surrounded. Bertha declared enthusiastically that it was "perfectly lovely," although it was obvious to all unprejudiced eyes that it resembled nothing so much as a piece of wrinkled beef of bad colour! Astrid declared that it had "such a wise look," despite the evident fact that its expression was little short of idiotical! Karlsefin said nothing, but he smiled a good deal, and chucked it under the place where its chin ought to have been with his great forefinger in a timid way.

But when Snorro was deemed sufficiently far advanced in life to be handed out for public exhibition, then it was that the greatest number of falsehoods were uttered, with the quietest deliberation, although, to say truth, the greater number of the men said nothing, but contented themselves with taking the infant in their big rough hands as delicately as if they thought it was a bubble, and feared that it might burst and leave nothing to be handed back to Thora, who acted the part of nurse. Others merely ventured to look at it silently with their hairy lips parted and their huge eyes gazing in blank admiration.

Perhaps Krake made the most original remark in reference to the newcomer. "Ah," said he quite seriously, touching its cheek as softly as though he half feared it would bite, "only to think that myself was like *that* once!"

This was received with a shout of laughter, so loud that little Snorro was startled.

"Ah, then," cried Krake, with a look of great alarm, "what is it going to do?"

This question was occasioned by the sudden change on the infant's countenance, which became, if possible, redder than before, and puckered up into such a complicated series of wrinkles that all semblance to humanity was well-nigh lost. Suddenly a hole opened on the surface and a feeble squall came forth!

"Oh, you wicked men!" cried Thora, snatching the infant indignantly from them and hurrying back into the house.

"'Tis a sweet child," observed Swend tenderly, as he and his comrades sauntered away.

"You must have a good opinion of yourself, Krake," said Tyrker, "to fancy that you were once like it."

"So I have," replied Krake. "It's what my father had before me. It lies in the family, you see, and with good reason too, for we were the best of company, not to mention fighting. It was always said that we were uncommonly fine infants, though a trifle big and noisy for the peace of our neighbourhood — quite like Turks in that way, I believe!"

"I doubt it not, Krake," said Biarne, who came up in time to hear the concluding remark; "and since you are such a noisy fellow I am going to send you on an expedition in search of these vines, that seem to me to have rooted themselves out of the land and fled, from mere spite, since Leif named it Vinland. There is but one quarter that I can think of now which has not yet been explored; you may take a party of men, and let Tyrker go too; as he discovered them on his first visit, the stupid fellow ought to have rediscovered them long before now. You can discuss by the way the little matter you have in hand — only see that you don't fall out about it."

Thus instructed, Krake organised a party, and set off to search for the celebrated vines, which, as Biarne said, had not up to that time been found.

That day they searched far and wide without success. Then they sat down to rest and eat. While thus engaged, Krake and Tyrker returned to the subject of the reported noisiness of Turks, and the former became so caustic in his jests that the irascible little Tyrker lost temper, much to the amusement of his comrades.

After refreshing themselves, the explorers again set out and came to a part of the country which was broken up and beautifully diversified by rocky eminences crowned with trees, and shady hollows carpeted with wild-flowers. It was difficult here to decide as to which of the innumerable valleys or hollows they should traverse; they therefore sat down again for a little to consult, but the consultation soon became a discussion, and Krake, whose spirit of fun had got the better of him, gradually edged the talk round until it came again, quite in a natural way, to the Turks. At last Tyrker became so angry that he started up, declared he would follow the party no longer, plunged into a thicket and disappeared.

He was followed by a shout of laughter, and then the others, rising, resumed their search, not doubting that their irate companion would ere long rejoin them.

But Tyrker did not join them, and when evening drew on apace they became anxious, gave up the search for vines, and went about looking for him. At last it became too dark for them to continue the search, and they were obliged to return home without their comrade.

On leaving them Tyrker had no definite idea what he meant to do or where he meant to go. He just walked straight before him in high dudgeon, taking no notice of the route by which he journeyed, or the flight of time. At length he awoke from his absent condition of mind and looked up. A vast amphitheatre of wooded hills surrounded him, and there, in the heart of a secluded dell, under a clump of trees, were the long sought and much-desired vines!

For some time Tyrker stood gazing at them in silent admiration and delight. He rubbed his eyes and looked again. Yes; there could be no question as to their reality. There hung the rich purple clusters such as he had seen on his first visit to Vinland, and such as he had been wont to see in his own land in days long gone by. He pinched himself, pulled his hair, punched his eyeballs, but no — all that failed to awaken him; from which circumstance he naturally came to the conclusion that he was awake already. He then uttered a wild, probably a Turkish, cheer, and rushed upon the spoil.

Filling both hands with the fruit he crammed his mouth full. Then he raised his eyes upwards in ecstasy and did it again. He repeated it! After which he paused to sigh, and leaped up to cheer and sat down again to — guzzle! Pardon the word, good reader, it is appropriate, for there is no disguising the fact that Tyrker was a tremendous glutton, and did not care a fig — or a grape — for appearances.

After eating for a long time he was satisfied and sat down to rest. By that time the shades of evening were falling. They proved to be soporific, for he gradually reclined backwards on the green turf and fell asleep, surrounded by and partially covered with grapes, like a drunken and disorderly Bacchus.

Now Tyrker was a man in robust health; full of energy and high spirits. Sleep therefore was to him a process which, once begun, continued till morning. Even the puckered little Snorro did not rest more soundly in his kneading-trough crib than did Tyrker on the greensward under his vinous canopy.

When next he opened his eyes, groaned, rolled over, sat up, and yawned, the sun was beginning to peep above the eastern sea.

"Ho!" exclaimed Tyrker. "I have forgot myself." To refresh his memory he scratched his head and shook it; then he raised his eyes, saw the grapes, leaped up and burst into a fit of joyous laughter.

Thereafter he again sat down and breakfasted, after which he filled his cap, his wallet, his various pockets, the breast of his coat — every available compartment, in fact, outside as well as in — with grapes, and hastened homeward at his utmost speed in order to communicate the joyful news to his comrades.

Now the disappearance of Tyrker had caused no small amount of anxiety to his friends at the hamlet, especially to Karlsefin, who was very fond of him, and who feared that his strength might have given way, or that he had fallen into the hands of savages or under the paws of bears. He sat up the greater part of the night watching and hoping for his return, and when the first grey light of dawn appeared he called up a number of the men, and, dividing them into several bands, organised a systematic search.

Placing himself at the head of one band he went off in the direction in which, from Krake's account of what had taken place, it seemed most probable that Tyrker might be found. They advanced so rapidly that when the sun rose they had got to within a mile or so of the spot where Krake and his party had given up their search on the previous evening. Thus it came to pass that before the red sun had ascended the eastern sky by much more than his own height, Karlsefin and Tyrker met face to face in a narrow gorge.

They stopped and gazed at each other for a few moments in silence, Karlsefin in astonishment as well — and no wonder, for the figure that stood before him was a passing strange one. To behold Tyrker thus dishevelled and besmeared was surprising enough, but to see him with grapes and vine-leaves stuffed all about him and twined all round him was absolutely astounding. His behaviour was little less so, for, clapping his hands to his sides, he shut his eyes, opened his big mouth, and burst into an uproarious fit of laughter.

The men who came up at that moment did so also for laughter is catching.

"Why, Tyrker, where have you been?" demanded Karlsefin.

"Grapes!" shouted Tyrker, and laughed again.

"Are these grapes?" asked Karlsefin, regarding the fruit with much interest.

"Ay, grapes! vines! Vinland! hurrah!"

"But are you sure?"

Instead of answering, Tyrker laughed again and began to talk, as he always did when greatly moved, in Turkish. Altogether he was so much excited that Krake said he was certainly drunk.

"Drunk!" exclaimed Tyrker, again using the Norse language; "no, that is not possible. A man could not get drunk on grapes if he were to eat a shipload of them. I am only joyful — happy, happy as I can be. It seems as if my young days had returned again with these grapes. I am drunk with old thoughts and memories. I am back again in Turkey!"

"Ye couldn't be in a worse place if all accounts be true," said Krake, with a grin. "Come, don't keep all the grapes to yourself; let us taste them."

"Ay, let us taste them," said Karlsefin, advancing and plucking a bunch from Tyrker's shoulders.

The others did the same, tasted them, and pronounced the fruit excellent.

"Now, lads, we will make the strong drink from the grapes," said Tyrker. "I don't know quite how to do it, but we will soon find out."

"That you certainly shall not if I can prevent it," said Karlsefin firmly.

Tyrker looked a little surprised, and asked why not.

"Because if the effect of eating grapes is so powerful, drinking the strong drink of the grape must be dangerous. Why do you wish to make it?"

"Why? because — because — it *does* make one so happy."

"You told us just now," returned Karlsefin, "that you were *as happy as you could be*, did you not? You cannot be happier than that — therefore, according to your own showing, Tyrker, there is no need of strong drink."

"That's for you," whispered Krake to Tyrker, with a wink, as he poked him in the side. "Go to sleep upon that advice, man, and it'll do ye good — if it don't do ye harm!"

"Ease him of part of his load, boys, and we shall go back the way we came as fast as may be."

Each man relieved Tyrker of several bunches of grapes, so that in a few minutes he resumed his own ordinary appearance. They then retraced their steps, and soon afterwards presented to the women the first grapes of Vinland. Karlsefin carried a chosen bunch to Gudrid, who, after thanking him heartily, stuffed a grape into the hole in Snorro's puckered visage and nearly choked him. Thus narrowly did the first Yankee (for such one of his own countrymen has claimed him to be) escape being killed by the first-fruits of his native land!

CHAPTER XV.

Greenland Again — Flatface Turns up, Also Thorward, who
Becomes Eloquent and Secures Recruits for Vinland.

Who has not heard of that solitary step which lies between the sublime and the ridiculous? The very question may seem ridiculous. And who has not, at one period or another of life, been led to make comparisons to that step? Why then should we hesitate to confess that the step in question has been suggested by the brevity of that other step which lies between the beautiful and the plain, the luxuriant and the barren, the fruitful and the sterile — which step we now call upon the reader to take, by accompanying us from Vinland's shady groves to Greenland's rocky shores.

Leif Ericsson is there, standing on the end of the wharf at Brattalid — bold, stalwart, and upright, as he was when, some years before, he opened up the way to Vinland. Flatface the Skraelinger is there too — stout, hairy, and as suggestive of a fryingpan as he was when, on murderous deeds intent, not very long before, he had led his hairy friends on tiptoe to the confines of Brattalid, and was made almost to leap out of his oily skin with terror.

But his terror by this time was gone. He and the Norsemen had been reconciled, very much to the advantage of both, and his tribe was, just then, encamped on the other side of the ridge.

Leif had learned a little of the Skraelinger tongue; Flatface had acquired a little less of the Norse language — and a pretty mess they made of it between them! As we are under the necessity of rendering both into English, we beg the reader's forbearance and consideration.

"So you are going off on a sealing expedition, are you?" said Leif, turning from the contemplation of the horizon, and regarding the Skraelinger with a comical smile.

"Yis, yo, ha, hooroo!" said Flatface, waving his arms violently to add force to his reply.

"And when do you go?" asked Leif.

"W'en? E go skrumch en cracker smorrow."

"Just so," replied Leif, "only I can't quite make that cracker out unless you mean *tomorrow*."

"Yis, yo, ha!" exclaimed the hairy man. "Kite right, kite right, smorrow, yis, tomorrow."

"You're a wonderful man," remarked Leif, with a smile. "You'll speak Norse like a Norseman if you live long enough."

"Eh!" exclaimed the Skraelinger, with a perplexed look.

"When are you to be back?" asked Leif.

Flatface immediately pointed to the moon, which, although it was broad daylight at the time, showed a remarkably white face in the blue sky, and, doubling his fist, hit himself four blows on the bridge of his nose, or rather on the spot where the bridge of that feature should have been, but where, as it happened, there was only a hollow in the fryingpan, with a little blob below it.

"Ha, four months. Very good. It will be a good riddance; for, to say truth, I'm tired of you and your noisy relations."

Leif said this more as a soliloquy than a remark, for he had no intention of hurting the feelings of the poor savage, who, he was aware, could not understand him. Turning again to him, he said — "You know the kitchen, Flatface?" Flatface said nothing, but rolled his eyes, nodded violently, and rubbed that region which is chiefly concerned with food.

"Go," said Leif, "tell Anders to give you food — food — food!"

At each mention of the word Flatface retreated a step and nodded. When Leif stopped he turned about, and with an exclamation of delight, trundled off to the kitchen like a good-natured polar bear.

For full half an hour after that Leif walked up and down the wharf with his eyes cast down; evidently he was brooding over something. Presently Anders came towards him.

Anders was a burly middle-aged Norseman, with a happy-looking countenance; he was also cook, steward, valet, and general factotum to Leif.

"Well, Anders, hast had a visit from Flatface?" asked Leif.

"Ay — he is in the kitchen now."

"Hast fed him?"

"Ay, gorged him," replied Anders, with a grin.

"Good," said Leif, laughing; "he goes off tomorrow, it seems, for four months, which I'm right glad to hear, for we have had him and his kindred long enough beside us for this time. I am sorry on account of the Christian teachers, however, because they were making some progress with the language, and this will throw them back."

Leif here referred to men who had recently been sent to Greenland by King Olaf Tryggvisson of Norway, with the design of planting Christianity there, and some of whom appeared to be very anxious to acquire the language of the natives. Leif himself had kept somewhat aloof from these teachers of the new faith. He had indeed suffered himself to be baptized, when on a visit to Norway, in order to please the King; but he was a very reserved man, and no one knew exactly what opinions he held in regard to religion. Of course he had been originally trained in the Odin-worship of his forefathers, but he was a remarkably shrewd man, and people said that he did not hold by it very strongly. No one ever ventured to ask him what he held until the teachers above mentioned came. When they tried to find out his opinions he quietly, and with much urbanity, asked to be informed as to some of the details of that which they had come to teach, and so managed the conversation that, without hurting their feelings, he sent them away from him as wise as they came. But although Leif was silent he was very observant, and people said that he noted what was going on keenly — which was indeed the case.

"I know not what the teachers think," said Anders, with a careless air, "but it is my opinion that they won't make much of the Skraelingers, and the

Skraelingers are not worth making much of."

"There thou art wrong, Anders," said Leif, with much gravity; "does not Flatface love his wife and children as much as you love yours?"

"I suppose he does."

"Is not his flesh and blood the same as thine, his body as well knit together as thine, and as well suited to its purposes?"

"Doubtless it is, though somewhat uglier."

"Does he not support his family as well as thou dost, and labour more severely than thou for that purpose? Is he not a better hunter, too, and a faster walker, and fully as much thought of and prized by his kindred?"

"All that may be very true," replied Anders carelessly.

"Then," pursued Leif, "if the Skraelingers be apparently as good as thou art, how can ye say that they are not worth making much of?"

"Truly, on the same ground that I say that I myself am not worth making much of. I neither know nor care anything about the matter. Only this am I sure of, that the Skraelingers do not serve you, master, as well as I do."

"Anders, thou art incorrigible!" said Leif, smiling; "but I admit the truth of your last remark; so now, if ye will come up to the house and do for me, to some extent, what ye have just done to Flatface, ye will add greatly to the service of which thou hast spoken."

"I follow, master," said Anders; "but would it not be well, first, to wait and see which of our people are returning to us, for, if I mistake not, yonder is a boat's sail coming round the ness."

"A *boat's* sail!" exclaimed Leif eagerly, as he gazed at the sail in question; "why, man, if your eyes were as good as those of Flatface, ye would have seen that yonder sail belongs to a ship. My own eyes have been turned inward the last half hour, else must I have observed it sooner."

"It seems to me but a boat," said Anders.

"I tell thee it is a ship!" cried Leif; "ay, and if my eyes do not deceive, it is the ship of Karlsefin. Go, call out the people quickly, and see that they come armed. There is no saying who may be in possession of the ship now."

Anders hastened away, and Leif, after gazing at the approaching vessel a little longer, walked up to the house, where some of his house-carls were hastily arming, and where he received from the hands of an old female servant his sword, helmet, and shield.

The people of Brattalid were soon all assembled on the shore, anxiously awaiting the arrival of the ship, and an active boy was sent round to Heriulfness, to convey the news to the people there — for in Greenland the arrival of a ship was of rare occurrence in those days.

As the ship drew near, all doubt as to her being Karlsefin's vessel was removed, and, when she came close to land, great was the anxiety of the people to make out the faces that appeared above the bulwarks.

"That is Karlsefin," said one. "I know his form of face well."

"No, it is Biarne," cried another. "Karlsefin is taller by half a foot."

"'Tis Thorward," said a third. "I'd know his face among a thousand."

"There seem to be no women with them," observed Anders, who stood at the end of the wharf near his master.

"Does any one see Olaf?" asked Leif.

"No — no," replied several voices.

When the ship was near enough Leif shouted — "Is Olaf on board?"

"No!" replied Thorward, in a stentorian voice.

Leif's countenance fell.

"Is all well in Vinland?" he shouted.

"All is well," was the reply.

Leif's countenance brightened, and in a few minutes he was shaking Thorward heartily by the hand.

"Why did ye not bring my son?" said Leif, somewhat reproachfully, as they went up to the house together.

"We thought it best to try to induce you to go to him rather than bring him to you," answered Thorward, smiling. "You must come back with me, Leif. You cannot conceive what a splendid country it is. It far surpasses Iceland and Norway. As to Greenland, it should not be named in the same breath."

Leif made no reply at that time, but seemed to ponder the proposal.

"Now we shall feast, Thorward," said Leif, as he entered the hall. "Ho! lay the tables, good woman. Come, Anders, see that ye load it well. Have all the house-carls gathered; I will go fetch in our neighbours, and we shall hear what Thorward has to say of this Vinland that we have heard so much about of late."

Leif's instructions were promptly and energetically carried out. The tables were spread with all the delicacies of the season that Greenland had to boast of, which consisted chiefly of fish and wild-fowl, with seal's flesh instead of beef, for nearly all the cattle had been carried off by the emigrants, as we have seen, and the few that were left behind had died for want of proper food. The banquet was largely improved by Thorward, who loaded the table with smoked salmon. After the dishes had been removed and the tankards of beer sent round, Thorward began to relate his story to greedy ears.

He was very graphic in his descriptions, and possessed the power of detailing even commonplace conversations in such a way that they became interesting. He had a great deal of quiet humour, too, which frequently convulsed his hearers with laughter. In short, he gave such a fascinating account of the new land, that when the people retired to rest that night, there was scarcely a man, woman, or child among them who did not long to emigrate without delay. This was just what Thorward desired.

Next day he unloaded the ship, and the sight of her cargo fully confirmed many parts of his story. The upshot of it was that Leif agreed to go and spend the winter in Vinland, and a considerable number of married men made up their minds to emigrate with their wives and families.

Having discharged cargo and taken in a large supply of such goods as were most needed at the new colony, Thorward prepared for sea. Leif placed Anders in charge of his establishment, and, about grey dawn of a beautiful morning, the *Snake* once again shook out her square sail to the breeze and set sail for Vinland.

CHAPTER XVI.

Joyful Meetings and Hearty Greetings.

Need we attempt to describe the joy of our friends in Vinland, when, one afternoon towards the end of autumn, they saw their old ship sweep into the lake under oars and sail, and cast anchor in the bay? We think not.

The reader must possess but a small power of fancy who cannot, without the aid of description, call up vividly the gladsome faces of men and women when they saw the familiar vessel appear, and beheld the bulwarks crowded with well-known faces. Besides, words cannot paint Olaf's sparkling eyes, and the scream of delight when he recognised his father standing in sedate gravity on the poop.

Suffice it to say that the joy culminated at night, as human joys not unfrequently do, in a feast, at which, as a matter of course, the whole story of the arrival and settlement in Vinland was told over again to the newcomers, as if it had never been told before. But there was this advantage in the telling, that instead of all being told by Thorward, each man gave his own version of his own doings, or, at all events, delegated the telling to a friend who was likely to do him justice. Sometimes one or another undertook that friendly act, without having it laid upon him. Thus, Krake undertook to relate the discovery of the grapes by Tyrker, and Tyrker retaliated by giving an account of the accident in connexion with a mud-hole that had happened to Krake. This brought out Biarne, who went into a still more minute account of that event with reference to its bearing on Freydissa, and that gentle woman revenged herself by giving an account of the manner in which Hake had robbed Biarne of the honour of killing a brown bear, the mention of which ferocious animal naturally suggested to Olaf the brave deed of his dear pet the black bull, to a narrative of which he craved and obtained attention. From the black bull to the baby was an easy and natural transition — more so perhaps than may appear at first sight — for the bull suggested the cows, and the cows the milk, which last naturally led to thoughts of the great consumer thereof.

It is right to say here, however, that the baby was among the first objects presented to Leif and his friends after their arrival; and great was the interest with which they viewed this first-born of the American land. The wrinkles, by the way, were gone by that time. They had been filled up so completely that the place where they once were resembled a fair and smooth round ball of fresh butter, with two bright blue holes in it, a knob below them, and a ripe cherry underneath that.

Snorro happened to be particularly amiable when first presented to his new friends. Of course he had not at that time reached the crowing or smiling age. His goodness as yet was negative. He did not squall; he did not screw up his face into inconceivable formations; he did not grow alarmingly red in the face; he did not insist on having milk, seeing that he had already had as much as he could possibly hold — no, he did none of these things, but lay in Gudrid's arms, the very embodiment of stolid and expressionless indifference to all earthly things — those who loved him best included.

But this state of "goodness" did not last long. He soon began to display what may be styled the old-Adamic part of his nature, and induced Leif, after much long-suffering, to suggest that "that would do," and that "he had better be taken away!"

The effervescence of the colony caused by this infusion of new elements ere long settled down. The immigrants took part in the general labour and duties. Timber-cutting, grape-gathering, haymaking, fishing, hunting, exploring, eating, drinking, and sleeping, went on with unabated vigour, and thus, gradually, autumn merged into winter.

But winter did not bring in its train the total change that these Norsemen had been accustomed to in their more northern homes. The season was to them comparatively mild. True, there was a good deal of snow, and it frequently gave to the branches of the trees that silvery coating which, in sunshine, converts the winter forest into the very realms of fairyland; but the snow did not lie deep on the ground, or prevent the cattle from remaining out and finding food all the winter. There was ice, also, on the lake, thick enough to admit of walking on it, and sledging with ponies, but not thick enough to prevent them cutting easily through it, and fishing with lines and hooks, made of bone and baited with bits of fat, with which they caught enormous trout, little short of salmon in size, and quite as good for food.

Daring the winter there was plenty of occupation for every one in the colony. For one thing, it cost a large number of the best men constant and hard labour merely to supply the colonists with firewood and food. Then the felling of timber for export was carried on during winter as easily as in summer, and the trapping of wild animals for their furs was a prolific branch of industry. Sometimes the men changed their work for the sake of variety. The hunters occasionally took to fishing, the fishers to timber felling and squaring, the timber-cutters to trapping; the trappers undertook the work of the firewood-cutters, and these latter relieved the men who performed the duties of furniture-making, repairing, general home-work and guarding the settlement. Thus the work went on, and circled round.

Of course all this implied a vast deal of tear and wear. Buttons had not at that time been invented, but tags could burst off as well as buttons, and loops were not warranted to last for ever, any more than buttonholes. Socks were unknown to those hardy pioneers, but soft leather shoes, not unlike mocassins, and boots resembling those of the Esquimaux of the present day, were constantly wearing out, and needed to be replaced or repaired; hence the women of the colony had their hands full, for, besides these renovating duties which devolved on them, they had also the housekeeping — a duty in itself calling for an amount of constant labour, anxiety, and attention which that ridiculous creature *man* never can or will understand or appreciate — at least so the women say, but, being a man, we incline to differ from them as to that!

Then, when each day's work was over, the men returned to their several abodes tired and hungry. Arrangements had been made that so many men should dwell and mess together, and the women were so appointed that each mess was properly looked after. Thus the men found cheerful fires, clean hearths, spread tables, smoking viands, and a pleasant welcome on their return home; and, after supper, were wont to spend the evenings in recounting their day's experiences, telling sagas, singing songs, or discussing general principles – a species of discussion, by the way, which must certainly have originated in Eden after the Fall!

In Karlsefin's large hall the largest number of men and women were nightly assembled, and there the time was spent much in the same way, but with this difference, that the heads of the settlement were naturally appealed to in disputed matters, and conversation frequently merged into something like orations from Leif and Biarne Karlsefin and Thorward, all of whom were far-travelled, well-informed, and capable of sustaining the interest of their audiences for a prolonged period.

In those days the art of writing was unknown among the Norsemen, and it was their custom to fix the history of their great achievements, as well as much of their more domestic doings, in their memories by means of song and story. Men gifted with powers of composition in prose and verse undertook to enshrine deeds and incidents in appropriate language at the time of their occurrence, and these scalds or poets, and saga-men or chroniclers, although they might perhaps have *coloured* their narratives and poems slightly, were not likely to have falsified them, because they were at first related and sung in the presence of actors and eyewitnesses, to attempt imposition on whom would have been useless as well as ridiculous. Hence those old songs and sagas had their foundation in truth. After they were once launched into the memories of men, the form of words, doubtless, tended to protect them to some extent from adulteration, and even when all allowance is made for man's well-known tendency to invent and exaggerate, it still remains likely that *all* the truth would be retained, although surrounded more or less with fiction. To distinguish the true from the false in such cases is not so difficult a process as one at first sight might suppose. Men with penetrating minds and retentive memories, who are trained to such work, are swift to detect the chaff amongst the wheat, and although in their winnowing operations they may frequently blow away a few grains of wheat, they seldom or never accept any of the chaff as good grain.

We urge all this upon the reader, because the narratives and poems which were composed and related by Karlsefin and his friends that winter, doubtless contained those truths which were not taken out of the traditional state, collected and committed to writing by the Icelandic saga-writers, until about one hundred years afterwards, at the end of the eleventh or beginning of the twelfth century.

On these winter evenings, too, Karlsefin sometimes broached the subject of the new religion, which had been so recently introduced into Greenland. He told them that he had not received much instruction in it, so that he could not presume to explain it all to them, but added that he had become acquainted with the name and some of the precepts of Jesus Christ, and these last, he said, seemed to him so good and so true that he now believed in Him who taught them, and would not exchange that belief for all the riches of this world, "for," said he, "the world we dwell in is passing away — that to which we go shall never pass away." His chief delight in the new religion was that Jesus Christ was described as a Saviour from sin, and he thought that to be delivered from wicked thoughts in the heart and wicked deeds of the body was the surest road to perfect happiness.

The Norsemen listened to all this with profound interest, for none of them were so much wedded to their old religion as to feel any jealousy of the new; but although they thought much about it, they spoke little, for all were aware that the two religions could not go together — the acceptance of the one implied the rejection of the other.

Frequently during the winter Karlsefin and Leif had earnest conversations about the prospects of the infant colony.

"Leif," said Karlsefin, one day, "my mind is troubled."

"That is bad," replied Leif; "what troubles it?"

"The thoughts that crowd upon me in regard to this settlement."

"I marvel not at that," returned Leif, stopping and looking across the lake, on the margin of which they were walking; "your charge is a heavy one, calling for earnest thought and careful management. But what is the particular view that gives you uneasiness?"

"Why, the fact that it does not stand on a foundation which is likely to be permanent. A house may not be very large, but if its foundation be good it will stand. If, however, its foundation be bad, then the bigger and grander it is, so much the worse for the house."

"That is true. Go on."

"Well, it seems to me that the foundation of our settlement is not good. It is true that some of us have our wives here, and there is, besides, a sprinkling of young girls, who are being courted by some of the men; nevertheless it remains a stubborn truth that far the greater part of the men are those who came out with Thorward and me, and have left either wives or sweethearts in Norway and in Iceland. Now these may be pleased to remain here for a time, but it cannot be expected that they will sit down contentedly and make it their home."

"There is truth in what you say, Karlsefin. Have any of your men spoken on that subject?"

"No, none as yet; but I have not failed to note that some of them are not so cheerful and hearty as they used to be."

"What is to prevent you making a voyage to Iceland and Norway next spring," said Leif, "and bringing out the wives and families, and, if you can, the sweethearts of these men?"

Karlsefin laughed heartily at this suggestion. "Why, Leif," he said, "has your sojourn on the barren coast of Greenland so wrought on your good sense, or your feelings, that you should suppose thirty or forty families will agree at once to leave home and kindred to sail for and settle in a new land of the West that they have barely — perhaps never — heard of; and think you that sweethearts have so few lovers at home that they will jump at those who are farthest away from them? It is one thing to take time and trouble to collect men and households that are willing to emigrate; it is another thing altogether to induce households to follow men who have already emigrated."

"Nay, but I would counsel you to take the men home along with you, so that they might use their persuasions," returned Leif; "but, as you say, it is not a likely course to take, even in that way. What, then, do you think, is wisest to be done?"

"I cannot yet reply to that, Leif. I see no course open."

"Tell me, Karlsefin, how is it with yourself?" asked Leif, looking earnestly at his friend. "Are you content to dwell here?"

Karlsefin did not reply for a few seconds.

"Well, to tell you the truth," he said at length, "I do not relish the notion of calling Vinland *home*. The sea is my home. I have dwelt on it the greater part of my life. I love its free breezes and surging waves. The very smell of its salt spray brings pleasant memories to my soul. I cannot brook the solid earth. While I walk I feel as if I were glued to it, and when I lie down I am too still. It is like death. On the sea, whether I stand, or walk, or lie, I am ever bounding on. Yes; the sea is my native home, and when old age constrains me to forsake it, and take to the land, my home must be in Iceland."

"Truly if that be your state of mind," said Leif, laughing, "there is little hope of your finally coming to an anchor here."

"But," continued Karlsefin, less energetically, "it would not be right in me to forsake those whom I have led hither. I am bound to remain by and aid them as long as they are willing to stay — at least until they do not require my services."

"That is well spoken, friend," said Leif. "Thou art indeed so bound. Now, what I would counsel is this, that you should spend another year, or perhaps two more years, in Vinland, and at the end of that time it will be pretty plain either that the colony is going to flourish and can do without you, or that it is advisable to forsake it and return home. Meanwhile I would advise that you give the land a fair trial. Put a good face on it; keep the men busy — for that is the way to keep them cheerful and contented, always being careful not to overwork them — provide amusements for their leisure hours if possible, and keep them from thinking too much of absent wives and sweethearts — if you can."

"*If I can*," repeated Karlsefin, with a smile; "ay, but I don't think I can. However, your advice seems good, so I will adopt it; and as I shall be able to follow it out all the better with your aid, I hope that you will spend next winter with us."

"I agree to that," said Leif; "but I must first visit Greenland in spring, and then return to you. And now, tell me what you think of the two thralls King Olaf sent me."

Karlsefin's brow clouded a little as he replied that they were excellent men in all respects — cheerful, willing, and brave.

"So should I have expected of men sent to me by the King," said Leif, "but I have noticed that the elder is very sad. Does he pine for his native land, think ye?"

"Doubtless he does," answered Karlsefin; "but I am tempted to think that he, like some others among us, pines for an absent sweetheart."

"Not unlikely, not unlikely," observed Leif, looking gravely at the ground. "And the younger lad, Hake, what of him? He, I think, seems well enough pleased to remain, if one may judge from his manner and countenance."

"There is reason for that," returned Karlsefin, with a recurrence of the troubled expression. "The truth is that Hake is in love with Bertha."

"The thrall?" exclaimed Leif.

"Ay, and he has gone the length of speaking to her of love; I know it, for I heard him."

"What! does Karlsefin condescend to turn eavesdropper?" said Leif, looking at his friend in surprise.

"Not so, but I chanced to come within earshot at the close of an interview they had, and heard a few words in spite of myself. It was in summer. I was walking through the woods, and suddenly heard voices near me in the heart of a copse through which I must needs pass. Thinking nothing about it I advanced and saw Hake and Bertha partially concealed by the bushes. Suddenly Hake cried passionately, 'I cannot help it, Bertha. I *must* tell you that I love you if I should die for it;' to which Bertha replied, 'It is useless, Hake; neither Leif nor Karlsefin will consent, and I shall never oppose their will.' Then Hake said, 'You are right, Bertha, right — forgive me — .' At this point I felt ashamed of standing still, and turned back lest I should overhear more."

"He is a thrall — a thrall," murmured Leif sternly, as if musing.

"And yet he is a Scottish earl's son," said Karlsefin. "It does seem a hard case to be a thrall. I wonder if the new religion teaches anything regarding thraldom."

Leif looked up quickly into his friend's face, but Karlsefin had turned his head aside as if in meditation, and no further allusion was made to that subject by either of them.

"Do you think that Bertha returns Hake's love?" asked Leif, after a few minutes.

"There can be no doubt of that," said Karlsefin, laughing; "the colour of her cheek, the glance of her eye, and the tones of her voice, are all tell-tale. But since the day I have mentioned they have evidently held more aloof from each other."

"That is well," said Leif, somewhat sternly. "Bertha is free-born. She shall not wed a thrall if he were the son of fifty Scottish earls."

This speech was altogether so unlike what might have been expected from one of Leif's kind and gentle nature that Karlsefin looked at him in some astonishment and seemed about to speak, but Leif kept his frowning eyes steadily on the ground, and the two friends walked the remainder of the road to the hamlet in perfect silence.

CHAPTER XVII.

*Treats of the Friendship and Adventures of Olaf and Snorro,
and of Sundry Surprising Incidents.*

We must now pass over a considerable period of time, and carry our story forward to the spring of the third year after the settlement of the Norsemen in Vinland.

During that interval matters had progressed much in the same way as we have already described, only that the natives had become a little more exacting in their demands while engaged in barter, and were, on the whole, rather more pugnacious and less easily pleased. There had been a threatening of hostilities once or twice, but, owing to Karlsefin's pacific policy, no open rupture had taken place.

During that interval, too, Leif had made two trips to Greenland and back; a considerable amount of merchandise had been sent home; a few more colonists had arrived, and a few of the original ones had left; Thorward's ship had been also brought to Vinland; and last, but not least, Snorro had grown into a most magnificent baby!

Things were in this felicitous condition when, early one beautiful spring morning, Snorro resolved to have a ramble. Snorro was by that time barely able to walk, and he did it after a peculiar fashion of his own. He had also begun to make a few desperate efforts to talk; but even Gudrid was forced to admit that, in regard to both walking and talking, there was great room for improvement.

Now, it must be told that little Olaf was particularly fond of Snorro, and, if one might judge from appearances, Snorro reciprocated the attachment. Whenever Snorro happened to be missed, it was generally understood that Olaf had him. If any one chanced to ask the question, "Where is Snorro?" the almost invariable reply was, "Ask Olaf." In the event of Olaf *not* having him, it was quite unnecessary for any one to ask where he was, because the manner in which he raged about the hamlet shouting, howling, absolutely yelling, for "O'af!" was a sufficient indication of his whereabouts.

It was customary for Olaf not only to tend and nurse Snorro, in a general way, when at home, but to take him out for little walks and rides in the forest — himself being the horse. At first these delightful expeditions were very short, but as Snorro's legs developed, and his mother became more accustomed to his absences, they were considerably extended. Nevertheless a limit was marked out, beyond which Olaf was forbidden to take him, and experience had proved that Olaf was a trustworthy boy. It must be remembered here, that although he had grown apace during these two years, Olaf was himself but a small boy, with the clustering golden curls and the red chubby cheeks with which he had left Greenland.

As we have said, then, Snorro resolved to have a walk one fine spring morning of the year one thousand and ten — or thereabouts. In the furtherance of his design he staggered across the hall, where Gudrid had left him for those fatal "few minutes" during which children of all ages and climes have invariably availed themselves of their opportunity! Coming to a serious impediment in the shape of the doorstep, he paused, plucked up heart, and tumbled over it into the road. Gathering himself up, he staggered onward through the village shouting his usual cry — "O'af! O'af! O'AF! O-o-o!" with his wonted vigour.

But "O'af" was deaf to the touching appeal. He chanced to have gone away that morning with Biarne and Hake to visit a bear-trap. A little black bear had been found in it crushed and dead beneath the heavy tree that formed the *drop* of the trap. This bear had been slung on a pole between the two men, and the party were returning home in triumph at the time that Snorro set up his cry, but they were not quite within earshot.

Finding that his cries were not attended to, Snorro staggered out of the village into the forest a short way, and there, standing in the middle of the path, began again — "O'af! O'af! O'AF! O-o-o!"

Still there was no reply; therefore Snorro, stirred by the blood which had descended to him through a long line of illustrious and warlike sea-kings, lost his temper, stamped his feet, and screeched with passion.

Nothing resulting, he changed his mood, shouted "O'af!" once more, in heartrending accents, and — with his eyes half shut and mouth wide open, his arms and hands helplessly pendent, his legs astraddle, and his whole aspect what is expressively styled in the Norse tongue begrutten — howled in abject despair!

In this condition he was found by the bear party not many minutes later, and in another moment he was sobbing out his heart and sorrows into the sympathetic bosom of his dearly-loved friend.

"What is it, Snorrie? What's the matter?" inquired Olaf tenderly.

"Hik! — Me — hup! — O! — want — hif! — wak," replied the sobbing child.

"It wants to walk, does it? So it shall, my bold little man. There, dry its eyes and get on my back, hup! — now, away we go! I'll be back soon," he said to Biarne, who stood laughing at them. "Be sure that you keep the claws of the bear for me. Now, Snorrie, off and away! hurrah!"

"Hoo'ah!" echoed Snorro, as, holding tight with both his fat arms round Olaf's neck, he was borne away into the wilderness.

Olaf's usual mode of proceeding was as follows:

First he dashed along the track of the woodcutters for about half a mile. It was a good broad track, which at first had been cleared by the axe, and afterwards well beaten by the constant passage of men and horses with heavy loads of timber. Then he stopped and set Snorro on his legs, and, going down on his knees before him, laughed in his face. You may be sure that Snorro returned the laugh with right good-will.

"Whereaway next, Snorrie?"

"Away! a-way!" shouted the child, throwing up his arms, losing his balance, and falling plump — in sedentary fashion.

"Ay, anywhere you please; that means, no doubt, up to the sun or moon, if possible! But come, it must walk a bit now. Give me its hand, old man."

Snorro was obedient to Olaf — and, reader, that was an amazing triumph of love, for to no one else, not even to his mother, did he accord obedience. He quietly took his guide's hand, trotted along by his side, and listened wonderingly while he chatted of trees, and flowers, and birds, and squirrels, and wild beasts, just as if he understood every word that Olaf said.

But Snorro's obedience was not perfect. Olaf's pace being regulated by his spirits, Snorro soon began to pant, and suddenly pulled up with a violent "'Top!"

"Ho! is it tired?" cried Olaf, seizing him and throwing him over his shoulder into the old position. "Well, then, off we go again!"

He not only went off at a run, but he went off the track also at this point, and struck across country straight through the woods in the direction of a certain ridge, which was the limit beyond which he was forbidden to go.

It was an elevated ridge, which commanded a fine view of the surrounding country, being higher than the treetops, and was a favourite resort of Olaf when he went out to ramble with Snorro. Beyond it lay a land that was unknown to Olaf, because that part of the forest was so dense that even the men avoided it in their expeditions, and selected more open and easier routes. Olaf, who was only allowed to accompany the men on short excursions, had never gone beyond the ridge in that direction. He longed to do so, however, and many a time had he, while playing with Snorro on the ridge, gazed with ever increasing curiosity into the deep shades beyond, and wondered what was there! To gaze at a forbidden object is dangerous. We have already said that Olaf was a trustworthy boy, but he was not immaculate. He not only sometimes wished to have his own way, but now and then took it. On this particular occasion he gave way, alas! to temptation.

"Snorro," said he, after sitting under a tree for a considerable time basking in the checkered sunshine with the child beside him, "Snorro, why should not you and I have a peep into that dark forest?"

"Eh?" said Snorro, who understood him not.

"It would be great fun," pursued Olaf. "The shade would be so pleasant in a hot day like this, and we would not go far. What does it think?"

"Ho!" said Snorro, who thought and cared nothing at all about it, for he happened to be engaged just then in crushing a quantity of wild-flowers in his fat hands.

"I see it is not inclined to talk much today. Well, come, get on my back, and we shall have just one peep — just one run into it — and then out again."

Error number one. Smelling forbidden fruit is the sure prelude to the eating of it!

He took the child on his back, descended the hill, and entered the thick forest.

The scene that met his gaze was indeed well calculated to delight a romantic boy. He found that the part of the woods immediately around him consisted of tall straight trees with thick umbrageous tops, the stems of which seemed like pillars supporting a vast roof; and through between these stems he could see a vista of smaller stems which appeared absolutely endless. There was no grass on the ground, but a species of soft moss, into which he sank ankle-deep, yet not so deep as to render walking difficult. In one direction the distance looked intensely blue, in another it was almost black, while, just before him, a long way off, there was a bright sunny spot with what appeared to be the glittering waters of a pond in the midst of it.

The whole scene was both beautiful and strange to Olaf, and would have filled him with intense delight, if he could only have got rid of that uncomfortable feeling about its being forbidden ground! However, having fairly got into the scrape, he thought he might as well go through with it.

Error number two. Having become impressed with the fact that he had sinned, he ought to have turned back *at once*. "In for a penny, in for a pound," is about the worst motto that ever was invented. Interpreted, it means, "Having done a little mischief, I'll shut my eyes and go crashing into all iniquity." As well might one say, "Having burnt my finger, I'll shove my whole body into the fire!"

But Olaf did not take time to think. He pushed boldly forward in the direction of the lake. As he drew near he found the moss becoming softer and deeper, besides being rather wet. Going a few steps further, he found that it changed into a swamp.

"Ho! Snorrie, this is dangerous ground," he said, turning back; "we'll take a round-about and try to get to the lake by a drier way."

He did so, but the more he diverged towards dry ground the more did the swamp force him to one side, until it compelled him to go out of sight of the pond altogether.

"Now, isn't that vexin'?" he said, looking about him.

"Iss," replied Snorro, who was becoming sleepy, and had laid his head on his friend's shoulder.

"Well, as we can't get to the lake, and as this is rather a wild place, we'll just turn back now and get out of it as fast as we can."

"Iss," murmured Snorro, with a deep sigh.

Olaf turned back and made for the edge of the wood. He was so long of coming to it that he began to be somewhat surprised, and looked about him a little more carefully, but the tall straight stems were all so much alike that they afforded him no clue to his way out of the wood. Young though he was, Olaf knew enough of woodcraft to be able to steer his course by the sun; but the sky had become clouded, and the direction of the sun could not be ascertained through the dense foliage overhead. He now became seriously alarmed. His heart beat against his ribs as if it wanted to get out, and he started off at a run in the direction in which, he felt sure, the ridge lay. Becoming tired and still more alarmed, he changed his course, eagerly advanced for a short time, hesitated, changed his course again, and finally stopped altogether, as the terrible fact flashed upon him that he was really lost in the woods. He set Snorro on the ground, and, sitting down beside him, burst into tears.

We need scarcely say that poor Olaf was neither a timid nor an effeminate boy. It was not for himself that he thus gave way. It was the sudden opening of his eyes to the terrible consequences of his disobedience that unmanned him. His quick mind perceived at once that little Snorro would soon die of cold and hunger if he failed to find his way out of that wilderness; and when he thought of this, and of the awful misery that would thus descend on the heads of Karlsefin and Gudrid, he felt a strange desire that he himself might die there and then.

This state of mind, however, did not last long. He soon dried his eyes and braced himself up for another effort. Snorro had gone to sleep the instant he was laid on the ground. As his luckless guide raised him he opened his eyes slightly, murmured "O'af," and again went off to the land of Nod.

Olaf now made a more steady and persevering effort to get out of the wood, and he was so far successful that he came to ground that was more open and broken — more like to that through which he had been accustomed to travel with the men. This encouraged him greatly, for, although he did not recognise any part of it, he believed that he must now be at all events not far distant from places that he knew. Here he again looked for the sun, but the sky had become so thickly overcast that he could not make out its position. Laying Snorro down, he climbed a tall tree, but the prospect of interminable forest which he beheld from that point of vantage did not afford him any clue to his locality. He looked for the ridge, but there were many ridges in view, any of which might have been *his* ridge, but none of which looked precisely like it.

Nevertheless, the upward bound which his spirits had taken when he came to the more open country did not altogether subside. He still wandered on manfully, in the hope that he was gradually nearing home.

At last evening approached and the light began to fade away. Olaf was now convinced that he should have to spend the night in the forest. He therefore wisely resolved, while it was yet day, to search for a suitable place whereon to encamp, instead of struggling on till he could go no farther. Fortunately the weather was warm at the time.

Ere long he found a small hollow in a sandbank which was perfectly dry and thickly overhung with shrubs. Into this he crept and carefully laid down his slumbering charge. Then, going out, he collected a large quantity of leaves. With these he made a couch, on which he laid Snorro and covered him well over. Lying down beside him he drew as close to the child as he could; placed his little head on his breast to keep it warm; laid his own curly pate on a piece of turf, and almost instantly fell into a profound slumber.

The sun was up and the birds were singing long before that slumber was broken. When at last Olaf and his little charge awoke, they yawned several times and stretched themselves vigorously; opened their eyes with difficulty, and began to look round with some half formed notions as to breakfast. Olaf was first to observe that the roof above him was a confused mass of earth and roots, instead of the customary plank ceiling and cross-beams of home.

"Where am I?" he murmured lazily, yet with a look of sleepy curiosity.

He was evidently puzzled, and there is no saying how long he might have lain in that condition had not a very small contented voice close beside him replied:

"You's here, O'af; an' so's me."

Olaf raised himself quickly on his elbow, and, looking down, observed Snorro's large eyes gazing from out a forest of leaves in quiet satisfaction.

"Isn't it nice?" continued Snorro.

"Nice!" exclaimed Olaf in a voice of despair, when the whole truth in regard to their lost condition was thus brought suddenly to his mind. "Nice! No, Snorrie, my little man, it isn't nice. It's dreadful! It's awful! It's — but come, I must not give way like a big baby as I did yesterday. We are lost, Snorrie, lost in the woods."

"Lost! What's lost?" asked Snorro, sitting up and gazing into his friend's face with an anxious expression — not, of course, in consequence of being lost, which he did not understand, but because of Olaf's woeful countenance.

"Oh! you can't understand it, Snorrie; and, after all, I'm a stupid fellow to alarm you, for that can do no good. Come, my mannie, you and I are going to wander about in the woods today a great long way, and try to get home; so, let me shake the leaves off you. There now, we shall start."

"Dat great fun!" cried Snorro, with sparkling eyes; "but, O'af, me want mik."

"Milk — eh? Well, to be sure, but —"

Olaf stopped abruptly, not only because he was greatly perplexed about the matter of breakfast thus suggested to him, but because he chanced at that moment to look towards the leafy entrance of the cave, and there beheld a pair of large black eyes glaring at him.

To say that poor Olaf's heart gave a violent leap, and then apparently ceased to beat altogether, while the blood fled from his visage, is not to say anything disparaging to his courage. Whether you be boy or man, reader, we suspect that if you had, in similar circumstances, beheld such a pair of eyes, you might have been troubled with somewhat similar emotions. Cowardice lies not in the susceptibility of the nervous system to a shock, but in giving way to that shock so as to become unfit for proper action or self-defence. If Olaf had been a coward, he would, forgetting all else, have attempted to fly, or, that being impossible, would have shrunk into the innermost recesses of the cave. Not being a coward, his first impulse was to start to his feet and face the pair of eyes; his second, to put his left arm round Snorro, and, still keeping his white face steadily turned to the foe, to draw the child close to his side.

This act, and the direction in which Olaf gazed, caused Snorro to glance towards the cave's mouth, where he no sooner beheld the apparition, than shutting his own eyes tight, and opening his mouth wide, he gave vent to a series of yells that might have terrified the wildest beast in the forest!

It did not, however, terrify the owner of the eyes, for the bushes were instantly thrust aside, and next instant Snorro's mouth was violently stopped by the black hand of a savage.

Seeing this, Olaf's blood returned to its ordinary channels with a rush. He seized a thick branch that lay on the ground, and dealt the savage a whack on the bridge of his nose, that changed it almost immediately from a snub into a superb Roman! For this he received a buffet on the ear that raised a brilliant constellation in his brain, and laid him flat on the ground.

Rising with difficulty, he was met with a shower of language from the savage in a voice which partook equally of the tones of remonstrance and abuse, but Olaf made no reply, chiefly because, not understanding what was said, he could not. Seeing this plainly indicated on his face, the savage stopped speaking and gave him a box on the other ear, by way of interpreting what he had said. It was not quite so violent as the first, and only staggered Olaf, besides lighting up a few faint stars. Very soon little Snorro became silent, from the combined effects of exhaustive squeezes and horror.

Having thus promptly brought matters to what he seemed to consider a satisfactory condition, the savage wiping his Roman nose, which had bled a little, threw Snorro over his shoulder and, seizing Olaf by the collar of his coat, so as to thrust him on in advance, left the cavern with rapid strides.

Words cannot describe the condition of poor Olaf's mind, as he was thus forced violently along through the forest, he knew not whither. Fearful thoughts went flashing swiftly through his brain. That the savage would take him and Snorro to his home, wherever that might be, and kill, roast, and eat him, was one of the mildest of these thoughts. He reflected that the hatred of the savage towards him must be very intense, in consequence of his recent treatment of his nose, and that the pain of that feature would infallibly keep his hatred for a long time at the boiling-point; so that, in addition to the roasting and eating referred to, he had every reason to expect in his own case the addition of a little extra torture. Then he thought of the fact, that little Snorro would never more behold his mother, and the torture of mind resulting from this reflection is only comparable to the roasting of the body; but the worst thought of all was, that the dreadful pass to which he and Snorro had come, was the consequence of his own wilful *disobedience*! The anguish of spirit that filled him, when he reflected on this, was such that it caused him almost to forget the pain caused by savage knuckles in his neck, and savage prospects in the future.

Oh how he longed for a knife! With what fearful gloating did he contemplate the exact spot in the savage groin into which he would have plunged it until the haft should have disappeared! And this, not so much from a feeling of revenge — though that was bad enough — as from an intense desire to rescue Snorro ere it should be too late.

Several times he thought of a final dying effort at a hand-to-hand struggle with his captor, but the power of the grip on the back of his neck induced him to abandon that idea in despair. Then he thought of a sudden wrench and a desperate flight, but as that implied the leaving of Snorro to his fate, he abandoned that idea too in disdain. Suddenly, however, he recurred to it, reflecting that, if he could only manage to make his own escape, he might perhaps find his way back to the settlement, give the alarm, and lead his friends to Snorro's rescue. The power of this thought was so strong upon him, that he suddenly stooped and gave his active body a twist, which he considered absolutely awful for strength, but, much to his astonishment, did not find himself free. On the contrary, he received such a shake, accompanied by such a kick, that from that moment he felt all hope to be gone.

Thus they proceeded through the woods, and out upon an open space beyond, and over a variety of ridges, and down into a number of hollows, and again through several forests not unlike the first, until poor Olaf began to wonder whether they had not passed the boundaries of the world altogether and got into another region beyond — until his legs, sturdy though they were, began to give way beneath him — until the noonday sun shone perpendicularly down through the trees, and felt as if it were burning up his brain. Then they came to a rivulet, on the banks of which were seen several tents of a conical form, made of skins, from the tops of which smoke was issuing.

No sooner did the savage come in sight of these tents than he uttered a low peculiar cry. It was responded to, and immediately a band of half naked savages, like himself, advanced to meet him.

There was much gesticulation and loud excited talking, and a great deal of pointing to the two captives, with looks expressive of surprise and delight, but not a word could Olaf understand; and the gestures were not definite in their expression.

When Snorro was placed sitting-wise on the ground — nearly half dead with fatigue, alarm, and hunger — he crept towards Olaf, hid his face in his breast, and sobbed. Then did Olaf's conscience wake up afresh and stab him with a degree of vigour that was absolutely awful — for Olaf's conscience was a tender one; and it is a strange, almost paradoxical, fact, that the tenderer a conscience is the more wrathfully does it stab and lacerate the heart of its owner when he has done wrong!

There was, however, no uncertainty as to the disposition of the savages, when, after a thorough inspection of the children, they took them to the tents and set before them some boiled fish and roast venison.

Need we remark that, for the time, Olaf and Snorro forgot their sorrow? It would scarcely be an exaggeration to say that Snorro was as ravenous as any wolf in Vinland. From the day of his birth that well-cared-for child had, four times a day, received regular nutriment in the form of milk, bread, eggs, and other substances, and never once had he been permitted to experience the *pangs* of hunger, though the *intimations* thereof were familiar. No wonder, then, that after an evening, a night, and half a day of abstinence, he looked with a longing gaze on victuals, and, when opportunity offered, devoured them desperately. Olaf, though trained a little in endurance, was scarcely less energetic, for his appetite was keen, and his fast had been unusually prolonged.

When they had eaten as much as they could — to the delight of the natives, excepting, of course, the man with the temporary Roman nose — they were ordered by signals, which even Snorro understood, to remain still and behave themselves. Thereafter the natives struck their tents, packed up their goods and chattels, embarked in sixteen large canoes, and descended the rivulet a hundred yards or so to the spot where it flowed into a large river. Here they turned the canoes upstream, and silently but swiftly paddled away into the interior of the land.

CHAPTER XVIII.

Anxious Times — A Search Organised and Vigorously Carried Out.

It is not easy to conceive the state of alarm that prevailed in the settlement of the Norsemen when it came to be known that little Snorro and Olaf were lost. The terrible fact did not of course break on them all at once.

For some hours after the two adventurers had left home, Dame Gudrid went briskly about her household avocations, humming tunefully one of her native Icelandic airs, and thinking, no doubt, of Snorro. Astrid, assisted by Bertha, went about the dairy operations, gossiping of small matters in a pleasant way, and, among other things, providing Snorro's allowance of milk. Thora busied herself in the preparation of Snorro's little bed; and Freydissa, whose stern nature was always softened by the sight of the child, constructed, with elaborate care, a little coat for Snorro's body. Thus Snorro's interests were being tenderly cared for until the gradual descent of the sun induced the remark, that "Olaf must surely have taken a longer walk than usual that day."

"I must go and meet them," said Gudrid, becoming for the first time uneasy.

"Let me go with you," said Bertha.

"Come, child," returned Gudrid.

In passing the spot where the little bear had been cut up and skinned, they saw Hake standing with Biarne.

"Did you say that Olaf took the track of the woodcutters?" asked Gudrid.

"Ay, that was their road at starting," answered Biarne. "Are they not later than usual?"

"A little. We go to meet them."

"Tell Olaf that I have kept the bear's claws for him," said Biarne.

The two women proceeded a considerable distance along the woodcutters' track, chatting, as they went, on various subjects, but, not meeting the children, they became alarmed and walked on in silence.

Suddenly Gudrid stopped.

"Bertha," said she, "let us not waste time. If the dear children have strayed a little out of the right road, it is of the utmost importance to send men to search and shout for them before it begins to darken. Come, we will return."

Being more alarmed than she liked to confess, even to herself, Gudrid at once walked rapidly homewards, and, on approaching the huts, quickened her pace to a run.

"Quick, Swend, Hake, Biarne!" she cried; "the children must have lost their way — haste you to search for them before the sun goes down. Shout as ye go. It will be ill to find them after dark, and if they have to spend the night in the woods, I fear me they will —"

"Don't fear anything, Gudrid," said Biarne kindly. "We will make all haste, and doubtless shall find them rambling in the thickets near at hand. Go, Hake, find Karlsefin, and tell him that I will begin the search at once with Swend, while he gets together a few men."

Cheered by Biarne's hearty manner, Gudrid was a little comforted, and returned to the house to complete her preparation of Snorro's supper, while Hake gave the alarm to Karlsefin, who, accompanied by Leif and a body of men, at once went off to scour the woods in every direction.

Of course they searched in vain, for their attention was at first directed to the woods near home, in which it was naturally enough supposed that Olaf might have lost his way in returning. Not finding them there, Karlsefin became thoroughly alive to the extreme urgency of the case, and the necessity for a thorough and extended plan of search.

"Come hither, Hake," said he. "This may be a longer business than we thought for. Run back to the huts, call out all the men except the home-guards. Let them come prepared for a night in the woods, each man with a torch, and one meal in his pouch at least —"

"Besides portions for the twenty men already out," suggested Hake.

"Right, right, lad, and tell them to meet me at the Pine Ridge. Away! If ever thy legs rivalled the wind, let them do so now."

Hake sprang off at a pace which appeared satisfactory even to the anxious father.

In half an hour Karlsefin was joined at the Pine Ridge by all the available strength of the colony, and there he organised and despatched parties in all directions, appointing the localities they were to traverse, the limits of their search, and the time and place for the next rendezvous. This last was to be on the identical ridge whence poor Olaf had taken his departure into the unknown land. Karlsefin knew well that it was his favourite haunt, and intended to search carefully up to it, never dreaming that the boy would go beyond it after the strict injunctions he had received not to do so, and the promises he had made.

"I'm not so sure as you seem to be that Olaf has not gone beyond the ridge," observed Leif to Karlsefin, after the men had left them.

"Why not?" asked the latter. "He is a most trustworthy boy."

"I know it — who should know it so well as his own father?" returned Leif; "but he is very young. I have known him give way to temptation once or twice before now. He may have done it again."

"I trust not," said Karlsefin; "but come, let us make direct for the ridge, while the others continue the search; we can soon ascertain whether he has wandered beyond it. I know his favourite tree. Doubtless his footsteps will guide us."

Already it had begun to grow dark, so that when they reached the ridge it was necessary to kindle the torches before anything could be ascertained.

"Here are the footsteps," cried Karlsefin, after a brief search.

Leif, who was searching in another direction, hurried towards his friend, torch in hand.

"See, there is Olaf's footprint on that soft ground," said Karlsefin, moving slowly along, with the torch held low, "but there is no sign of Snorro's little feet.

Olaf always carried him — yet — ah! here they are on this patch of sand, look. They had halted here — probably to rest; perhaps to change Snorro's position. I've lost them again — no! here they are, but only Olaf's. He must have lifted the child again, no doubt."

"Look here," cried Leif, who had again strayed a little from his friend. "Are not these footsteps descending the ridge?"

Karlsefin hastily examined them.

"They are," he cried, "and then they go down towards the wood — ay, *into* it. Without doubt Olaf has broken his promise; but let us make sure."

A careful investigation convinced both parents that the children had entered that part of the forest, and that therefore all search in any other direction was useless. Karlsefin immediately reascended the ridge, and, putting both hands to his mouth, gave the peculiar halloo which had been agreed upon as the signal that some of the searchers had either found the children or fallen upon their tracks.

"You'll have to give them another shout," said Leif.

Karlsefin did so, and immediately after a faint and very distant halloo came back in reply.

"That's Biarne," observed Karlsefin, as they stood listening intently. "Hist! there is another."

A third and fourth halloo followed quickly, showing that the signal had been heard by all; and in a very short time the searchers came hurrying to the rendezvous, one after another.

"Have you found them?" was of course the first eager question of each, followed by a falling of the countenance when the reply "No" was given. But there was a rising of hope again when it was pointed out that they must certainly be in some part of the tract of dense woodland just in front of them. There were some there, however — and these were the most experienced woodsmen — who shook their heads mentally when they gazed at the vast wilderness, which, in the deepening gloom, looked intensely black, and the depths of which they knew must be as dark as Erebus at that hour. Still, no one expressed desponding feelings, but each spoke cheerfully and agreed at once to the proposed arrangement of continuing the search all night by torchlight.

When the plan of search had been arranged, and another rendezvous fixed, the various parties went out and searched the live-long night in every copse and dell, in every bush and brake, and on every ridge and knoll that seemed the least likely to have been selected by the lost little ones as a place of shelter. But the forest was wide. A party of ten times their number would have found it absolutely impossible to avoid passing many a dell and copse and height and hollow unawares. Thus it came to pass that although they were once or twice pretty near the cave where the children were sleeping, they did not find it. Moreover, the ground in places was very hard, so that, although they more than once discovered faint tracks, they invariably lost them again in a few minutes. They shouted lustily, too, as they went along, but to two such sleepers as Olaf and Snorro in their exhausted condition, their wildest shouts were but as the whisperings of a sick mosquito.

Gradually the searchers wandered farther and farther away from the spot, until they were out of sight and hearing.

We say sight and hearing, because, though the children were capable of neither at that time, there was in that wood an individual who was particularly sharp in regard to both. This was a scout of a party of natives who chanced to be travelling in that neighbourhood at the time. The man — who had a reddish-brown body partially clad in a deerskin, glittering black eyes, and very stiff wiry black hair, besides uncommonly strong and long white teeth, in excellent order — chanced to have taken up his quarters for the night under a tree on the top of a knoll. When, in the course of his slumbers, he became aware of the fact that a body of men were going about the woods with flaring torches and shouting like maniacs, he awoke, *not* with a start, or any such ridiculous exclamation as "Ho!" "Ha!" or "Hist!" but with the mild operation of opening his saucerlike eyes until they were at their widest. No evil resulting from this cautious course of action, he ventured to raise his head an inch off the ground — which was his rather extensive pillow — then another inch and another, until he found himself resting on his elbow and craning his neck over a low bush. Being almost black, and quite noiseless, he might have been mistaken for a slowly-moving shadow.

Gradually he gained his knees, then his feet, and then, peering into space, he observed Biarne and Krake, with several others, ascending the knoll.

For the shadow to sink again to its knees, slope to its elbows, recline on its face, and glide into the heart of a thick bush and disappear, did not seem at all difficult or unnatural. At any rate that is what it did, and there it remained observing all that passed.

"Ho! hallo! Olaf! Snorro! hi-i-i!" shouted Biarne on reaching the summit of the knoll.

"Hooroo!" yelled Krake, in a tone that must have induced the shadow to take him for a half-brother.

"Nothing here," said Biarne, holding up the torch and peering round in all directions.

"Nothing whatever," responded Krake.

He little knew at the time that the shadow was displaying his teeth, and loosening in its sheath a long knife or dagger made of bone, which, from the spot where he lay, he could have launched with unerring certainty into the heart of any of those who stood before him. It is well for man that he sometimes does not know what *might* be!

After a brief inspection of the knoll, and another shout or two, they descended again into the brake and pushed on. The shadow rose and followed until he reached a height whence he could see that the torch-bearers had wandered far away to the westward. As the friends and relatives for whom he acted the part of scout were encamped away to the eastward, he returned to his tree and continued his nap till daybreak, when he arose and shook himself, yawned and scratched his head. Evidently he pondered the occurrences of the night, and felt convinced that if so many strange men went about looking for something with so much care and anxiety, it must undoubtedly, be something that was worth looking for. Acting on this idea he began to look.

Now, it must be well-known to most people that savages are rather smart fellows at making observations on things in general and drawing conclusions therefrom. The shouts led him to believe that lost human beings were being sought for. Daylight enabled him to see little feet which darkness had concealed from the Norsemen, whence he concluded that children were being sought for. Following out his clue, with that singular power of following a trail for which savages are noted, he came to the cave, and peered through the bushes with his great eyes, pounced upon the sleepers, and had his pug nose converted into a Roman — all as related in the last chapter.

Sometime after sunrise the various searching parties assembled at the place of rendezvous — fagged, dispirited, and hungry.

"Come," said Karlsefin, who would not permit his feelings to influence his conduct, "we must not allow ourselves to despond at little more than the beginning of our search. We will breakfast here, lads, and then return to the ridge where we first saw their footsteps. Daylight will enable us to track them more easily. Thank God the weather is warm, and I daresay if they kept well under cover of the trees, the dear children may have got no harm from exposure. They have not been fasting *very* long, so — let us to work."

Leif and Biarne both fell in with Karlsefin's humour, and cheered the spirits of the men by their tone and example, so that when the hurried meal was finished they felt much refreshed, and ready to begin the work of another day.

It was past noon before they returned to the ridge and began the renewed search. Daylight now enabled them to trace the little footsteps with more certainty, and towards the afternoon they came to the cave where the children had slept.

"Here have they spent the night," said Leif, with breathless interest, as he and Karlsefin examined every corner of the place.

"But they are gone," returned the other, "and it behoves us to waste no time. Go, Biarne, let the men spread out — stay! — Is not this the foot of a man who wears a shoe somewhat different from ours?"

"'Tis a savage," said Biarne, in a tone of great anxiety.

Karlsefin made no reply, and the party being now concentrated, they followed eagerly on, finding the prints of the feet quite plain in many places.

"Unquestionably they have been captured by a savage," said Leif.

"Ay, and he must have taken Snorro on his shoulder, and made poor Olaf walk alongside," observed Biarne.

Following the trail with the perseverance and certainty of bloodhounds, they at last came to the deserted encampment on the banks of the rivulet. That it had been forsaken only a short time before was apparent from the circumstance of the embers of the fires still smoking. They examined the place closely and found the little footmarks of the children, which were quite distinguishable from those of the native children by the difference in the form of the shoes.

Soon they came to marks on the bank of the stream which indicated unmistakeably that canoes had been launched there. And now, for the first time, the countenances of Leif and Karlsefin fell.

"You think there is no hope?" asked the latter.

"I won't say that," replied Leif; "but we know not what course they have taken, and we cannot follow them on foot."

"True," observed Karlsefin, in bitter despondency.

"The case is not so bad," observed Heika, stepping forward at this point. "You know we have a number of canoes captured from the savages; some of us have become somewhat expert in the management of these. Let a few of us go back and fetch them hither on our shoulders, with provisions for a long journey, and we shall soon be in a position to give chase. They cannot have gone far yet, and we shall be sure to overtake them, for what we lack in experience shall be more than made up by the strength of our arms and wills."

"Thou art a good counsellor, Heika," said Karlsefin, with a sad smile; "I will follow that advice. Go thou and Hake back to the huts as fast as may be, and order the home-guard to make all needful preparation. Some of us will follow in thy steps more leisurely, and others will remain here to rest until you return with the canoes."

Thus directed the brothers turned their powers of speed to good account, so that, when some of their comrades returned footsore and jaded for want of rest, they not only found that everything was ready for a start, but that a good meal had been prepared for them.

While these remained in the settlement to rest and protect it, the home-guards were ordered to get ready for immediate service. Before night had closed in, the brothers, with torches in their hands, headed a party of fresh men carrying three canoes and provisions on their shoulders. They reached the encampment again in the early morning, and by daybreak all was ready for a start. Karlsefin, Thorward, and Heika acted as steersmen; Krake, Tyrker, and Hake filled the important posts of bowmen. Besides these there were six men in each canoe, so that the entire party numbered twenty-four strong men, fully armed with bow and arrow, sword and shield, and provisioned for a lengthened voyage.

"Farewell, friends," said Karlsefin to those who stood on the banks of the little stream. "It may be that we shall never return from this enterprise. You may rest assured that we will either rescue the children or perish in the attempt. Leif and Biarne have agreed to remain in charge of the settlement. They are good men and true, and well able to guide and advise you. Tell Gudrid that my last thoughts shall be of her — if I do not return. But I do not anticipate failure, for the God of the Christians is with us. Farewell."

"Farewell," responded the Norsemen on the bank, waving their hands as the canoes shot out into the stream.

In a few minutes they reached the great river, and, turning upstream, were soon lost to view in the depths of the wide wilderness.

CHAPTER XIX.

New Experiences — Difficulties Encountered and Overcome —
Thorward and Tyrker Make a Joint Effort,
with Humbling Results.

It may be as well to remark here, that the Norsemen were not altogether ignorant of the course of the great river on which they had now embarked. During their sojourn in those regions they had, as we have said, sent out many exploring parties, and were pretty well acquainted with the nature of the country within fifty miles or so in all directions. These expeditions, however, had been conducted chiefly on land; only one of them by water.

That one consisted of a solitary canoe, manned by four men, of whom Heika was steersman, while Hake managed the bow-paddle, these having proved themselves of all the party the most apt to learn the use of the paddle and management of the canoe. During the fight with the savages, recorded in a previous chapter, the brothers had observed that the man who sat in the bow was of quite as much importance in regard to steering as he who sat in the stern; and when they afterwards ascended the river, and found it necessary to shoot hither and thither amongst the surges, cross-currents, and eddies of a rapid, they then discovered that simple steering at one end of their frail bark would not suffice, but that it was necessary to steer, as it were, at both ends. Sometimes, in order to avoid a stone, or a dangerous whirlpool, or a violent shoot, it became necessary to turn the canoe almost on its centre, as on a pivot, or at least within its own length; and in order to accomplish this, the steersman had to dip his paddle as far out to one side as possible, to draw the stern in that direction, while the bowman did the same on the opposite side, and drew the bow the other way — thus causing the light craft to spin round almost instantly. The two guiding men thus acted in unison, and it was only by thoroughly understanding each other, in all conceivable situations, that good and safe steering could be achieved.

The canoes which had been captured from the savages were frail barks in the most literal sense of these words. They were made of the bark of the birch-tree, a substance which, though tough, was very easily split insomuch that a single touch upon a stone was sufficient to cause a bad leak. Hence the utmost care was required in their navigation. But although thus easily damaged they were also easily repaired, the materials for reparation — or even, if necessary, reconstruction — being always at hand in the forest.

Now although Heika and his brother were, as we have said, remarkably expert, it does not follow that those were equally so who managed the other two canoes of the expedition. On the contrary, their experience in canoeing had hitherto been slight. Karlsefin and his bowman Krake were indeed tolerably expert, having practised a good deal with the Scottish brothers, but Thorward turned out to be an uncommonly bad canoe-man; nevertheless, with the self-confidence natural to a good seaman, and one who was expert with the oar, he scouted the idea that anything connected with freshwater voyaging could prove difficult to *him*, and resolutely claimed and took his position as one of the steersmen of the expedition. His bowman, Tyrker, as ill luck would have it, turned out to be the worst man of them all in rough water, although he had shown himself sufficiently good on the smooth lake to induce the belief that he might do well enough.

But their various powers in this respect were not at first put to the test, because for a very long way the river was uninterrupted by rapids, and progress was therefore comparatively easy. The scenery through which they passed was rich and varied in the extreme. At one part the river ran between high banks, which were covered to the water's edge with trees and bushes of different kinds, many of them being exceedingly brilliant in colour. At another part the banks were lower, with level spaces like lawns, and here and there little openings where rivulets joined the river, their beds affording far-reaching glimpses of woodland, in which deer might occasionally be seen gambolling. Elsewhere the river widened occasionally into something like a lake, with wooded islets on its calm surface, while everywhere the water, earth, and air teemed with animal life – fish, flesh, fowl, and insect. It was such a sight of God's beautiful earth as may still be witnessed by those who, leaving the civilised world behind, plunge into the vast wildernesses that exist to this day in North America.

Beautiful though it was, however, the Norsemen had small leisure and not much capacity to admire it, being preoccupied and oppressed by anxiety as to the fate of the children. Still, in spite of this, a burst of admiration would escape them ever and anon as they passed rapidly along.

The first night they came to the spot where the natives had encamped the night before, and all hands were very sanguine of overtaking them quickly. They went about the encampment examining everything, stirring up the embers of the fires, which were still hot, and searching for little footprints.

Hake's unerring bow had supplied the party with fresh venison and some wild geese. While they sat over the fires that night roasting steaks and enjoying marrowbones, they discussed their prospects.

"They have got but a short start of us," said Karlsefin, looking thoughtfully into the fire, before which he reclined on a couch of pine-branches, "and if we push on with vigour, giving ourselves only just sufficient repose to keep up our strength, we shall be sure to overtake them in a day or two."

"It may be so," said Thorward, with a doubtful shake of the head; "but you know, brother, that a stern chase is usually a long one."

Thorward was one of those unfortunate men who get the credit of desiring to throw wet blankets and cold water upon everything, whereas, poor man, his only fault was a tendency to view things critically, so as to avoid the evil consequences of acting on the impulse of an over-sanguine temperament. Thorward was a safe adviser, but was not a pleasant one, to those who regard all objection as opposition, and who don't like to look difficulties full in the face. However, there is no question that it would have been better for him, sometimes, if he had been gifted with the power of holding his tongue!

His friend Karlsefin, however, fully appreciated and understood him.

"True," said he, with a quiet smile, "as you say, a stern chase is a long one; nevertheless we are not *far* astern, and that is what I count on for shortening the chase."

"That is a just remark," said Thorward gravely, applying a marrowbone to his lips, and drinking the semi-liquid fat therefrom as if from a cup; "but I think you might make it (this is most excellent marrow!) a still shorter chase if you would take my advice. Ho! Krake, hand me another marrowbone. It seems to me that Vinland deer have a peculiar sweetness, which is not so obvious in those of Norway, though perchance it is hunger which gives the relish; and yet can I truly say that I have been hungered in Norway. However, I care not to investigate reasons too closely while I am engaged in the actual practice of consumption."

Here he put another marrowbone to his lips, and sucked out the contents with infinite gusto.

"And what may your advice be?" asked his friend, laughing.

"I'll wager that Hake could tell you if his mouth were not too full," replied Thorward, with a smile.

"Say, thou thrall, before refilling that capacious cavern, what had best be done in order to increase our speed?"

Hake checked a piece of wild-fowl on its passage to his mouth, and, after a moment's consideration, replied that in his opinion lightening the load of the canoe was the best thing to be done.

"And say," continued Thorward, beginning to eat a large drumstick, "how may *that* be done?"

"By leaving our provisions behind," answered Hake.

"Ha! did not I say that he could tell you?" growled Thorward between his teeth, which were at that moment conflicting with the sinewy part of the drumstick.

"There is something in that," remarked Karlsefin.

"*Something* in it!" exclaimed Thorward, resting for a moment from his labours in order to wash all down with a cataract of water; "why, there is everything in it. Who ever heard of a man running a race with a full stomach – much less winning it? If we would win we must voyage light; besides, what need is there to carry salt salmon and dried flesh with us when the woods are swarming with such as these, and when we have a man in our company who can bring down a magpie on the wing?"

"And that's true, if anything ever was," observed Krake, who had been too busy up to that point to do more than listen.

Hake nodded his approval of the sentiment, and Karlsefin said that he quite agreed with it, and would act upon the advice next day.

"Just take a *very* little salmon," suggested Tyrker, with a sigh, "for fear this good fortune should perhaps come suddenly to an end."

There was a general laugh at Tyrker's caution, and Karlsefin said he was at liberty to fill his own pockets with salmon for his own use, if he chose.

"Sure it would be much better," cried Krake, "to eat a week's allowance all at once, and so save time and trouble."

"If I had your stomach, Krake, I might try that," retorted Tyrker, "but mine is not big enough."

"Well, now," returned Krake, "if you only continue to over-eat for a week or two, as you're doing just now, you'll find it big enough – and more!"

"We must sleep tonight, and not talk," said Karlsefin gravely, for he saw that the dispute was likely to wax hot. "Come, get you all to rest. I will call you two hours hence."

Every man of the expedition was sound asleep in a few minutes after that, with the exception of their leader, who was to keep the first half hour watch – Thorward, Heika, and Hake being appointed to relieve him and each other in succession.

The moon was shining brightly when the two hours had elapsed. This was very fortunate, because they expected to arrive at the rapids ere long, and would require light to ascend them. Owing to recent heavy rains, however, the current was so strong that they did not reach the rapids till sunrise. Before starting, they had buried all their provisions in such a way that they might be dug up and used, if necessary, on their return.

"'Tis as well that we have daylight here," observed Karlsefin, as he, Thorward, and Hake stood on a rocky part of the bank just below the rapids, and surveyed the place before making the attempt.

It might have been observed that Thorward's face expressed some unusual symptoms of feeling, as he looked up the river, and saw there nothing but a turbulent mass of heaving surges dashing themselves wildly against sharp forbidding rocks, which at one moment were grinning like black teeth amidst the white foam, and the next were overwhelmed by the swelling billows.

"You don't mean to say we have to go up that maelstrom?" he said, pointing to the river, and looking at Hake.

"I would there were any other road," answered Hake, smiling, "but truly I know of none. The canoes are light, and might be carried by land to the still water above the rapids, but, as you see, the banks here are sheer up and down without foothold for a crow, and if we try to go round by the woods on either side, we shall have a march of ten miles through such a country that the canoes will be torn to pieces before the journey is completed."

"Have you and Heika ever ascended that mad stream?" cried Thorward.

"Ay – twice."

"Without overturning?"

"Yes – without overturning."

Again Thorward bestowed on the river a long silent gaze, and his countenance wore an expression of blank surprise, which was so amusing that Karlsefin forgot for a moment the anxiety that oppressed him, and burst into a hearty fit of laughter.

"Ye have little to laugh at," said Thorward gravely. "It is all very well to talk of seamanship – and, truly, if you will give me a good boat with a stout pair of oars, and the roughest sea you ever saw, I will show you what I can do – but who ever heard of a man going afloat in an eggshell on a monstrous kettle of boiling water?"

"Why, Hake says he has done it," said Karlsefin.

"When I see him do it I will believe it," replied Thorward doggedly.

"You will not, I suppose, object to follow, if I lead the way?" asked Hake.

"Go to, thrall! Dost think I am afraid?" said Thorward sternly; and then, as if he thought such talk trifling, turned on his heel with a light laugh, and was about to descend the bank of the river to the spot where the men stood in a group near the canoes, when Karlsefin called him back.

"Softly, not so fast, Thorward. Although no doubt we are valiant sailors — and woe betide the infatuated man who shall venture to deny it! — yet must we put our pride in our pouches for once, and accept instruction from Hake. After all, it is said that wise men may learn something from babes — if so, why may not sea-kings learn from thralls? — unless, indeed, we be not up to the mark of wise men."

"I am all attention," said Thorward.

"This, then," said Hake, pointing to a large rock in the middle of the stream, "is the course you must pursue, if ye would reach the upper end of the rapid in a dry skin. See you yonder rock — the largest — where the foam breaks most fiercely, as if in wrath because it cannot overleap it? Well, that is our first resting-place. If you follow my finger closely, you will see, near the foot of the rapid, two smaller rocks, one below the other; they only show now and then as the surges rise and fall, but each has an eddy, or a tail of smooth water below it. Do you see them?"

"I see, I see," cried Thorward, becoming interested in spite of himself; "but, truly, if thou callest that part of the river smooth and a 'tail,' I hope I may never fall into the clutches of the smooth animal to which that tail belongs."

"It is smooth compared with the rest," continued Hake, "and has a back-draught which will enable us to rest there a moment. You will observe that the stone above has also a tail, the end of which comes quite down to the head of the tail below. Well, then, you must make such a bold dash at the rapid that you shall reach the lower eddy. That gained, the men will rest a space and breathe, but not cease paddling altogether, else will you be carried down again. Then make a dash into the stream and paddle might and main till you reach the eddy above. You will thus have advanced about thirty yards, and be in a position to make a dash for the long eddy that extends from the big rock."

"That is all very plain," observed Thorward; "but does it not seem to you, Hake, that the best way to explain matters would be to go and ascend while we look on and learn a lesson through our eyes?"

"I am ready," was the youth's brief reply; for he was a little hurt by the seaman's tone and manner.

"Thorward is right, Hake," said Karlsefin. "Go, take your own canoe up. We will watch you from this spot, and follow if all goes well."

The young Scot at once sprang down the bank, and in a few minutes his canoe with its six men, and Heika steering, shot out from the bank towards the rapid.

All tendency to jest forsook Thorward as he stood beside his friend on the cliff with compressed lips and frowning brow, gazing upon the corklike vessel which danced upon the troubled waters. In a minute it was at the foot of the broken water. Then Heika's voice rose above the roar of the stream, as he gave a shout and urged on his men. The canoe sprang into the boiling flood. It appeared to remain stationary, while the men struggled might and main.

"'Tis too strong for them!" cried Thorward, becoming excited.

"No; they advance!" said Karlsefin in a deep, earnest tone.

This was true, but their progress was very small. Gradually they overcame the power of the stream and shot into the first eddy, amid the cheers of their comrades on shore. Here they waited only a moment or two, and then made a dash for the second eddy. There was a shout of disappointment from the men, because they swept down so fast that it seemed as if all the distance gained had been lost; but suddenly the canoe was caught by the extreme tail of the eddy, the downward motion of its bow was stopped, it was turned straight upstream, and they paddled easily towards the second rock. Another brief pause was made here, and then a dash was made for the eddy below the large rock. This was more easily gained, but the turbulence of the water was so great that there was much more danger in crossing from one eddy to the other than there had been before.

Under the large rock they rested for a few minutes, and then, dashing out into the rapid, renewed the struggle. Thus, yard by yard, taking advantage of every available rock and eddy, they surmounted the difficulty and landed at the head of the rapids, where they waved their caps to their friends below.

"It's Krake that wishes he was there!" observed that worthy, wiping the perspiration from his brow and drawing a long deep breath; for the mere sight of the struggle had excited him almost as much as if he had engaged in it.

"'Tis Krake that will soon be there if all goes well," remarked Karlsefin, with a laugh, as he came forward and ordered his canoe to be pushed off. "I will be ready to follow, but you had better go first, Thorward. If anything befalls you I am here to aid."

"Well, come along, lads," cried Thorward. "Get into the bow, Tyrker, and see that you do your duty like a man. Much depends on you — more's the pity!" He added the last words in a low voice, for Thorward, being a very self-reliant man, would like to have performed all the duties himself, had that been possible.

"Shove off!"

They shot from the bank and made for the rapid gallantly. Thorward's shout quite eclipsed that of Heika on taking the rapid. Truly, if strength of lung could have done it, he might have taken his canoe up single-handed, for he roared like a bull of Bashan when Tyrker missed a stroke of his paddle, thereby letting the bow sweep round so that the canoe was carried back to the point whence it had started.

Tremendous was the roar uttered by Thorward when they faced the rapid the second time, and fierce was the struggle of the men when in it, and anxious was Tyrker to redeem his error — so anxious, in fact, that he missed another stroke and well-nigh fell overboard!

It is said that "Fortune favours the brave." There was no lack of bravery in Tyrker — only lack of experience and coolness — and Fortune favoured him on this occasion. If he had *not* missed a stroke and fallen forward, his miscalculation of aqueous forces would have sent the canoe past the mark in the opposite direction from the last time; but the missed stroke was the best stroke of all, for it allowed the canoe to shoot into the first eddy, and converted a terrific roar of wrath from Thorward into a hearty cheer.

Resting a few moments, as Heika and his crew had done, they then addressed themselves to the second part of the rapid. Here Thorward steered so well that the canoe took the stream at the proper angle; but Tyrker, never having perceived what the right angle was, and strongly impressed with the belief that the bow was pointing too much up the river, made a sudden stroke on the wrong side! The canoe instantly flew not only to the tail of the eddy, but right across it into the wild surges beyond, where it was all but upset, first to one side then to the other, after which it spun round like a teetotum, and was carried with fearful violence towards one of those rocky ridges which we have described as being alternately covered and uncovered by the foam. On the crest of a bulging cascade they were fortunately borne right over this ridge, which next moment showed its black teeth, as if grinning at the dire mischief it might have done if it had only chosen to bite! Next instant the canoe overturned, and left the men to flounder to land, while it went careering down towards the gravelly shallows below.

Now Karlsefin had anticipated this, and was prepared for it. In the first place, he had caused the arms, etc., to be removed from Thorward's canoe before it set out, saying that he would carry them up in his canoe, so that his friend's might go light. Then, having his vessel ready and manned, he at once pushed out and intercepted the other canoe before it reached the gravelly shallows, where it would have been much damaged, if not dashed to pieces.

"That is bad luck," observed Thorward, somewhat sulkily, as, after swimming ashore, he wrung the water from his garments.

"Not worse than might have been expected on a first trial," said Karlsefin, laughing. "Besides, that rascal Tyrker deceived me. Had I known he was so bad, you should have had Krake."

Poor Tyrker, very much crestfallen, kept carefully away from the party, and did not hear that remark.

"Now it is my turn," continued Karlsefin. "If we get up safely I will send Heika down to take the bow of your canoe."

Karlsefin, as we said, was somewhat more expert than most of the men in managing canoes, and Krake, besides having had more experience than many of his fellows, had once before visited and ascended this rapid. They therefore made the ascent almost as well as the Scots had done.

Arrived at the upper end, Hake and Heika were ordered to remove everything out of their canoe, and, with a full crew, to run down to the aid of their friends. Karlsefin himself went with them as one of the crew, so that he might take the steering paddle when Heika should resign it in order to act as Thorward's bowman. Thus manned, the second attempt was crowned with success, and, not long afterwards the three canoes swept into a smooth reach of the river above the rapids, and proceeded on their way.

But a great deal of time had been lost in this way, and Karlsefin felt that it must be made up for by renewed diligence and protracted labour.

CHAPTER XX.

Remarkable Experiences of Olaf and Snorro —
The Former Suffers the Pangs of Remorse.

A camp of savages is, in some respects, exceedingly unattractive. Indeed, it may truly be said to be in many respects repulsive. There are usually odours in such a camp which are repellent to the nose, dishes that are disgusting to the taste, sights that are disagreeable to the eyes, sounds that are abhorrent to the ear, and habits that are uncongenial to the feelings.

Nevertheless there is much in such a camp that is deeply interesting. The student of nature, the mental and moral philosopher, the anthropologist, and the philanthropist — ay, even the cynic — might each find much food here suited to his particular tastes and powers of mental digestion. At present, however, we have chiefly to do, good reader, with that which interests you and me — namely, Olaf and Snorro, who were prisoners of war in a savage camp.

The camp referred to was not the small affair already described as having taken sudden flight from the rivulet which flowed into the great river, where we have left the Norsemen doing battle with the waters. It was the great parent, of which that little camp was but an offshoot — the headquarters of a whole tribe of savages, who dwelt in it to the extent of many hundreds. Yet it was not a fixed camp. It was a moving village of leathern tents, or wigwams, pitched without any regard to order, on the margin of what appeared to be a small lake, but which was in reality a mere widening of the great river.

Hither Olaf and Snorro were brought by their captors, and immediately conveyed to the tent of the chief, who was an aged and white-haired though vigorous and strong-boned savage. Whitepow, for such, curiously enough, was his name, opened his eyes uncommonly wide when he saw the children of the Norsemen, and, sitting up on the couch of furs on which he had been reclining, gazed at them for about five minutes without speaking, almost without winking.

Snorro did not appear to relish this, for he crept close to Olaf's side and tried to turn away his eyes, but found this to be impossible, for a sort of fascination kept them riveted on the countenance of the aged Whitepow.

At last the savage chief opened his mouth as well as his eyes, and spoke to the savage who had brought the children into the royal presence. That worthy rapidly related the circumstances of the capture — at least so it is to be presumed, but no one can now tell for certain — after which Whitepow turned to Olaf and said something which as near as possible resembled the words:

"Whardeekum froyoul ittlsiner?"

"I don't understand you," answered Olaf humbly. Whitepow repeated the words, and Olaf reiterated his assurance that he could make nothing of them whatever.

This concluded the interview at that time, and Whitepow gave an order which resulted in the children being conveyed to a tent where there were several women, old and young, to whom they were handed over with a message which we cannot record, not knowing what it was.

The reception which they met with from these native women was flattering, if not in all respects pleasant. First, they were placed in the centre of the group and gazed at in wondering admiration. Then they were seized and kissed and hugged all round the circle. Then they were examined carefully all over, and under as well, their white skins being as much a matter of interest as their clothing. After that their fair hair was smoothed and parted by not untender hands, and they were hugged again — just as two new dolls might have been by a group of sisters on first making their acquaintance.

Of course there was an immense deal of talking and chatting and commenting, also no small amount of giggling, and once or twice one of the women addressed Olaf; but Olaf shook his head and stuck to his first assurance that their words were incomprehensible.

All this was borne by the captives with wonderful equanimity, because neither was old enough to be much affected by dirtiness of person or garments, and both were thoroughly able to appreciate kindness.

Finally, a stout and not bad-looking young woman took possession of Snorro, and robbed her own offspring in order to bestow on him a very acceptable drink of milk. This last act quite reconciled him to his fate, and Olaf, though not so easily won over, was somewhat mollified by a kindly old woman, who placed him at her side, and set before him a dish of dried berries.

When this feeding process was concluded, and the first blush of novelty began to wear off, the children were turned out in front of the women's tent, where, seated together on a bit of wood, they underwent the inspection of the whole tribe, old and young, male and female. This was a much more trying ordeal, but in about an hour an order was issued which resulted in the dispersion of every one save a few boys, who were either privileged individuals or rebellious subjects, for they not only came back to gaze at the children, but ventured at length to carry them off to play near the banks of the river.

Olaf was so far reconciled to his new friends that he did not object to witness and take an interest in their games, though he resolutely refused to join, fearing that if he did so his little charge might be spirited away while he was not watching.

At last one of the boys, whose head was very small and round, and whose name appeared to be Powlet, came forward with a little red paint, and offered to apply it to Olaf's face. All the boys' faces were, we may observe, more or less painted with black, red, white, and blue colours, and their heads were decorated more or less with feathers. Indeed, these feathers constituted, with the exception of a trifling shred of leather about the loins, and some feathers in their hair, all the clothing they wore at that season of the year.

Olaf refused to be painted, whereupon Powlet rubbed the red paint on the point of his own nose, an operation which so tickled the fancy of Snorro, that he burst into a hearty fit of laughter, to Olaf's ineffable joy.

"That's right, Snorrie," he cried, setting the child on his knee, "laugh again;

do it heartily; it will cheer us both."

"It am so funny, O'af," said Snorro, repeating the laugh as he looked at the native boy.

Observing the success of his efforts to please, Powlet put a spot of the red paint under each eye, and Snorro laughed so much at this that all the other boys came crowding round to ascertain and enjoy the joke.

Powlet now offered to anoint Snorro in the same way, but Snorro objected, and, pointing to his protector said, with a look of glee —

"Do O'af."

Nothing else would have induced Olaf to submit, but Snorro's wish was law to him. He therefore consented at once, and Powlet, dipping his finger in the red paint which he carried in the hollow of his hand, drew a thick stroke from Olaf's forehead down to the point of his nose, where he made it terminate in a large, round spot.

There was a tremendous shout at this, not only from Snorro, but from all the other boys; and Olaf was so pleased to see Snorro happy, that he turned to Powlet, pointed to his face, and nodded his head by way of inviting further decoration.

Powlet was an intelligent boy. He understood him at once, and went on with his work, a boy coming up at the moment with some white paint in his hand, and another with some blue. A white diamond was immediately planted on each cheek, and a blue circle under each eye, with a red spot in the centre of each. So far, the work was very striking and suggestive, but when Powlet finished off by drawing a series of blue, red, and white lines over Olaf's eyes, in the forms that usually indicate astonishment, added a red oval to the chin, with a blue spot in the middle of it, and stuck some feathers in his hair, the effect was absolutely tremendous, for it caused the native boys to yell with delight, and Snorro almost to fall off his protector's knee in a fit of juvenile hysterics.

"Don't overdo it, Snorrie," said Olaf in some alarm.

"Oh! O'af, 'oo *is so* funny!" he cried again, giving way to mirth till the tears ran down his cheeks.

At this point a tall savage came rushing out of the chief's tent with glaring eyes, and made for the spot where the boys were assembled. They seemed to know at once what was his errand, for, with one consent, they scattered and fled. The tall savage singled out Powlet, caught him, punched his head, and flung him into the river, after which he turned, and, without taking any notice of the captives further than to gaze at them, returned leisurely to the regal tent.

Meanwhile Powlet came to the surface, swam like an otter to the shore, and, clambering up the bank, ran into the woods, seemingly none the worse of his bath.

Thus left alone, Olaf put Snorro on his back and sauntered away into the woods along the banks of the river. Forgetting his ridiculous appearance, he began to think of home and to feel very sad, while his charge, overcome with his late exertions, fell asleep on his back. The longer he walked the sadder he grew, and at last he groaned rather than said, "What *shall* I do?"

Suddenly it occurred to him, that as the savages appeared to be very careless about watching him, he might run away. It could do no harm to try, and he would not be in a much worse position than when lost in the woods before. Under the influence of this thought he stopped and looked cautiously round in all directions. No one was to be seen. He breathed hard, turned off the track on tiptoe until he had got into what appeared to him to be a very dense and sequestered part of the woods, then suddenly took to his heels and ran for his life!

A loud laugh sounded in the bushes in front of him, and he stopped short just as Powlet appeared, wagging his small head and laughing inordinately.

Poor Olaf guessed at once that the boy had been set to watch him; he therefore wheeled about and walked back to the river, where, going out on a spit of land that he might not be overheard, he sat down on the ground and communed bitterly with himself.

"Oh why, why did I break my promise?" he murmured in deep despondency.

After a long silence he began to think aloud.

"It all comes of *disobedience!*" he muttered.

"Father used to say, 'If you love me, obey me. If you want to prove that you love Gudrid, *obey* her.' That's it, Olaf. It's there that the sin lies. He told me never to pass the ridge, and I *did* pass the ridge, even though I had promised not to; and so, owing to that little bit of disobedience, here you are, Olaf — and Snorrie too — poor Snorrie — and we're likely to remain here for ever, as far as I can see. Oh that I had not done it! But what good can wishing do *now*? If I had loved father better, perhaps I would have obeyed him better."

It would almost seem as if Olaf had heard of such a word as this — "If ye love me, keep my commandments!"

After a few minutes he broke forth again — "Yes, I know that I did not intend to disobey; nevertheless I *did* it. And I did not think such awful things would follow — but that does not mend the matter. What *shall* I do? Snorrie, I think I could gladly lay down my life, if I could give you back once more to your mother."

Snorro heard not the remark. He was as sound as a top, and Olaf looked sadly at the little head that lay on his shoulder. Then it struck him that it was high time to have the child put to bed, so he rose and hurried back to the women's tent, where he was received with as much kindness as before.

Very soon Snorro's little head reposed upon a pillow of rabbit-skins, and not long after that Olaf went to rest beside him on a deerskin couch, where, lying on his back, he could see the sky through the hole in the top of the tent whence the smoke of the fire escaped. As he lay there the burden of his thoughts was ever the same — "Oh *why* did I do it? Why did I disobey?" Thus the poor boy lay, self-condemned, and gazed upwards and pondered, until sweet sleep came and carried heart and brain to the blessed refuge of oblivion.

CHAPTER XXI.

Reinforcements Sent off to Karlsefin — Foes Discovered in the Woods — A Night Attack, and other Warlike Matters.

We must return now for a little to the settlement of the Norsemen, which, by the way, had by this time come to be called by the name of Leifsgaard.

Here, from Thorward's house, there issued tones which indicated the existence of what is popularly known as a "breeze." Human breezes are usually irregular, and blow after the manner of counter-currents; but in Thorward's habitation the breezes almost invariably blew in one direction, and always issued from the lungs of Freydissa, who possessed a peculiar knack of keeping and enjoying all the breeze to herself, some passive creature being the butt against which it impinged.

On the present occasion that butt was Bertha. Indeed, Bertha was a species of practising-butt, at which Freydissa exercised herself when all other butts failed, or when she had nothing better to do.

"Don't say to me that you can't help it!" she cried, in her own amiably shrill tones. "You can help it well enough if you choose. You are always at it, morning, noon, and night; I'm quite sick of you, girl; I'm sorry I brought you here; I'd send you back to Greenland tomorrow if I could. If the ship sank with you on the passage, I'd rejoice — I *would*! There! don't say it again, now; you're going to — I can see that by your whimpering look. *Don't* say you can't help it. Don't! don't! Do you hear?"

"Indeed, *indeed* I can't —"

"There! I knew you would," shrieked Freydissa, as she raised herself from the washtub in which she had been manipulating some articles of clothing as if she were tearing Bertha to pieces — "*why* can't you?"

"It isn't easy to help weeping," whimpered Bertha, as she continued to drive her spinning-wheel, "when one thinks of all that has passed, and poor —"

"Weeping! weeping!" cried Freydissa, diving again into the tub; "do you call that weeping? *I* call it downright blubbering. Why, your face is as much *begrutten* as if you were a mere baby."

This was true, for what between her grief at the sudden disappearance of Olaf and Snorro, and the ceaseless assaults of her mistress, who was uncommonly cross that morning, Bertha's pretty little face was indeed a good deal swelled and inflamed about the eyes and cheeks. She again took refuge in silence, but this made no difference to Freydissa, or rather it acted, if anything, as a provocative of wrath. "Speak, you hussy!" was usually her irate manner of driving the helpless little handmaid out of that refuge.

"What were you going to say? Poor what?" she asked sharply, after a few minutes' silence.

"I was going to say that poor Snorro and —"

"Oh! it's all very well to talk of poor Snorro," interrupted her mistress;

"you know quite well that you took to snivelling long before Snorro was lost. You're thinking of Hake, you are. You know you are, and you daren't deny it, for your red face would give you the lie if you did. Hake indeed! Even though he *is* a thrall, he's too good for such a silly thing as you. There, be off with you till you can stop your *weeping*, as you call it. Go!"

Freydissa enforced her command by sending a mass of soapy cloth which she had just wrung out after the retreating Bertha. Fortunately she was a bad shot. The missile flew past its intended object, and, hitting a hen, which had ventured to intrude, on the legs, swept it with a terrific cackle into the road, to the amazement, not to say horror, of the cock and chickens.

As Bertha disappeared Biarne entered the room — "Hallo! Freydissa, stormy weather — eh?"

"You can go outside and see for yourself," answered Freydissa angrily.

"So I mean to," returned Biarne, with a smile, "for the weather is pleasanter outside than in; but I must first presume to put the question that brought me here. Do you chance to know where Leif is this morning?"

"How should I know?"

"By having become acquainted with the facts of the case somehow," suggested Biarne.

"Well, then, I don't know; so you can go study the weather."

"Oho! mistress: I see that it is time we sent to Iceland for another cat!"

This allusion to her husband's former treatment of her pet was almost the only thing that could calm — or at least restrain — the storm! Freydissa bit her lips and flushed as she went on with her washing, but she said nothing more.

"Well, good-morning," said Biarne as he left the house to search for Leif.

He found him busily engaged in executing some repairs on board the 'Snake'.

"I have a thought in my head," said Biarne.

"Out with it then," replied Leif, wiping his brow, "because thoughts, if kept long in the brain, are apt to hatch, and the chicken-thoughts are prone to run away at the moment of birth, and men have a tendency to chase the chickens, to the utter forgetting of the original hens! What is thy thought, Biarne?"

"That I should take as many of the men as you can spare," he replied, "and go off by water to reinforce Karlsefin."

"That is strange," said Leif. "I sometimes think that there must be a mysterious influence which passes between mind and mind. The very same thought came into my head this morning when I was at work on this oar, and I had intended to talk with you on the subject. But why do you think this course of action needful?"

"Just because the party of savages may turn out to be larger than we imagined, or they may be joined by others, and it has occurred to me that the force which is out with Karlsefin is barely sufficient to make a good stand against heavy odds. With a small party heavy odds against you is a serious matter; but with a large party heavy odds on the side of the enemy makes little weight — unless, indeed, their men are willing to come on and be killed in large numbers, which my experience of savages assures me that they are never willing to do."

"Your reasons, Biarne, are very much the same as my own; therefore, being of one mind, we shall go about the business without delay, for if our aid is to reach them at all it must be extended at once. Go, then, select and collect your men; I will be content to guard the place with the half of those that are now here; and make haste, Biarne, the more I think of it the more I fear delay."

Biarne was not slow to act. In a remarkably brief space of time he had selected his men, prepared the canoes, loaded them with arms and food, and got everything ready; so that before the afternoon had far advanced he was enabled to set off with four canoes and thirty-two men.

Meanwhile Leif had set those that remained to complete a small central point of defence – a sort of fortalice – which had been for some time in preparation as a last refuge for the colonists in the event of their ever being attacked by overwhelming numbers.

Karlsefin had long seen the propriety of building some such stronghold; but the friendly relations that had existed for a considerable period between the Norsemen and the natives had induced him to suspend building operations, until several annoying misunderstandings and threats on the part of the savages had induced him to resume the work. At the time of which we write it was almost completed.

This fortress was little more than a strong palisade of stout planks about twelve feet high, placed close together, with narrow slits on every side for the discharge of arrows, and a platform all round the top inside, on which men could stand to repel an assault or discharge stones and other missiles over the wall. But the chief strength of the place lay in its foundation, which was the summit of a small isolated rocky mound in the centre of the hamlet. The mound was not more than thirty feet high, but its sides were so steep that the top could not be reached without difficulty, and its area was so small that the little fortification embraced the whole of it. It was large enough, however, to contain the whole population of the place, exclusive of the cattle.

To the completion, then, of this place of refuge, Leif addressed himself with all the energy of his nature. A large shed was erected in one corner of it, with a strong plank roof, to protect the women from stones, arrows, and javelins, which were the only projectiles in vogue at that period of the world's history. Another shed was built just under the fortalice, on the lake side, for the safe housing of the live stock. Arrows were made in great numbers by some of the men, while others gathered and stored an immense supply of heavy ammunition in the shape of stones. Besides this a large quantity of dried provisions was stored in the women's shed, also a supply of water; but in regard to the last, being near the lake, and within easy bow-shot of their vessel, they trusted to bold night-sallies for additional supplies of the indispensable fluid. Finally, the work was carried on with such vigour that eight days after Biarne's departure it was finished.

Finished – and not a moment too soon! At the time when Biarne started on his voyage, the woods were, unknown to the Norsemen, alive with savages. Fortunately these had not observed the departure of the canoes, the whole of them being engaged at the time deep within the woods, holding a council of war, in which it was resolved to attack the white invaders of their land, kill them all, and appropriate their property.

Leif committed a slight mistake in not sending out scouts at this time to guard against surprise, but he was so eager to have the works completed that he grudged sending away any of his small body of men.

On the day when everything had been got ready, he sent a man named Hengler, who was an expert bowman, to procure some venison. In less than an hour Hengler was seen running towards the hamlet at break-neck speed, with his eyes almost starting out of his head, his hair streaming in the breeze, and two savages close on his heels.

"To arms, men!" shouted Leif, as he snatched up a bow, and, without waiting to put on helmet or sword, ran out to meet Hengler.

Seeing this, the savages stopped, hastily fitted arrows to their bowstrings and discharged them, the one at Hengler, the other at Leif. The first just grazed the flying Norseman's ear; the other fell short, but before a second discharge was possible Leif had sent an arrow whizzing at the first savage. It pierced his thigh. Uttering a fierce yell, he plucked the shaft out of the wound, and turning round fled back to the woods followed by his companion.

"Not a moment to lose," gasped Hengler, as he ran into the hamlet. "There are hundreds of them everywhere."

"Coming towards us?" asked Leif.

"Not when I saw them, but doubtless when these two return they will come down like a mountain foss."

"Quick, get into the fort, lads! — Stay, Hengler, assist me with the women."

"Do you think they really mean to attack us?" asked Gudrid, who, with Bertha and Freydissa, came forward at the moment.

"Assuredly they do," answered Leif; "come, follow Hengler to the fort. Whatever they intended before, the arrow in that fellow's leg will settle the question. Where are Thora and Astrid?"

"In the dairy," replied Gudrid.

"Away, then; I go to fetch them."

"Would that I were a man!" exclaimed Freydissa, catching up a spear and shaking it as she strode along with the rest. "*I'd* teach them to think twice before coming here to disturb peaceable folk!"

"Peaceable," thought Leif, with a grim smile, as he hurried towards the dairy; but he said nothing, for he deemed that to be a time for silence and action.

In a few minutes nearly all the population of the place had taken refuge in the fort, and soon afterwards the livestock was driven into the shed beside the rock. The gate was then shut and the men mounted the battlements, or breastwork, to watch for the expected foe.

But no foe made his appearance. Hour after hour passed away; the sun descended behind the treetops and below the horizon; the grey mantle of evening overspread the scene; still the watchers stood on the battlements and gazed intently into the forest — still there was not the slightest sound or symptom of an enemy in the vast sleeping wilderness.

"Now this is passing strange," observed Hengler, who had been appointed second in command, and stood beside Leif.

"Not so strange as ye suppose," replied Leif. "Many a time have I fought with men in the mountains of Norway and on the plains of Valland, and invariably have I found that a surprise is never attempted save in the night."

"True," returned Hengler, "but when a very strong foe stands before a very weak one, it seems to me childish to delay the assault."

"Thine ignorance of war must be great, Hengler," returned Leif, regarding the man with a smile, "if thou hast yet to learn that a body of men weak in numbers becomes passing strong when posted behind good walls, with plenty of missiles and provender."

"My knowledge of war is not great," said the man, who was quite a youth, "but methinks it is like to improve now."

"I fear it is," returned Leif sadly, "but now I will give thee a job to perform that is necessary. From my experience of such matters I feel well assured that the savages intend an assault during the night, when they doubtless expect that their numbers will more easily cope with and overcome us; but in my judgment it is likely that they understand nothing of this fort-work, therefore I shall give *them* a surprise, instead of receiving one at their hands. Go thou, then, with six of the most active among the men, and slip as quietly as may be into the forest; gather there as many pine cones as shall fill your shields to overflowing, and bring them hither, along with a quantity of birch bark. If ye are attacked fight your way back, and we will cover your retreat from the ramparts."

While Hengler and six men were absent on this duty, another small party was sent to fetch into the fort a log about eighteen feet long, which lay on the ground close at hand; at the same time they were ordered to run down to the lake and bring up three or four old planks which had lain for a long time in the water, and were quite sodden. These things were all secured and carried into the fortress in the course of a few minutes. The log was then set up on end and sunk deep into a hole in the ground, so that it remained standing in the centre of the fort with the top just reaching a little above the walls. Pegs were driven into it all the way up, so that a man could easily ascend it. On the top of this pole was affixed a platform made of the soaked planks, about six feet square, with a hole left near the head of the pole through which a man could thrust himself. These Norsemen were smart in using their hands and axes. The contrivance which we have taken so long to describe was erected in a very few minutes. It was well-nigh completed when Hengler and his party returned with the pine cones and birch bark, both of which substances are exceedingly resinous and inflammable. Leif made the men carry them to the top of the pole, and pile them on the platform. He then ordered a small fire to be kindled in a corner of the fort, but to be kept very low and small, so that the tiny wreath of smoke which arose from it might be dissipated before it reached the battlements. After that he called all the men to him.

"Now, my lads," said he, "it is likely that these savages will try to take us by surprise. This they will not find it easy to do. From what I know of them they will come like the fox — slily — and try to pounce upon us. We will let them come; we will let them pounce, and not show face until such time as I give the word — then ye will know how to quit you like men. Away, all of you, to rest — each man with his shield above him and his sword by his side. I myself will do the part of sentinel."

The men quietly obeyed this order. Leif did not think it necessary to say more to them, but to Hengler and two others who had been selected as leaders he revealed more minutely the intended plan of action before they lay down.

Leaving Hengler for a few minutes to guard the walls, he entered the shed where the women were seated.

"You must keep well under cover, Gudrid," he said, "for it is likely that these fellows will shower some arrows upon us — perhaps something heavier; but we are well prepared to receive them."

"Are our enemies numerous?" asked Gudrid anxiously.

"So it is said, but that will do them little service so long as we are behind these walls."

"I wish I had my fingers in their chief's hair!" muttered Freydissa between her teeth.

"I echo the wish you expressed not long ago," said Leif laughing. "Would that thou wert a man, Freydissa, for assuredly a spirit like thine is invaluable on the field of battle."

"Thankful am I that there are other fields besides battlefields where women may be useful," observed Bertha, who was seated on a box beside Astrid, with her arm round her waist.

Freydissa merely cast on her handmaid a look of scorn, for she was aware that neither the time nor place was suited to the exercise of her peculiar talents.

"I just looked in to assure you that all goes well," said Leif, addressing the women generally, "and that you have nothing to fear."

"We fear *nothing*!" said Freydissa, answering for the rest.

The somewhat flippant remark, "Speak for yourself," might have been appropriately made by some of her sisterhood, but they were all too anxious about the impending danger to heed what she said.

When Leif rejoined Hengler on the walls, the shades of night had fallen on the forest. He advised his lieutenant to lie down, but Hengler begged and obtained permission to share his vigil.

There was no moon that night, and it became extremely dark — just such a night as was suited to the purpose of the natives. Leif stood motionless, like a statue, leaning on his spear. His man sat on the rampart; both gazed and listened with painful intensity.

At last Leif pointed to what appeared to be a moving object on the space of cleared ground that intervened between the slight wall of the hamlet and the edge of the forest.

"Awake the men," he whispered, "and let not a sound of voice or clank of sword be heard."

Hengler made no reply, but glided silently away. One by one the men came up with the light tread of cats, and manned the walls, keeping well under cover of the parapet – each taking his appointed station beside his particular pile of stones and sheaf of arrows, which lay on the platform, while below a man with a bow was stationed at every slit.

Suddenly there arose on the night air a yell so fierce, so prolonged, and so peculiar, that it made even the stout hearts of the Norsemen quail for a moment – it was so unearthly, and so unlike any war-cry they had ever before heard. Again and again it was repeated, then a rushing sound was heard, and hundreds of dark objects were indistinctly seen leaping over the slight wall of felled trees that surrounded the hamlet.

With furious shouts the savages surrounded the houses, burst open the doors, and rushed in; but they rushed out again almost immediately, and their yells were exchanged for exclamations of surprise as they went about searching in the dark for their concealed enemies. Of course they came to the rock-fortress almost immediately after, and another war-cry was uttered as they surrounded the place in hundreds, but as there was still no sound or appearance of their expected foe, they became suddenly silent, as if under the impression that there was something mysterious in the affair which was not in accordance with their past experiences.

They nevertheless clambered to the top of the rock, and began to feel round the bottom of the wooden palisades for a door.

At that moment, while they were clustering thick as bees round the base of the building, Leif gave a preconcerted signal. One of the men applied a light to the pile of bark and fir-cones, and a bright flash of flame shot upward as Leif said – "Up, lads!" in deep stern tones.

Instantly a shower of heavy stones descended on the pates of the savages, who rolled down the steep sides of the mound with shrieks and cries and yells very different indeed from those which had characterised their assault. From all directions the savages now concentrated on the fortress. At the same time the fire suddenly shot up with such a glare that the whole scene was made nearly as light as day, and from the parapets and every loop-hole of the fortress a very hail of arrows poured forth into the midst of them, while their own shafts either quivered in the palisade or fell harmless from the shields and helmets of the Norsemen.

Even in that hour of extreme danger, Leif's desire to spare life, with a view to future proposals of peace, was exemplified in his ordering the men to draw their bows slightly, so as to wound without killing, as much as possible, and to aim as well as they could at the legs of the foe! One result of this was, that the wounded men were soon very numerous, and, as they fled away, filled the woods with such howls of agony that their still unhurt comrades were more alarmed than they would probably have been if the ground had been strewn with the dead.

At this point a vigorous sally from the fortress, and a deep-toned Norse cheer, settled the question for the time being. The entire army of dark-skinned warriors turned and fled into its native wilderness!

There was not, it may be well to remark here, so much danger in this sally as we moderns might suppose, for, even though the savages had not run, but had faced and surrounded their enemy, these Norsemen, with their massive limbs, sweeping swords, large shields, and defensive armour, could have cut their way back again to the fort through hundreds of such half naked foes.

Of course Leif had expected them to fly, and had no intention of retiring immediately to the fort. He merely went the length of the outer wall, and then, with half of his men, kept up a vigorous shouting to expedite the flight of the foe, while the other half picked up as many arrows as they could find. Leif was glad to learn, on returning to the fort, that only two dead men had been discovered on the ground.

But the savages had not given in by any means, as became pretty clear from the noise they made in the woods soon afterwards. This continued all night, and Leif ordered the fire to be extinguished, lest they should be tempted by its light to send a flight of arrows among them, which might wound some of his people when off their guard.

When the first grey light of dawn appeared, it became evident to the beleaguered Norsemen what the savages had been about. Not very far from the fortress an enormous pile of dry timber had been raised, and, although it was within easy bowshot, the savages managed, by dodging from tree to tree, to get under its shelter with fresh logs on their shoulders, and thus increased the pile continually.

"They mean to burn us out!" exclaimed Hengler anxiously.

"Rather to smoke us out," observed one of the men. "Fire can never reach us from that distance."

Leif, who was very grave, shook his head and said:

"If they make the pile very big it may reach us well enough. They have plenty of hands and no lack of wood. See, they are piling it to windward. God grant that the breeze may not increase, else shall we have to forsake the fortress. Nevertheless our good ship is at hand," he added, in a more cheerful tone, "and they will find us tough to deal with when we get upon the water. Come, lads, we will at all events harass if we cannot stop them."

So saying, Leif ordered the men to keep up a constant discharge of arrows whenever they obtained a glimpse of the savages, and he himself headed a sally and drove them back to the woods. But as soon as he and his men had returned to the fortress, out came the savages again like a swarm of bees, and continued their work vigorously.

Thus the morning passed away, and the pile of the intended bonfire, despite the arrows and the frequent sallies of the Norsemen, continued slowly but steadily to grow.

CHAPTER XXII.

Hake Makes a Bold Venture, but does not Win — The Norsemen Find that There is Many a Slip 'twixt the Cup and the lip.

When Karlsefin and his men had surmounted the rapid, as before described, they found their future advance unimpeded, and, in the natural course of things — or of the river — arrived, not long after the children, at the lakelike expansion on the shores of which the native village stood.

This village, it must be understood, was not a permanent one. The natives were nomads. Their tents were merely poles cut as required from the neighbouring woods, tied together at the top, spread out in a circle at the base, and covered with leather, which coverings were the only parts of their habitations the natives deigned to carry about with them. They were here today and away tomorrow, stopping a longer or shorter time in each encampment according to fancy, or to the measure of their success in procuring food. The particular tribe of natives which had captured the Norsemen's children had only just come to the locality; they therefore knew nothing of the arrival of the white strangers in their land, except what they had recently learned from their scouts, as we have seen.

Karlsefin's canoe led the way; hence, on turning sharp round a point of rock that jutted out into the stream, Krake was the first who caught sight of the smoke that rose above the treetops.

"Hist! hold on," he exclaimed in a hoarse whisper, looking over his shoulder as he backed water suddenly. Karlsefin and the men instantly did the same, and sent the canoe back under the shelter of the point. The other canoes of course followed suit.

"The Skraelingers!" whispered Krake. "I saw the smoke of their fires."

"Did you see tents?" asked the leader.

"No; there was scarce time to see anything before we got back here."

"What do you advise?" asked Karlsefin, looking at Thorward.

"Go ashore and attack them at once," he replied.

"Ay, that's it, there's nothing like fighting it out at once!" muttered Krake in an undertone.

"My advice," said Karlsefin, "is, that we cross the river and get on yonder height, which from its position must needs overlook the camp of the savages, and there reconnoitre and form our plans."

"Well, I daresay your advice is best after all," rejoined Thorward, with a smile. "You were always a cautious and peaceful man; though I'm bound in fairness to admit that you can fight passing well when it comes to that."

"Thanks for your good opinion," said Karlsefin, laughing quietly. "So now, lads, turn about and follow me closely. Keep silence, and dip your paddles as lightly as may be."

Saying this, he returned a considerable way down the river; keeping very close in to the banks, which were overhung with bushes, until he reached a point where it seemed likely that the party could cross without being observed. There was a slight rapid at the place, so that they had only to enter it at an angle with the bank and were swept across in a few moments, almost without requiring to use their paddles.

Landing at the edge of a dense thicket, they hauled the canoes out of the water, secreted them carefully, and then, taking their arms, made a detour through the forest in the direction of the cliff before referred to by Karlsefin. In less than half an hour they reached it, and found, as had been anticipated, that it commanded a view of the native encampment, which to their dismay they now discovered was an immense one, filled with many hundreds of men, besides women and children.

Here, prone on their breasts, and scarce venturing to raise their heads above the grass, the two leaders held a consultation, while their men kept well in the background.

"This is an unfortunate business," said Karlsefin.

"Truly it is," replied Thorward; "but the question is, can this be the set of rascals who carried off the children? It seems to me that, being a small band, as we know, they did not belong to the same set."

"That may be so, Thorward; — but I incline to the belief that the small party was but an offshoot from the large one, and that our dear little ones are even now with the people before us."

As if to put the matter beyond doubt, Olaf, with Snorro on his back, issued at that moment from the woods on the opposite side of the river, and went out upon the identical spit of sand where, on the previous evening, he had held such bitter communings with his own spirit. The Norseman leaders recognised the children at once, being almost within hail of them, and it was with difficulty they restrained the impulse to spring to their feet and shout.

"Thanks be to God for the sight of them at all events," said Karlsefin fervently; "see, the dear boy has brought my darling there to amuse him. Ah! little dost thou know, Olaf, the hold that thy kindness has given thee of his father's heart!"

"'Twould be well if he had a hold of the father's hand just at this time," drily observed Thorward, who was not gifted with much of a sentimental temperament.

"That is not easy of accomplishment," returned the other. "Even you would scarcely, methinks, advise so small a band of men to make an open attack on five or six hundred savages."

"I would not advise it," replied Thorward; "nevertheless, if it came to the worst I would *do* it. But what, then, is your advice?"

"Why, *until* it comes to the worst we must try strategy," answered Karlsefin. "I will call Hake to our council; the youth, I have observed, is a deep thinker, and clear-sighted."

When Hake was summoned, and had laid himself down beside his leaders, he remained for some time silently gazing on the busy scene below, where some men in canoes were spearing fish in the bay, and others were skinning and cutting up deer near the edge of the woods, while women were cooking and engaged in other domestic duties at the doors of the tents, and children and dogs were romping about everywhere.

"Could we not get into our canoes," suggested Thorward, "make a dash at the spit of sand, and carry off the children at a swoop before the brown-skinned rascals were well aware of us?"

"They would see us before we got halfway to the spit," replied Karlsefin, "carry the children into the woods, and then be ready to receive us in hundreds on shore. What think you, Hake; can you suggest any plan of outwitting these savages?"

"I have a plan," answered the Scot, "but I fear you will deem it foolish."

"Out with it, man, foolish or otherwise," said Thorward, who was beginning to chafe under difficulties that appeared to be insurmountable, even by his favourite method — force of arms.

"If ye approve of it," returned Hake, "I will cross the river alone and unarmed, and walk straight to the spot where the children are now seated. Much of the way is concealed by shrubs, and when I saunter across the open part, it may be that I shall scarce be noticed until I am near them. If I be, then will I make a dash, catch them up, make for the rapid, plunge in, and, on gaining the opposite bank, run to meet you. We can then hasten to the canoes — fight our way to them if need be — and sweep down the river. We shall probably get a fair start; and if so, it will go hard but we reach Leifsgaard before they overtake us. If not, why —"

Hake touched the hilt of his sword by way of completing the sentence.

"A rare plan!" said Thorward with a suppressed chuckle; "and how, my bold youth, if thou art observed and caught before getting hold of the children?"

"I will then set my wits to devise some other plan. It may be of some advantage to them that I should be a captive along with the children, and at most it is but one man lost to the expedition."

"Ay, but that would be a heavy loss," said Karlsefin; "nevertheless the plan seems to me not so unlikely — only there are one or two points about which I have my doubts. In the first place, although your legs are marvellously good, I fear that with the additional weight of Olaf and Snorro on them, the fleet runners among the savages, of whom there must be many, would soon overtake thee."

"With Olaf on my back, Snorro under my left arm, and the right arm free to swing — I think *not*," replied Hake, quietly but decidedly.

"Then as to crossing: how do you —"

"I would swim," replied Hake.

"What! with the weight and drag of wet garments to cumber you!" exclaimed Thorward; "besides making it clear to the savages, if they caught you, that you had come from the opposite bank of the river, where your *friends* might be expected to be waiting for you!"

"I would tie my clothes in a tight bundle on the top of my head," said Hake. "Many a time have I crossed the streams of my native land in this manner."

"Well, ye have a ready answer for everything," returned Thorward; "nevertheless I like not the plan."

"If you cannot suggest a better, I am disposed to let Hake try it," said Karlsefin.

Thorward had no better plan to suggest. Indeed, the more he thought of it the more did he feel inclined to make a tremendous onslaught, cut as many men to pieces as he could before having his own life taken, and so have done with the whole affair for ever. Fortunately for Olaf and Snorro his counsels were not followed.

In a few minutes Hake was ready. His brother was ordered to lead the men back to the canoes, there to keep in close hiding and await further orders. Meanwhile Karlsefin remained on the cliff to watch the result.

Hake felt it to be a desperate venture, but he was possessed of that species of spirit which rejoices in such, and prefers danger to safety. Besides, he saw at a glance that there would be no chance whatever of success if his leaders made up their minds to attempt an open attack against such fearful odds.

With a light step the young Scot descended to the river, thinking of Bertha as he went. A few minutes afterwards he was seen — or rather his head with a bundle on it — was seen crossing the river by the watchers on the cliff. A few minutes later, and he was on the opposite shore rapidly putting on his light garments. Thereafter he entered the bushes, and a glimpse could be caught of him ever and anon as he glided swiftly, like the panther towards his prey.

When the last point capable of affording concealment was gained, Hake assumed a careless air, and, with his head down, as if in meditation, sauntered towards the spit of land where Olaf and Snorro were still playing.

"Well done!" exclaimed Thorward, with a look of admiration; "cleverly, bravely done!"

There is no doubt that such was the case, and that Hake would have reached the children unobserved by the natives had not Olaf chanced to notice him while he was yet about fifty yards off. He recognised him at once, and, with a shout of joy, ran to meet him.

Hake dashed past him, sprang toward Snorro, whom he caught up, and, stooping, cried — "Up, Olaf! up for your life!"

Olaf understood at once, sprang on his back, and held on tight, while Hake, bending low, sped away at a pace that defied pursuit, though by that time a hundred savages were almost at his heels!

It was obvious from the first that the lithe Scot was well able to achieve his purpose. He was already nearing the rapid. His pursuers were far behind, and Karlsefin could scarcely restrain a shout of exultation as he rose to run round to his canoes, when he observed that a party of more than a dozen natives, who chanced to be ascending the river's bank on foot, met the fugitive. Observing that he was a stranger, and pursued by natives, they crossed his path at once.

Hake stopped abruptly, glanced at the bushes, then turned to the river, and was on the point of plunging in, when a canoe, with four savages in it, shot out from the bank just below him.

He saw at once that escape was impossible. Feeling intuitively that submission was his best policy, he set the children on the ground and quietly suffered himself to be taken prisoner.

"I knew it! I *said* it!" growled Thorward between his teeth, as he sprang up, drew his sword, and slashed down two small trees at a single stroke in his wrath, then rushing through the woods, he made for the canoes.

Karlsefin followed in a state of mind almost as furious. It was such a bitter disappointment to fail so signally on the very eve of success!

The canoes were already in the water and manned when the leaders reached them, for Heika, who had been left in charge, knew well that whatever might be the result of the enterprise, prompt action would be necessary.

"Quick, shove off!" cried Karlsefin, taking his place, and driving his paddle into the water with such force that the light craft shot from the bank like an arrow.

The men were not slow to obey. The fierce spirit of their leader seemed to be catching, and the foam curled from their respective bows, leaving a long white track behind, as they rushed up the river and swept out upon the broad expanse above.

Of course they had been seen before reaching that point, and the savages immediately lined the banks with armed men. They did not, however, go out upon the spit of sand where Olaf and Snorro had first been observed by their friends. That point was so high up the stream, that it did not seem to be considered by any one as worthy of attention. This Karlsefin observed at once, and formed his plans accordingly. He advanced as if he were about to land below the spit, but made no hostile demonstrations of any kind, and paddled so quietly on nearing the shore, that the savages did not seem to understand him, and, although ready with their arrows for instant action, they remained passive.

When within a short distance of the land, Karlsefin suddenly, but still quietly, turned the head of his canoe up the stream, and made for the spit of sand. The other canoes followed. The natives, perceiving the intention of the strangers, uttered a wild shout, and made for the same place along the shore, but before they reached it Karlsefin had landed with all his men, and, with their stalwart figures and strange arms, presented such an imposing front that the natives stopped short.

At this point the crowd opened a little to let some one pass, and Whitepow came to the front. Judging him to be the chief, Karlsefin at once laid down his sword, and, stepping a few paces in front of his men, held up his hands and made demonstrations of a peaceful kind.

But Whitepow was not peacefully inclined. Although aged, he was a sturdy fellow, stood erect, and carried a heavy club on his shoulder. To the Norseman's demonstrations he replied by frowning fiercely and shaking his head savagely, as though to intimate that he was much too old a bird to be taken in with such chaff. Then, turning to those beside him, he gave an order, which resulted in Hake being led to the front with his arms tightly bound to his sides.

"Ah!" thought Karlsefin, "if you had only brought the children to that spot, I would have rescued them at all hazards."

He did not, however, think it wise to make so desperate an attempt merely to rescue Hake, while the children were still concealed and at the mercy of the savages. He therefore put on his blandest looks and manner, and again invited confidence, but Whitepow again shook his head, pointed backwards as if in reference to the two children, and then at Hake, after which he flung his club with such violence and precision at Karlsefin's head that the stout Norseman would certainly have measured his length on the sand, if he had not been very much on the alert. As it was, he received the missile on his shield, from which it glanced with a loud clang, and went hissing into the river.

Karlsefin smiled, as if that sort of thing rather amused him than otherwise, and again held up his hands, and even advanced a step or two nearer, while the concourse of savages gave vent to a shout of surprise. It is probable that Whitepow was a hero whose artillery had hitherto been the messenger of certain death to foes. The failure of the club seemed to exasperate the old savage beyond endurance, for he instantly seized a bow, and let fly an arrow at the Norseman leader. It was well aimed, but was also caught on the shield, and fell broken to the ground.

Seeing this, some of the Norsemen hastily drew their bows, but Karlsefin, anticipating something of the kind, turned about and bade them forbear.

Meanwhile Whitepow had ordered his warriors to remove Hake, and to fall back a little. This they did, and appeared to be awaiting further orders from their chief, who had gone up towards the tents. The movement puzzled Karlsefin, who rejoined his men.

"It is my advice," said Thorward, "that we hesitate no longer. Stand or fall, we are in for a fight now, so the sooner we begin the better. No doubt the odds are great, but they don't seem to be able for much — at least if that old chap gave us a good specimen of their powers."

Most of the Norsemen appeared to agree with this advice, but Karlsefin did not.

"You forget," said he, "that this would not be a mere trial of strength. If we once begin, and chance to fail, every man of us must die, and our colony, thus left so weak, would stand a small chance of surviving in the midst of so many savages. Besides — the children would be lost *for ever*! It is my opinion that we should wait a little to see what this movement implies. Perhaps that white-haired old savage may have recovered his temper and senses by this time, and is making up his mind to have peace instead of war. God grant that it may be so."

Instead of replying Thorward frowned darkly, and with something of a savage sneer on his lip pointed to a bend in the river above them, round which, at that moment, a hundred canoes swept, and came swiftly towards them.

"Looks *that* like peace?" he said bitterly.

Karlsefin's countenance fell.

"All is lost!" he muttered, in a tone that was rather sad than fierce. "Oh my tender little child!"

Crushing down his feelings with a mighty effort, he turned to the men, and quietly but quickly arranged them in a circle, with their faces outwards, so that they presented a front in all directions.

"Now, ye men of Norway and Iceland," he said, "the day has come at last when ye must prove yourselves worthy descendants of a noble race. Our cause this day is a right cause, and God is with the right, whether it please Him to send death or victory. Quit you like men, and let us teach these Skraelingers how to fight — if need be, how to die."

Taking his stand on the landward side of his men, and ordering Thorward to do the same in the direction of the water, he calmly awaited the onset.

And now, indeed, it seemed as if a fierce and bloody battle were about to begin, for when the canoes of their comrades swept round the point of land, as already described, the savages on shore, constantly reinforced by new arrivals, began to move steadily down in an overwhelming mass towards the spit of sand, and the heroes who stood there, though comparatively so few in number, were, with their superiority of weapons and courage, certain to make a fearfully prolonged and bloody resistance.

Affairs had reached this critical point, when a sudden and loud shout was heard down the river. All eyes were turned in that direction, and there several canoes were seen coming round the bend of the river, full of armed men. The descent of the native fleet was checked. The Norsemen at once recognised their comrades, and greeted their approach with a lusty cheer. In another minute the newcomers had leaped upon the sand.

"Welcome, welcome, Biarne!" exclaimed Thorward, seizing and wringing his friend's hand in great delight. "Why, man, we had all but taken leave of each other, but we shall have another tale to tell now."

"May God bless you, Biarne, for coming so opportunely," said Karlsefin. "Let your men join and extend the circle. There, spread it out wider; that will do. I won't trouble you with questions just now, Biarne, as to what made you think of coming. We have more pressing work on hand."

Thus saying, the leader busied himself in arranging his reinforcements, while the savages held back, and awaited the result of a consultation between Whitepow and the chief men of the tribe.

CHAPTER XXIII.

Difficulties Regarding Intercommunication — The Power of Finery Displayed — Also the Power of Song and Sentiment.

The additional force thus opportunely gained by the Norsemen, although hailed with so much enthusiasm, did not very materially alter their position. True, they now formed a company of above fifty stout and well-armed men, who, in the hour of extremity, could make a formidable resistance to any foe, however numerous; but what chance had they of ultimately escaping from upwards of a thousand savages, every man of whom was an adept at bush-warfare; could dart from tree to tree, and harass and cut off in detail an enemy whom he would not dare, or did not care, to face in the open field — which latter mode of warfare was more natural and congenial to the Norsemen?

This truth soon began to force itself upon Karlsefin's understanding; but as he feared to damp the spirits of his less thoughtful comrades, he kept his anxieties to himself, and made the best disposition of his force that was possible in the circumstances.

Very soon there was a movement among the savages on shore, and its object was not long of being apparent, for presently a fleet of canoes was seen ascending the river. At the same time the other fleet renewed its advance from above, while the men on shore moved once more towards the spit of sand.

"They mean to attack on all sides at once," said Biarne.

"Let them come," growled Thorward. "'Tis death or victory now, lads."

No one spoke, but the eagle glances of the men, and their firm grasp of sword and spear, told that they were ready; and once more it seemed as if the bloody fight were about to begin, when again it was interrupted by a shout. This time the shout came from the woods, from which, a few minutes later, a solitary savage was seen to issue. He appeared to be in haste, and ran through the crowd of warriors, who made way for him, straight towards the white-haired chief, to whom he appeared to speak with great fervour and many gesticulations, though he was too far off to be heard, or his countenance to be distinctly seen, by the Norsemen.

"That fellow brings news of some sort or other. I should say," remarked Biarne.

"Whatever his news may be," replied Karlsefin, "I don't think it will be likely to do much for us."

"The rascal's figure seems not unfamiliar to me," said Thorward.

At that moment the crowd of chiefs around Whitepow shouted the word "Ho!" apparently in approbation of something that he had just remarked, and immediately after the man whom Thorward had styled a rascal began to talk and gesticulate again more violently than ever.

"What *is* the man after now?" said Thorward. "It seems to me that he is mad."

The savage did indeed appear to be slightly deranged, for, in the midst of his talk, he took an arrow and went through the pantomime of discharging it; then he applied the point of it to his own back, and fell down as if wounded; whereupon he rose quietly and kneeled with a tender air, as if in the act of succouring a wounded man; and thereafter went on to perform other pantomimic acts, which at last induced Thorward to open his eyes very wide and whistle, as he exclaimed — "Why, 'tis Utway, that fellow who was half killed in our first brush with the Skraelingers."

"Ay, and who was so tenderly nursed by Bertha," added Biarne.

"There can be no doubt of it," said Karlsefin, in a cheerful voice; "and now have I some hope of a peaceful end to this affair, for what else can he be doing but pleading our cause?"

"I'm not so sure of that," replied Thorward. "He may just as likely be telling them what lots of good things might be got by killing us all and taking possession of Leifsgaard."

"The question will soon be settled, Thorward, for here comes the savage," said Biarne.

This was true. Having finished his talk, whatever it was, and heard a brief reply from Whitepow, Utway turned round and ran fearlessly towards the Norsemen.

"I will go meet him," said Karlsefin.

"There may be danger in that," suggested Biarne.

"Greater danger in showing distrust," replied Karlsefin. "Confidence should beget confidence."

Without more words he flung down sword and shield, and advanced unarmed to meet the savage, whom he shook warmly by the hand — a style of salutation which Utway thoroughly understood, having learned it while lying wounded in Leifsgaard.

They could not of course make use of speech, but Utway was such a powerful gesticulator that it was not difficult to make out his meaning. After shaking hands he put his hand on his heart, then laid it on Karlsefin's breast, and pointed towards the old chief with an air that would have done credit to a courtier.

Karlsefin at once took the hand of the savage, and walked with him through the midst of the native chiefs, above whose heads he towered conspicuously, until he stood before Whitepow. Taking off his iron helmet he bowed to the old chief, an act which appeared to afford that worthy much satisfaction, for, although he did not venture to return the bow, he exclaimed "Ho!" with solemn emphasis.

This was all very pleasant, but it was not much. Karlsefin, therefore, tried his hand at a little gesticulation, while the natives gazed at him with speechless interest. Whitepow and Utway then replied with a variety of energetic demonstrations, some of which the Norseman understood, while of others he could make nothing at all, but the result of it all was, that Utway made a final proposal, which was very clear, to the effect that the Norsemen should approach the savages, mingle with them, and be friends.

To this Karlsefin returned a decided negative, by shaking his head and frowning portentously. At the same time he stooped and held his hand about two feet from the ground, as if to indicate something that stood pretty nearly that height. Then he tenderly patted the top of the imaginary thing, whatever it was, and took it up in his arms, kissed it, and laid it on his breast. After that he indicated another thing somewhat higher, which he also patted on the top. Thereafter he pressed his arms close to his side and struggled as if to get loose from something, but could not until he had taken hold of an imaginary knife, cut the something which bound him, and set his arms free.

All this was apparently understood and immensely relished by the natives, who nodded to each other and vociferated "Ho!" to such an extent that the repetition caused it to sound somewhat like a fiendish laugh. But here Whitepow put in his veto, shook his head and appeared inexorable, whereupon Karlsefin crossed his arms on his breast and looked frowningly on the ground.

Things had just reached this uncomfortable pass, when Karlsefin's eye chanced to fall on the end of a piece of bright scarlet cloth with which Gudrid had smilingly ornamented his neck before he set out on this expedition – just as a young wife might, in chivalrous ages, have tied a scarf to her knight's arm before sending him off to the wars.

A sudden idea flashed upon him. He unfastened the strip of cloth, and, advancing, presented it to Whitepow, with a bland smile.

The aged chief was not proof against this. He gazed at the brilliant cloth with intense admiration, and expressed as much delight at receiving it as if he had been a child – which, by the way, he was, in regard to such fabrics and in his inability to restrain his feelings.

Rejoiced to observe the good effect thus produced, Karlsefin did his best to assure the chief that there was plenty more of the same in his possession, besides other things – all of which Utway corroborated – and signified that he, Whitepow, should have large quantities thereof if he would restore the captives to their friends. In order to add force to what he said, he drew from his pouch or wallet several small metal ornaments strung together like beads, and presented these also to Whitepow, as well as to several of the chiefs who stood nearest to him. At the same time he uncovered, as if inadvertently, a magnificent silver brooch which hung round his neck, under his leathern war-shirt.

This brooch was by no means a trifling bauble. It was massive, beautifully carved, and hung round with little silver cups and diamond-shaped pieces of silver about the size of a man's thumbnail. It was much prized by its owner on account of being an heirloom of his family, having been carried to Iceland by his forefathers when they were expatriated from Norway by King Harald Fairhair.

Whitepow's eye at once fell on the brooch, and he expressed a strong desire to possess it.

Karlsefin started as if in alarm, seized the brooch with both hands, held it aloft, and gazed at it in a species of veneration, then, clasping it to his breast, shook his head by way of an emphatic "No!"

Of course Whitepow became doubly anxious to have it; whereupon Karlsefin again stooped, and, placing his hand about two feet from the ground, patted the top of the thing indicated, and said that he might have the brooch for *that* and the other things previously referred to.

Whitepow pondered a few minutes, and Utway said something very seriously to him, which resulted in his giving an order to two of his chiefs, who at once left the group. They quickly returned, leading Hake and the children between them — the former being still bound at the elbows.

There was something quite startling in the shout of surprise that Olaf gave on observing Karlsefin. It was only equalled by the shriek of glee that burst from Snorro when he recognised his father.

Olaf instantly seized Snorro and ran towards him. Karlsefin met them more than halfway, and, with an expression of deep thankfulness, caught up his little one and strained him to his heart, while Olaf tightly embraced his leg!

But, recollecting himself instantly, he set Snorro down, removed the silver brooch from his neck and placed it in the hand of the old chief. At the same time he pointed to Hake's bonds. Whitepow understood him, and, drawing his stone knife, cut these asunder.

"Make no haste, Hake," said his leader, "but take Snorro in your arms and Olaf by the hand, and walk *slowly* but steadily towards your comrades. If any one offers to intercept you, resist not, but turn and come back hither."

Hake made no reply, but did as he was bid, and was soon in the midst of his comrades. Meanwhile Karlsefin, whose joy almost prevented him from maintaining the dignity that was appropriate to the occasion, took off every scrap in the shape of ornament that he possessed and presented all to Whitepow, even to the last bauble in the bottom of his wallet, and he tried to make the old man understand that all his men had things of a similar kind to bestow, which would be brought to him if he would order the great mass of his people to retire to a considerable distance, retaining only about his person a party equal in numbers to the Norsemen.

To this the chief seemed inclined to object at first, but again Utway's eloquence and urgency prevailed. The old man stood up, shouted an order in the voice of a Stentor, and waved his hand. The whole multitude at once fell back to a considerable distance, leaving only a few of the principal men around their chief.

The active Scot instantly bounded towards him — not less with desire to serve his deliverer than with delight at finding himself once more free!

"Go back, Hake, and tell the men to come quietly hither in a compact body, leaving their bows and spears behind them, only carrying each man his sword and shield. Let a strong guard stay with the weapons and the children, and see that Biarne and Thorward also remain with them. Quietly place the children in a canoe, and do you and Heika stand ready to man it."

"That has already been done," said Hake.

"By whose orders?" demanded Karlsefin.

"At my suggestion," replied Hake.

"Thou art a wise man, Hake. I thank thee. Go; I need not explain that two canoes at least would require to accompany you, so as to repel attack by water, and, if it be necessary, to flee, while we guard the retreat."

"That has already been arranged," said Hake.

"Good, good. Then, whatever betide us, the dear children are like to be safe. Get you gone, Hake; and, harkee, if *we* should not return, be sure thou bear my love to Gudrid. Away."

Hake bowed in silence and retired. In a few minutes the greater part of the Norsemen stood before the old chief, and, by Karlsefin's command, every man who chanced to have any trifling ornament of any kind about him took it off and presented it to the savages.

Whitepow, in return, ordered a package of furs to be brought, and presented each man with a beautiful sable. Karlsefin then made Utway explain that he had seen much valuable cloth and many ornaments in the Norsemen's camp, and that these would be given in exchange for such furs — a piece of news which seemed to gratify the savages, for they possessed an immense number of furs, which were comparatively of little value to them.

Thus amicable relations were established; but when Whitepow invited the Norsemen to accompany him to his village and feast, Karlsefin intimated that he intended to sup and pass the night on the spit of sand, and that in the early morning he would return to his home, whither he hoped the savages would soon follow him with their furs. That, meanwhile, a small number might accompany him, if they chose, to view his habitation and take back a report. This was agreed to, and thus happily the conferences ended.

That night the Norsemen held high carousal on the spit of sand, partly because they were rejoiced at the successful issue of the expedition as far as it had gone, and partly because they wished to display a free-and-easy spirit to the savages. They drew a line at the narrowest part of the neck of land, and there posted armed sentinels, who resolutely refused to let any one pass. On the outward edge of the spit, other sentinels were placed, who checked all tendency to approach by water, and who — in one or two instances, when some obstinate natives attempted to force a landing — overturned the canoes and left the occupants to swim ashore the best way they could.

The only exception to this rule was made in favour of Utway and Whitepow, with the grandson of the latter, little Powlet. These three came down to the spit after the Norsemen had kindled a magnificent bonfire of dry logs, round which they sat and ate their supper, told sagas, sang songs, cracked jokes, and drank to absent friends in cans of pure water, with an amount of dash, fervour, and uproarious laughter that evidently raised quite a new idea in the savage minds, and filled them with amazement unutterable, but not inexpressible, for their glaring eyes, and lengthened jaws, and open mouths were the material embodiment of surprise. In fact, the entire population sat on the surrounding banks and heights nearly the whole night, with their hands and chins resting on their knees, listening and gazing in silent admiration at the proceedings of the Norsemen, as a vast audience might witness the entertainments of an amphitheatre.

The utmost hospitality was of course extended by the Norsemen to their three visitors, who partook of the food set before them with much relish. Fortunately some of the men who had been left to guard the arms still possessed a few trinkets and pieces of bright cloth, so that Karlsefin was again enabled to gratify his new friends with a few more presents.

"Snorro," said Karlsefin, who sat beside Whitepow in front of the fire with the child on his knee, "are you glad to see your father again?"

"Iss," said Snorro, responding *slightly* to the tender embrace which he received.

We are afraid that truth requires us to state, that Snorro had not quite reached the age of reciprocal attachment — at least in regard to men. Of course we do not pretend to know anything about the mysterious feelings which he was reported to entertain towards his mother and nurse! All we can say is, that up to this point in his history the affections of that first-born of Vinland appeared to centre chiefly in his stomach — who fed him best he loved most! It is but simple justice to add, however, that Olaf was, in Snorro's eye, an exception to the rule. We really believe that if Olaf had starved and beaten him during the first half of a day, by way of experiment, Snorro would have clung to him and loved him throughout the other half!

"Come hither, Olaf, take this bit of cloth in your hand, and present it to that little boy," said Karlsefin, pointing to Powlet. "He seems fond of Snorro, and deserves something."

"Fond of him!" exclaimed Olaf, laughing, as he presented the cloth according to orders, and then returned to Snorro's side. "You should have seen the way he made Snorro laugh one day by painting my face."

Here Olaf went into a minute account of the operation referred to, and told it with so much humour that the Norsemen threw back their wild heads and shook their shaggy beards in fits of uproarious laughter, which awakened the echoes of the opposite cliffs, and caused the natives to think, no doubt, that the very rocks were merry.

After this Krake told a story and sang a rollicking song, and of course Hake was made to sing, which he readily did, giving them one of his native airs with such deep pathos, that the very savages — unused though they were to music — could not refrain from venting a murmur of admiration, which rose on the night air like a mysterious throb from the hearts of the dark concourse.

Immediately after Hake's song the old chief and his friends took their leave. The sentinels were now changed and doubled, the fire was extinguished, each Norseman lay down with his hand on his sword-hilt, and his shield above him, and the vast multitude of savages melted away to their respective places of repose.

CHAPTER XXIV.

*The Burning on the Fortress — A Threatened Fight Ends
in a Feast, Which Leads to Friendship —
Happy Reunion and Proposed Desertion.*

Next morning, according to arrangement, the Norsemen were up and away by daybreak; but they did not start off alone. A much larger fleet than they had bargained for accompanied them. Karlsefin, however, made no objection, partly because objection would have been unavailing, and partly because the natives were so genuinely well-disposed towards him, that he felt assured there was no reason to distrust them or to fear their numbers.

Little did Karlsefin think, as they proceeded happily and leisurely down the stream at that time, the urgent need there was for haste, or the dire extremity to which his friends at Leifsgaard had been reduced. Knowing, of course, nothing about this, they descended by easy stages and encamped in good time at night, in order to have their fires lighted and food cooked before daylight had quite disappeared, so that they might have the more time to sit chatting by the light of the campfires and enjoying the fine summer weather.

On the other hand, had Leif only known how soon his friends were to return, he might have held the fortress longer than he did, by continuing his desperate sallies to check the raising of the pile that was meant to burn him out; but not being aware of this, and finding that the necessity for constant vigilance and frequent sallies was wearing out his men, he resolved to abandon the castle to its fate and take to the ship.

Watching his opportunity, he had everything portable collected, and, during the darkest hour of a dark night, quietly issued from the little fortress, descended to the beach, and got on board the *Snake*, with all the women and men, without the savages being aware of the movement.

Once on board, he fortified the vessel as well as he could, and hung the shields round the bulwarks.

Curiously enough, the savages had fixed on that very night for setting fire to their pile of timber, which by that time towered to a height that made it almost equal to the fortress it was about to consume. At grey dawn the torch was applied to it. At the very same hour Karlsefin and his men, accompanied by their savage friends, launched their canoes and left the encampment of the previous night.

The leader of the fleet had purposely encamped when not very far from the settlement, preferring, with such a large and unexpected party, rather to arrive in the morning than at night.

Great then was the surprise of the Norsemen when, soon after starting, they saw a dense cloud of smoke rising in the far distance, and deep was their anxiety when they observed that this cloud not only spread abroad and increased in density, but appeared to float exactly over the place where the settlement lay.

"Give way, lads! push on! There is something wrong at the gaard," shouted Karlsefin when he became thoroughly alive to the fact.

There was little necessity for urging the men. Each man became an impulsive volcano and drove his paddle into the water with such force and fury that the canoes almost leaped out of the river as well as over it.

Meanwhile the sun rose in splendour, and with it rose the mighty flames of the bonfire, which soon caught the neighbouring trees and licked them up as if they had been stubble. Such intense heat could not be long withstood. The wooden fortress was soon in flames, and then arose a yell of triumph from the savages, which sent dismay to the hearts of those who were approaching, and overawed the little band that still lay undiscovered on board the *Snake*.

But when it was ascertained that there was no one in the fortress, a cry of fury followed the shout of triumph, and the whole band, at once suspecting that their enemies had taken to their vessel, rushed down to the shores of the lake.

There they found the Norsemen ready to receive them; but they found more than they had expected, for, just then, Karlsefin and his men swept round the point above the bay with a tremendous cheer, and were followed by a continuous stream of the canoes of their savage friends whom they had outstripped in the mad race.

Karlsefin did not wait to ascertain how affairs stood. Enough for him that the village seemed to be in flames. Observing, as he passed, that his comrades and the women were safe on board the *Snake*, he ran the canoes high and dry on the beach and leaped ashore. Drawing quickly up into a compact line, the Norsemen rushed with wild shout upon the foe. The natives did not await the onset. Surprise alone had kept them waiting there as long as they did. With one consent, and a hideous yell, they turned and fled like autumn leaves before the wind.

Returning to the friendly savages, who had looked on at all this in some surprise and with no little concern, Karlsefin looked very sternly at them, pointed to the woods into which his enemies had vanished, shook his fist, and otherwise attempted by signs to indicate his displeasure, and to advise the instant interference of the friendly savages in the way of bringing about peaceful relations.

The natives were intelligent enough and prompt in action. A party of them at once started off to the woods, while Karlsefin went on board the *Snake*, where he found Leif and his friends right glad to meet him, and the women, in a state of the wildest delight, almost devouring Olaf and Snorro, who had been sent direct to the vessel when the men landed to attack the savages.

"'Tis good for the eyes to see thy sweet face, Gudrid," he said, giving his wife a hearty kiss, "and I am quite sure that Snorro agrees with me in that."

"He does, he does," cried Gudrid, hugging the child, who clung round her neck with a tenacity that he had never before exhibited, having learned, no doubt, that "absence makes the heart grow fonder."

"Oh! I am so happy, and so thankful. My sweet bairn! Where did you find him? How did you rescue him? I felt *sure* you would do it. How did he look when he saw you? and —"

"Hold, Gudrid," cried Karlsefin, laughing, "joy has upset thy judgment. I can answer but one question at a time."

Gudrid made no reply; indeed she did not seem to expect an answer to her queries, for she had turned again to Snorro and Olaf, whom she overwhelmed with embraces, endearing epithets, and questions, in all which she was ably assisted by Bertha, Astrid, and Thora. Even Freydissa became soft for once; kissed Olaf and Snorro several times in a passionate manner, and was unusually gracious to Thorward.

"Ye came in the nick of time," said Leif, as he and his friends retired to the poop for a brief consultation.

"So it would seem," said Biarne, "but it was more by good fortune than good planning, for I left you weak-handed; and if good luck had not brought us here just at the time we did, methinks there would have been heavy hearts among us."

"A higher Power than good luck brought us hither in time," said Karlsefin.

"That is true," said Leif, with a nod and an earnest look at his friend.

"I doubt it not," returned Biarne, "and the same Power doubtless led me to start off with a reinforcement in time to help you in the hour of need, Karlsefin. But it is my advice now that we go ashore and put the huts in a state of defence as quickly as may be."

"That is just my opinion," replied Karlsefin, "for it may be that the friendly natives will find it easier to be converted into foes than to turn our enemies into friends. What is your advice, Leif?"

"That we land and do as Biarne suggests without delay."

"And what if these villains come down in such overwhelming numbers — as they now can easily do — that they shall carry all before them and drive us into the lake?" asked Thorward.

"Why, man," cried Biarne, with a touch of ire, "if I did not know thee well I would say that thou wert timid."

"Knowing me well; then, as ye say," returned Thorward, "and reserving the matter of timidity for future discussion, what reply have ye to make to my question?"

"That we must make up our minds to be drowned, like Freydissa's cat," replied Biarne.

"Nay, not quite that," said Leif, with a smile; "we can at least have the comfort of leaving our bones on the land to mingle with those of as many savages as we can slay."

"The thought of that would prove a great comfort to the women, no doubt, when they were carried off by the savages," returned Thorward, with a touch of sarcasm in his tone.

"I see what you mean," said Karlsefin; "that we should have the *Snake* ready to fall back on if we chance to be beaten; but, to say truth, the idea of being beaten by such miserable savages never entered my head."

"The consideration of your head's thickness, then," said Thorward, "would be an additional element of comfort, no doubt, to the women in case of things going against us."

At this Karlsefin laughed, and asked Thorward what he would advise.

"My advice is," said he, "that we not only get the *Snake* ready for a long voyage, but that we haul round my ship also — which by good fortune is here just now — and get her ready. There is no need to put our goods and chattels on board, for if things went ill with us we could no doubt keep the savages at bay long enough to accomplish that by means of placing Biarne at the post of danger with orders to die rather than give in; but I would leave the women and children on board at any rate to keep them out of harm's way —"

"And it is *my* advice," cried Freydissa, coming up at the moment, "that ye set about it at once without more talk, else the women and children will have to set you the example."

There was a general laugh at the tone and manner in which this was said, and the four chiefs left the poop to carry out their plans. Meanwhile an immense concourse of natives assembled on the neighbouring heights, and for a long time carried on a discussion, which, to judge from the violence of their gesticulations, must have been pretty hot. At last their meeting came to an abrupt close, and a large band was seen to separate from the rest and move down towards the hamlet.

Before they reached it the Norsemen had manned the defences and awaited them.

"They come on a peaceful errand, I think," said Karlsefin, who stood at the principal opening. "At least it seems to me that they carry no arms. What say you, Hake? Your eyes are sharp."

"They are unarmed," replied Hake.

This was found to be the case; and when they had approached to within a long bowshot of the defences, all doubt as to their intention was removed by their holding up their hands and making other peaceful demonstrations.

Judging it wise to meet such advances promptly and without suspicion, Karlsefin at once selected a number of his stoutest men, and causing them to lay aside their arms, issued forth to meet the savages. There was, as on a former occasion, a great deal of gesticulation and talking with the eyes, the upshot of which was, that the brown men and the white men vowed eternal friendship, and agreed to inaugurate the happy commencement thereof with a feast — a sort of picnic on a grand scale — in which food was to be supplied by both parties, arms were to be left at home on both sides, and the scene of operations was to be a plot of open ground near to, but outside, the hamlet.

It is easy to record all this briefly, but it must not therefore be supposed that it was easy of arrangement, on the part of the high contracting parties, whose tongues were unavoidably useless in the consultation.

Krake proved himself to be the most eloquent speaker in sign-language, and the manner in which he made his meaning intelligible to the savages was worthy of philosophic study. It is, however, quite beyond the powers of description; a great deal of it consisting not only of signs which might indeed be described, but of sounds — guttural and otherwise — which could not be spelt. We are constrained, therefore, to leave it to the reader's imagination.

At the feast an immense quantity of venison and salmon was consumed, as you may easily believe, and a great number of speeches were made by both parties — the men of each side approving and applauding their own speakers, and listening to those of the other side with as much solemnity of attention as if they understood every word.

There were two points of great interest connected with this feast, which we must not omit to mention. One was, the unexpected arrival, in the middle of it, of the old chief, Whitepow, in a canoe, with Utway and a few of his principal men, and his grandson Powlet. These were hailed by both parties with great delight, because they formed an additional bond of union between them.

It had been arranged by Karlsefin, for the sake of security, that the savages and Norsemen should not intermingle, but that they should sit in two distinct groups opposite to each other. Whitepow, however, ignorant of, or indifferent to such arrangements, passed over at once to the Norsemen on his arrival, and went through the ceremony, which he had so recently acquired, of shaking hands all round. Powlet also followed his example, and so did Utway. They then sat down, and the latter did good service in the cause of peace by making an enthusiastic speech, which the Norsemen could see, from his pantomimic motions, related to his own good treatment at their hands in time past.

Powlet also unwittingly aided in the same good cause, by running up to Olaf and bestowing on him a variety of attentions, which were all expressive of good-will and joy at meeting with him again. He also shouted the name of Snorro several times with great energy, but Olaf could only reply by shaking his head and pointing towards the hamlet where Snorro and the women had been left under a strong and trusty guard.

The other point of interest to which we have alluded was, that a number of the savages became particularly earnest and eager, when the eating was concluded, in their endeavours to impress something on their new friends, which they could not for a long time be made to understand even by the most graphic and energetic signs.

"I fear, Krake, that you have eaten too much, or by some other means have spoilt your powers of interpretation," said Leif with a laugh, as the puzzled interpreter shook his head for the fifth time at an energetic young savage with a red spot on his chin, and a blue stripe on his nose, who had been gesticulating — we might almost say agonising — before him for some time.

"'Tis beyond my powers entirely," said Krake. "Try it again, Bluenose," he added, turning once more to the savage with resolute intensity of concentration; "drive about your limbs and looks a little harder. I'll make ye out if it's in the power of man."

Thus adjured, the young savage opened his mouth wide, pointed with his finger down his throat, then up at the sky, spread both hands abroad in a vague manner, and exclaimed "ho!" as though to say, "that's plain enough, surely!"

"Oh, for shame! Is it eaten too much ye have? Is that what ye want to say?"

That was evidently not what he wanted to say, for the poor savage looked round with quite a disconsolate aspect.

"Come hither, Powlet," cried Biarne; "you're a smart boy; see if you can make the matter somewhat plainer."

Powlet at all events understood his name, and Biarne's beckoning finger, for he rose and went to him. Biarne confronted him with the young savage, and told the two to talk with each other by means of signs, which consisted in his touching the lips of both and thrusting their heads together.

The young savage smiled intelligently and spoke to Powlet, who thereupon turned to Biarne, and, rolling his eyes for a few seconds, uttered a low wail.

"Sure it isn't pains you're troubled with?" asked Krake, in a voice of pity.

"I do believe it must be that they refer to some one whom we have wounded during the fight," suggested Leif, "and that they think we have him concealed in the hamlet."

"It seems to me," said Thorward, "that if they were troubled about a wounded or missing comrade, they would have asked for him sooner."

"That is true," replied Leif. "I wish we knew what it is they would communicate, for they appear to be very anxious about it."

As he spoke, a tall savage, with an unusually grave countenance, stalked from among his fellows, thrust Powlet and the young man whom Krake had styled Bluenose aside, and seated himself on the ground in imitation of the free-and-easy manner of the Norsemen. Suddenly his face lighted up. He clapped both hands to his chest and breathed hard, then raised his hands aloft, looked enthusiastically up at the sky, rolled his eyes in a fearful manner, opened his mouth wide, and gave utterance to a series of indescribable howls. Checking himself in the midst of one of these, he suddenly resumed his grave aspect, looked straight at Krake, and said "Ho!"

That he thought he had hit the mark, and conveyed the meaning of himself and his friends precisely, was made evident by the other savages, who nodded their heads emphatically, and exclaimed "Ho!" with earnestness.

"H'm! 'tis easy to say 'Ho!'" replied Krake, more perplexed than ever, "and if 'Ho' would be a satisfactory answer, I'd give ye as much as ye liked of that; but I can't make head or tail of what it is ye would be at."

"Stay," exclaimed Hake, stepping quickly forward, "I think I know what they want."

Saying this, he looked earnestly at the grave savage, and ran over one or two notes of a song.

No words in any language could convey such a powerful meaning as did the beam of intelligence and delight which overspread the faces of these sons of the wilderness. The "ho! ho! hos!" and noddings were repeated with such energy, that Krake advised them to "stop that, lest their heads should come off altogether!"

"I thought so," said Hake, turning away from them; "they want you to give them a song, Krake."

"They shall have that, and welcome," cried the jovial Norseman, striking up the "Danish Kings" at once, with all the fire of his nature.

The natives sat in rapt solemnity, and when the Norsemen joined laughingly in the chorus, they allowed a faint smile to play for a moment on their faces, and murmured their satisfaction to each other when the song was done. But it was evident that they wanted something more, for they did not seem quite satisfied until one of their number rose, and going up to Hake touched his lips with his finger.

"Ha! I thought so!" exclaimed Krake in contempt. "It's bad taste ye have to want a song from *him* after hearing *me*! But what else could we expect from ye?"

Hake willingly complied with their wish, and it then became evident that the savages had gained their point at last, for they listened with half closed eyes, and more than half opened mouths, while he was singing, and heaved a deep sigh when he had finished.

Thus pleasantly was the feast concluded, and thus they sealed their friendship.

But there was something still more satisfactory in store for the Norsemen, for it was soon afterwards discovered that the savages possessed a large quantity of beautiful furs, with which, of course, they were willing to part for the merest trifle, in the shape of a shred of brilliant cloth or an ornamental bauble.

This was not only fortunate, as affording an opportunity for the Norsemen to procure full and valuable cargoes for both their ships, but as creating a busy and interesting occupation, which would prevent the natives from growing weary of inaction, and, perhaps, falling into those forms of mischief which proverbially lie ready to idle hands.

"It seems to me, friends," said Leif one evening, shortly after the feast just described, while he was seated in the chief hall, polishing his iron headpiece, and occasionally watching the active hands of Gudrid and Thora as they busied themselves about domestic affairs, while Bertha sat beside him dandling Snorro on her knee — "It seems to me that we have got together such a rich cargo that the sooner we send our ships to Greenland the better. They can then return with fresh supplies of such things as are needed in good time. For myself, I will go with the ships, and overlook the loading of them in Greenland."

"Oh! may I go with you?" exclaimed Bertha, looking up suddenly with much eagerness.

Hake, who was seated at the lower end of the hall, busily engaged in making a bow, paused abruptly in his work, but did not raise his head.

"I have no objection, if Freydissa has none," answered Leif.

"Freydissa will be only too glad to get rid of her," replied that amiable woman, who was engaged in the manufacture of a leathern tunic for Snorro; "she is tired of milk-and-water."

"And yet milk-and-water is more likely to agree with you than anything resembling beer," said Biarne, with a laugh.

"I should be sorry to leave Vinland," returned Bertha, "but I am very *very* anxious to see my dear father again. Besides — I can return hither."

Hake's hand was suddenly released, and resumed its occupation.

"If you go, Leif," asked Karlsefin, "will you return and spend the winter with us?"

"I will not promise that," replied Leif with a smile.

There was silence for some minutes, which was broken at length by a very small voice saying:

"'Norro go to G'eenland too?"

Poor Snorro was as regardless of the *S* in his own name as he was of the *l* in Olaf's!

"'Norro may go, if Gudrid will allow him," answered Leif, patting the child's curly pate.

"And O'af too?" added Snorro.

"Of course *I* must go if Snorrie goes," cried Olaf who had just entered the hall. "We could not live separate – could we, Snorrie?" He caught up the child and placed him on his back in his wonted fashion. "Just think," he continued, "what would it do in Greenland without O'af to give it rides and take it out for long walks?"

"Ay, and go lost with it in the woods," added Biarne.

Olaf blushed, but replied promptly – "That would be impossible, Biarne, for there are no woods in Greenland."

"If Snorro goes so must I," said Thora. "He could not get on without his nurse."

"Methinks we had better all go together to Greenland," said Astrid, who was busy preparing supper.

"Not bad advice," observed Biarne, somewhat seriously.

"Do you mean what you say?" asked Karlsefin.

"I half mean it," replied Biarne.

There was a pause here. Karlsefin then said – "It seems to me, friends, that our minds are all jumping together. I have thought for a long time of leaving Vinland, for it is plain to me that as we stand just now we cannot make much headway. Many of our men are longing to get back to their families, some to their sweethearts, and some to their native land; while, from what you have said, it would seem that none of us are very anxious to remain."

"Do not speak for *all*," said Thorward.

"Well, dost *thou* wish to stay?"

"It may be that I do. At any rate, we have had much trouble in coming hither and settling ourselves, and it would be a pity to lose all our labours unless we can't help it. There may be others of my way of thinking in the colony. It is my advice that before we discuss such a matter we had better call a Thing,[8] and do it in an orderly way."

"By all means," said Karlsefin, "let us discuss the matter for *decision* in a

8   An assembly for discussion.

Thing; yet our discussing here for amusement is not disorderly."

After a little more conversation it was finally arranged that a Thing, or general assembly of the people, should be called on the following day, to discuss and decide on the propriety of forsaking Vinland and returning home.

CHAPTER XXV.

The First Congress and the Last Farewell.

At the gathering of the Vinland colonists next day a number of able speeches were made by various individuals; for the Norsemen of old were accustomed to the free discussion of public affairs, at a time when nearly all Europe was crushed under the yoke of feudalism. Some of the speeches were humorous, and some had a good deal of sound about them without much weight of matter — a peculiarity, by the way, which marks many of the speeches made in the national and general assemblies of mankind in the present day, not less, perhaps rather more, than in the olden time.

All the men of the colony were entitled to raise their voices in the council except the thralls, so that the brothers Hake and Heika took no part in the discussion. These two therefore held a private confabulation of their own on the margin of the lake.

Thorward was among the first speakers at the assembly.

"It is my opinion," he said, in the tone of a man who expects to have his opinion opposed, "that we have not yet given Vinland a fair trial. We are only just beginning to discover the value of the land. Ye know now that it is not a small island, as was at first supposed, but a vast country of unknown extent. Who knows but that it may be as large as Norway? This lake and river on which we dwell do not owe their birth to an insignificant country; any man with half the vision of one eye remaining may see that! The woods supply all that man can desire; the waters swarm with fish; the climate is delightful; our ships are even now loaded to the bulwarks with costly furs, and the natives are friendly. What would ye more? It seems to me that we might, if we chose, lay the foundation of a new nation that would rival Iceland, perchance equal old Norway itself, if we take advantage of the great opportunities that have fallen to our hands. But if we get frightened at the yell of every savage that makes his appearance, or grow weary of good, vigorous, hard work, and begin to sigh like children for home, then there is small chance of our doing anything, and it will doubtless be the fate of a bolder race of men to people this land at some future time."

There was a good deal of applause from some of the people when Thorward finished this speech, which was uttered with great decision, but it was observable that those who thought with him, though noisy, were not numerous.

The moment Thorward sat down Krake started up and said somewhat warmly — "'Tis all very well for Thorward to speak in this way, and ask 'What would ye more?' seeing that he has got in his house a handsome and sweet-tempered wife; but I will tell him of *something more* that I want, and that I haven't got just now, and am not likely to get as long as I remain in Vinland. There is a comely little woman in Iceland, who was born in that best of countries, Ireland, and who forsook the land, and her father and mother, and kith and kin, all for the sake of a red-headed thrall — for he was no better at that time — called Krake.

Now, *I* want that sweet little Irishwoman! Moreover, there's a stout curly-headed boy in Iceland who's an elegant chip of the ancient tree, and the born image of his mother — I want that curly-headed boy! Then there are six other curly-headed boys in Iceland — only that three of them are girls, and the youngest had the curls in prospect when I saw it last, bein' as bare on the head as the palm of my hand — all of them descending in size, one after another, from the first curly-headed boy — I want these. Besides which there is a sweet little hut in Iceland at the edge of a swamp, with the spouting waters not far off, and the boilin' waters quite handy to cook your dinner without firin', and a lovely prospect of the burnin' hill behind — I want all that; and I want to know how Thorward would feel if he wanted all that and couldn't get it, and was advised to go on wantin' it, and if he couldn't keep himself easy, to try his best to keep as easy as he could!"

There was some laughter and great applause at this point.

"Moreover," continued Krake, with increasing energy, "it don't give me a scrap of comfort to be told that this is a vast country, full of all that's desirable and the best of livin', when I can't enjoy it along with my sweet little Kathleen and the curly-headed boys and girls before mentioned. What does Krake care for stuffing his own ugly carcase full when mayhap the wife and bairns are dyin' for want — anyhow dyin' to see their husband an' father? And what does Krake care to be the beginning of a new nation? No more than he does to be the middle of it, and if left to himself he'd far sooner be the end of it by not beginning it at all! As for being frightened by the yells of savages, it's not worth my while to mention *that*, but when Thorward talks about beginning to sigh like children for home, he misses his mark entirely. It's not *sighing* I am for home, but roaring, bellowing, howling for it in my wearied spirit, and it's my opinion, comrades, as I gaze round upon your speaking faces, that there's a good many here howling along with me."

There could be no doubt that Krake's sentiments were largely entertained and appreciated, for his speech was followed by prolonged and enthusiastic applause, in which the Norsemen not only raised their voices, but rattled their arms on their shields by way of emphasis. Thorward smiled grimly and shrugged his shoulders, but made no reply.

After several others had spoken in various strains — a few in favour of Thorward's opinion, but many more in sympathy with Krake — Leif made a short speech, advising immediate return to Greenland, Biarne followed suit, and Karlsefin wound up with a few remarks, in which he urged, among other things, that although the savages were friendly just then, it was not likely they would remain so very long, and in the event of a quarrel it was certain, considering their great numbers, that the infant colony would be kept in perpetual hot water, if not actual warfare. He suggested, moreover, that the proper way to establish a colony, that would have some chance to survive and flourish, would be to organise it thoroughly in Iceland or Norway, and induce so many married men with their families to emigrate, that they would be able to *feel* at home in the new land, and thus *wish* to remain. He concluded by saying that those who now desired to remain in Vinland might join together and devote their energies to the getting up of such a band of colonists if so disposed. For his own part, since the majority were evidently in favour of returning home, he was free to confess that he had no taste for colonising. The ocean was *his* home, and when that failed him he hoped that God might permit him to end his days and lay his bones in Iceland.

It was finally agreed that the country should be abandoned, and that, having made up their minds, they should set about preparations without delay.

We have said that the Scottish brothers had gone to the margin of the lake to hold a little consultation by themselves, while the affairs of the nation were being settled in the grand parliament.

"What think you? Will these men of Iceland decide to return home or to remain here?" said Hake, seating himself on a bank of wild-flowers, which he began to pluck and scatter with an absent air.

"They will decide to forsake Vinland," answered Heika.

"You appear to be very sure, brother."

"I am; because I have been watching the men for some time past, and occasionally leading them on to talk about the matter."

"Which way do you hope they will decide?" asked Hake.

"I hope they will leave."

"Do you? For my part I care but little. It seems to me that we have as small a chance of escaping from Greenland as from this land."

"Brother, ye think in this way because you are content to remain where Bertha dwells. If Bertha were with Emma in bonny Scotland, your wits would be sharp enough to perceive that the voyage from Vinland to Scotland, with an unknown sea between, would be a more hazardous venture than a voyage from Greenland to Scotland, with Iceland between."

"That may be true, brother, but methinks my wits are sharp enough to perceive that neither voyage concerns us, seeing that we have no ship, and are not likely to succeed in persuading a whale to carry us over."

"Nevertheless," replied Heika, "I mean to go over to Scotland this summer if I can."

Hake looked earnestly in his brother's face.

"From your tones and words," said he, "I know that you have some plan in your head."

"That have I," rejoined Heika firmly, yet with a look of sadness. "Listen, Hake: the thought that I shall never more see Emma or my father is more than I can bear. I will now make the effort to escape from Greenland — for well assured am I that we shall soon be there again — or die in the attempt. Of what value is a thrall's life? The plan that I have in my head is this. You know that when in Greenland we were often sent out beyond the fiord to fish and to hunt the walrus and the seal — sometimes in large, sometimes in small, boats. The boats on Eric's fiord are numerous now. The absence of one for a time would not be much noticed. There is a man there whose life I saved not long before we set sail for Vinland. He has a good boat, which I will borrow, take it round to the western skerries, to which our men seldom go, and there quietly fit it out for a long voyage. When a fitting time arrives I will set sail for Scotland."

Hake shook his head.

"What wild thoughts are these, brother? Who ever heard of a man crossing the ocean in a small boat?"

"The thing may be done," replied Heika. "It is risky, no doubt; but is not everything more or less risky? Besides, I had rather die than remain in thraldom."

He paused, and Hake gazed at the ground in silence.

"I see," he continued sadly, "you do not like my project, and will not aid me in the enterprise. After all, how could I expect that you would be willing to forsake Bertha and face so great a danger?"

Hake still continued to gaze in silence, and with a strangely perplexed air, at the ground.

"Well, well, Hake," resumed the other, in a tone of reproach, "I did not expect that ye would go with me on this venture, but truly I had counted on your sympathy and counsel as well as your aid."

"Ye do wrong me," cried Hake, suddenly starting up and seizing his brother's hand; "I not only sympathise with you, but I will go with you. It is not easy all at once to make up one's mind on a point of such importance. Forsake Bertha I never will as long as one drop of Scottish blood flows in my veins, for I know that she loves me, though her sense of duty keeps her aloof — for which I love her all the more. Nevertheless, I will leave her for a time. I will make this venture with you. If we perish, we perish. If we succeed I will return to Greenland with a force that will either induce or compel the surrender of my bride."

"Thou art a bold lover," said Heika, smiling. "What! wilt thou carry her off whether she will or no?"

"Not so; but I will carry her off whether Leif or Karlsefin, or Biarne or Thorward, or all Greenland put together, will or no!"

"Nay, brother, that may not be. It were the maddest venture of all. I will run this risk alone."

For some time the brothers disputed upon this point and held out against each other pretty stoutly. At length Heika reluctantly gave in, and it was finally agreed that Hake should join him in the proposed attempt to regain his liberty.

It did not take long to make the necessary arrangements for leaving Vinland. The little colony had not struck its roots very deeply into the soil. They were easily torn out without damage to the feelings of any one, for little Snorro, as Krake said, was the only creature that had to bid farewell to his *native* land — always excepting some of the cattle and chickens — and he was too young to take it much to heart.

In a few weeks the *Snake*, and Thorward's ship, the *Dragon*, were loaded with everything that was of value in the colony, including much even of the rude furniture of the huts.

Before leaving, Karlsefin resolved to give a last grand feast to the savages. He therefore called them together and explained, as he best could, that he and his friends were going to leave them, but that perhaps some of them might return again with large supplies of the gay cloth and ornaments they were so fond of, and he recommended them in the meantime to make as large a collection of furs as they could, in order to be ready to trade when the white men returned. He then spread before them the most sumptuous feast the land could provide, including a large quantity of dairy produce, which the savages regarded as the most luxurious of fare.

After the feast he presented Whitepow, Utway, and Powlet with a large quantity of bright-coloured cloth and a few silver and iron ornaments, to be distributed among the members of the tribe as they should see fit after helping themselves. He also gave them a few cattle and domestic fowls, after which, weighing anchors, putting out the oars, and hoisting their sails, the Norsemen bade farewell to Leifsgaard. As they swept round the point which shut it out from view, they gave vent to one vigorous parting cheer, which was replied to by the savages with a feeble imitation and a waving of arms.

Dropping down the river, they passed the spit of sand where the first night in Vinland had been spent so pleasantly; caught an offshore breeze that carried them swiftly beyond the island betwixt which and the shore they had captured the whale, and finally leaped out upon the swell of the great ocean.

"Aha! now am I at home," exclaimed Karlsefin, with heightened colour and sparkling eyes, as he stood at the helm, and glanced from the bulging sail to the heaving swell, where Thorward's *Dragon* was bending over to the breeze about a cable's length to leeward – "Now am I at home once more!"

"So am not I," murmured poor Bertha, whose white face betrayed the miserable emotions – or commotions – within.

All the women, we may remark, had expressed a desire to keep together during the voyage, hence they had embarked in the *Snake*, which was a better seaboat than Thorward's vessel.

"Of course *you* are not at home. You are never contented or at home anywhere!" cried Freydissa sharply.

Hake wished with all his heart that Bertha was at home in Scotland, and that her home was his; and Snorro, who was seated on Olaf's knee, said –

"Never mind, Bert'a, oos be a tome soon."

There was a general laugh at this consolatory remark; even Bertha smiled faintly as she patted Snorro's head, while Astrid and Thora – not to mention Gudrid – agreed between themselves that he was the dearest, sweetest, and in every way the most delightful Vinlander that had ever been born.

"Of that there can be no doubt," said Leif, with a laugh, "since he is the only white Vinlander that ever *was* born."

But although the party assembled on the poop indulged at first in a few humorous remarks, they soon became silent and sad, for they were fast leaving behind them a spot which, with all its drawbacks, had been a pleasant and happy home for upwards of three years.

As they stood leaning on the rails that guarded the poop, and gazed regretfully on the lessening hills, each recalled many pleasant or stirring incidents which had occurred there, incidents which would remain – however far or long that land might be left behind — for ever engraven on their memories. And, long after twilight and distance had concealed the coast from view, the Norsemen continued to strain their vision towards the horizon, mentally bidding a long and last farewell to Vinland.

CHAPTER XXVI.

Changes in Brattalid — The Scots Continue to Plot and Plan.

Greenland again! Flatface standing on the wharf at Brattalid; Anders beside him; groups of Norse men, women, and children, and Skraelingers, around and scattered along the bay.

What a commotion there was in the colony, to be sure, when it was discovered that two large ships were sailing up the fiord; and what a commotion it created in the breasts of those on board these ships when it was discovered that two other large ships were already at anchor in the harbour!

It is not necessary to detain the reader with the details of question and reply, by which the truth was at last elicited on both sides. Suffice it to say that the two ships were found to be merchant-vessels from Iceland, and that, among other colonists, they had brought out several men whose purpose was to teach and plant the new religion. Already a small building had been set up, with a short tower on the roof, which the Norsemen were told was a church, and in which some of the services of the Christian religion were performed. Elsewhere several new houses had been built, and everywhere there were signs of increasing population and prosperity.

Leif was half pleased, half disappointed at all this. It was gratifying to find things prospering so well, but it was not pleasant to see the old place so greatly changed, and to have much of the old home-feeling done away.

However, little was said on the subject. The Vinland colonists were too busy at first, meeting with relations and old companions, and being introduced to new friends, to say or think much about the matter. After a few days they became reconciled to the change, and settled down into a regular busy life.

One evening Heika went to the house of his friend Edwinsson, who owned the boat that he wished to become possessed of. He found that the man was not at home, but there was a serving-woman in the house.

"Edwinsson no longer lives here," said the girl. "He has gone to live with old Haraldson and manage his boats, for the old man is not able for that work now."

"Do you mean Bertha's father?" asked Heika.

"Yes; Haraldson is Bertha's father."

Heika went at once to search for his friend. By the way he chanced to meet with his brother.

"Come, Hake," said he, "I want you to go with me to find Edwinsson."

"With all my heart," said Hake.

They soon came to old Haraldson's house, which lay at the extreme west of Brattalid; and when Heika opened the door, there he saw the old man seated in a large chair, propped up with eider-down pillows. Bertha was seated on a stool at his feet holding one of his hands.

"Come in, Heika," she cried, springing up and hasting forward with pleasure. "I have been trying to tell dear father about the whale you killed in Vinland."

She stopped abruptly on observing that Hake was behind his brother. Recovering herself quickly, however, she welcomed him also with a slight blush.

"I want you, Heika," she continued, "to tell the story to my father."

"Ay, sit down here, young man, and tell it me," said Haraldson, in a tremulous voice. "I love to hear anything about Vinland, especially what pleases Bertha. Dear Bertha! I have become very frail since she went away — very frail; and it has been a weary time — a weary time. But come, tell me about the whale."

"Gladly would I do that," said Heika; "but I have business with your man Edwinsson — business which I want to put out of hands at once. But Hake will tell the story of the whale. He is a better sagaman than I."

"Let Hake tell it, then," returned the old man. "You will find Edwinsson somewhere about among my boats."

Hake gladly sat down beside Bertha, and began the story of the whale, while his brother went down to the beach, where he found his friend.

"Edwinsson," said Heika, after some conversation had passed between them, "you have a good boat near Leif's wharf. Will you lend it to me?"

"Right willingly," replied his friend.

"But I am bound on an excursion that may chance to end in the wreck of the boat," said Heika. "Will you hold me responsible if I lose it?"

"'Twill be difficult to hold thee responsible," returned Edwinsson, laughing, "if ye lose your life along with it. But that matters not. I gift thee the boat if thou wilt have it. I count it a small gift to the man who saved my life."

"Thanks, Edwinsson — thanks. I accept the gift, and, if my venture is successful, I shall try to let you share the benefit in some way or other."

"Hast discovered a new fishing-ground, Heika? What venture do ye intend?" asked the other.

"That I will keep secret just now," said Heika, laughing carelessly. "I don't want to be followed at first. Ye shall know all about it soon. But hearken, friend, make no mention of it. One does not like to be laughed at if one fails, you know."

So saying, Heika went off to Leif's wharf, loosed the boat which he found there, hoisted the sail, and dropped down with the tide to the mouth of the fiord. Here a light breeze was blowing, under the influence of which he soon ran round the point of land that divided Ericsfiord from Heriulfness. In the course of another hour he reached the western skerries.

The skerries or islets in question were little better than bare rocks, which lay about fifty yards from the mainland, along which they formed a sort of breakwater for a distance of nearly a quarter of a mile. Within this breakwater there were several narrow and well-sheltered inlets. Into one of these Heika ran his boat, and made it fast in a place which was so well overshadowed by rocks, that the boat could neither be seen from the land nor from the sea.

On the landward side this inlet could be reached by a path, which, though it appeared somewhat rugged, was nevertheless easy to traverse. Up this path

Heika hastened after making the boat fast, intending to return to Brattalid by land. The distance over land was much shorter than by water, so that he could soon reach Leif's house, and his brief absence would attract no attention.

Just as the Scot issued from behind the rocks which concealed the path to the inlet, he was suddenly bereft almost of the power to move by the unexpected sight of Leif himself advancing towards him!

Poor Heika's heart died within him. He felt that all his long-cherished and deeply-laid plans were crushed, just as they were about to be carried into effect, and a feeling of fierce despair prompted him, for a moment, to commit some wild deed of violence, but he observed that Leif's head was bent forward and his eyes rested on the ground, as he advanced slowly, like one who meditates. Heika drew swiftly back behind the rock, from the shelter of which he had barely passed, and breathed freely again when Leif passed by, without showing any symptom of having observed him. Waiting till he had sauntered beyond the next turn in the path, he started at his utmost speed, and was soon beyond the reach of Leif's eyes, and back in Brattalid with a relieved mind.

Had the Scot waited to observe the motions of his master after passing the turn in the path above mentioned, he would not have experienced so much mental relief; for no sooner had Leif got behind a small but thick bush than he turned abruptly, raised his head with an intelligent smile, lay down behind the bush, and looked quietly through its foliage. He saw Heika issue from behind the rock, observed his cautious glances from side to side, and, with something like a chuckle, witnessed his rapid flight in the direction of the settlement.

"Hem! something i' the wind," muttered Leif, rising and walking towards the spot whence his thrall had issued.

He found the rugged path, descended to the inlet, discovered the boat, and stood looking at it with a perplexed air for full ten minutes. Thereafter he shook his head once or twice, smiled in a grave manner, and slowly sauntered home absorbed in meditation.

"Hake," whispered Heika to his brother that night, as they sat down together in the little sleeping-closet off Leif's hall, that had been allotted to their use, "all my hopes and plans were on the point of being ruined today."

"Ruined! brother. How was that?"

Heika related to him all that had occurred at the inlet near the western skerries.

"Art thou sure he saw thee not?" asked Hake earnestly.

"There can be no doubt of that," replied Heika, "for he had no cause to suspect that anything was wrong; and if he had seen me as I first stood before him, motionless with surprise, he would doubtless have hailed me. No, no; something was working very hard in his brain, for he passed on without the least sign of having seen me."

"That is well, brother, yet I do not feel easy, for it is well-known that Leif is a shrewd man, with great command over his feelings. But now, tell me how best I shall aid you in this enterprise."

"That is best done by using your bow well, for we shall require a large supply of dried meat for the voyage, and we must work diligently as well as secretly during our few hours of leisure, if we would get ready in time to sail before the rough winds of autumn set in. There are some tight casks in Leif's old store which I mean to take possession of, at the last, for water. Our service will more than pay for these and any other trifles we may find it needful to appropriate."

Hake thought in his heart that the enterprise was a wild and foolish one, but, having promised to engage in it, he resolved not to cast the slightest hindrance in the way, or to say a single word of discouragement. He therefore approved of all that Heika suggested, and said that he would give his aid most vigorously.

"Moreover," he continued, "I have had some consolation today which will spur me on, for I have got Bertha to admit that she loves me, and to promise that if I can obtain my freedom she will wed me. She even gave me to understand that she would wed me as a thrall, if only Leif and Karlsefin would give their consent. But that shall not be. Bertha shall never be a thrall's bride. I will return and claim her, as I have said."

Heika made no reply, but continued to gaze at the floor in silence.

"Methinks ye are perplexed by something, brother," said Hake.

"I am thinking," replied Heika, "that it is a pity we cannot use those curious marks made on skins, wherewith, we are told, men can communicate one with another when they are absent from each other."

"What causes the regret just now?"

"I grudge to quit Leif without a parting word," returned Heika, looking at his brother with peculiar earnestness; "it seems so ungrateful, so unkind to one who has ever treated us well."

"I think with you in that, brother," said Hake.

"It would be so easy too," continued Heika, "to have some method of letting him know what I think, if we could only agree about the signs or signals beforehand."

Hake laughed softly.

"That would not be easy; for we could scarcely go to him and say, 'Leif, when you see these particular marks on a certain stone, you are to understand that we take leave of you for ever with hearty good-will!' I fear that his suspicions might be aroused thereby."

"Nay, but I only express regret that we have not some such mode of intercourse," returned Heika, smiling. "Ye know the sign of the split arrow which tells of war. Why might we not multiply such signs? For instance, *by laying a billet of firewood across a man's bed*, one might signify that he bade him farewell with tender affection and goodwill!"

"Why, brother," said Hake, laughing, "ye look at me as earnestly as if you had said something smart; whereas I regard your idea as but a clumsy one. A billet of wood laid across your friend's bed might more fitly suggest that you wanted to knock out his brains, or damage his skin, or burn him alive!"

Heika laughed heartily, and said that he feared he had nothing of the spirit of the skald about him, and that his power of invention was not great.

"But I have more news to give thee, brother, besides that regarding Bertha," said Hake. "Do you know there is a countryman of ours on board of one of the ships that brought out the men of the new religion, and he has but lately seen our father and Emma?"

Heika started and laid his hand on his brother's arm, while he gazed earnestly into his face.

"It is ill jesting on such a subject," he said somewhat sternly.

"So think I, brother; therefore I recommend you not to jest," returned Hake gravely.

"Nay, but is it true?"

"Ay, true as that the sky is over our heads. I have had a long talk with him, and when he found I was a countryman he gave me a hug that made my ribs bend. His name is Sawneysson, a very giant of a man, with hair that might have grown on the back of a Greenland bear, only that it is red instead of white. He told me that he knew our father well by sight, and last saw him taking a ramble on Dunedin hill, whither he had walked from our village on the Forth, which shows that the old man's vigour has improved. Emma was with him too, so Sawneysson said, looking beautiful, but somewhat sad."

"How knew he her name?" asked Heika.

"He knew it not," replied Hake. "He did but say that a fair maiden walked with our father, and I knew at once from his description that it was Emma. But you can inquire for yourself at his own mouth, for this countryman of ours is an enthusiastic fellow, and fond of talking about home."

"Brother," said Heika, with a sad but earnest look, "I must give this man the cold shoulder."

"Nay, then, disappointment must have changed thee much," said Hake, in surprise, "for that is the last thing I had expected thee to say."

"It is not disappointment but caution that makes me speak and think as I do. If we seem to be too eager about our native land it may tend to make Leif more watchful of us, which of all things would be the greatest misfortune that could befall us just at this time."

"There is something in that," returned Hake; "but will it not suffice to exercise a little caution and self-restraint, without giving our countryman the cold shoulder?"

"I know not," replied Heika, with a troubled air; "but I would that he had not turned up just now, though I confess it gladdens me to hear of our father and Emma. Now, Hake, we must to bed if we would be up betimes to secure a little leisure for the carrying out of our enterprise."

Without further conversation the brothers threw off their coats and shoes, and lay down together with the rest of their clothing on, so as to be ready for an early start. The shield and helmet of each hung on the wall just over the bed, and their two swords leaned against the bed itself, within reach of their hands, for thus guardedly did men deem it necessary to take their rest in the warlike days of old.

CHAPTER XXVII.

Disappointment Terminates in Unlooked-for Success, and the Saga Comes to an End.

During some weeks after the events narrated in the last chapter, the Scottish brothers continued quietly, stealthily, and steadily to collect provisions and all things necessary for the projected voyage across the Atlantic.

During the same period the general business of the settlement was prosecuted with activity. The Christian missionaries not only instructed the people in the new faith, and baptized those that believed, but assisted and guided them in the building of huts and houses, the planning of wharves and the laying out of townships;[9] while the crews of the two recently arrived ships, having found it necessary to make up their minds to winter in Greenland, busied themselves in collecting fats, oil, skins, feathers, etc., to be packed and got ready for shipment in the following spring.

Karlsefin also made preparations for a voyage in spring to Iceland, and Thorward, Biarne, Krake, and the other Vinland heroes assisted in that work, or in some other of the multifarious duties that had to be attended to in the colony, while Olaf undertook the responsible duty of superintending the education, mental and physical, of that rampant little Vinlander, Snorro, the son of Karlsefin.

Leif Ericsson exercised a sort of general superintendence of the whole colony. It seemed to be tacitly agreed on and admitted that he was the national chief or governor, and as no one was disposed to dispute his claim to that position all was peace and harmony.

Nevertheless there was something unusual in Leif's manner at that time which rather perplexed his friends, and quite puzzled Anders, his major-domo.

---

9   An important Christian colony existed in Greenland for nearly 400 years — from some time in the tenth to near the end of the fourteenth century — a colony in which, in the fourteenth century, there were 190 townships and a town called Garda, in which were a cathedral, bishop's seat, and twelve or thirteen churches, besides other Christian establishments, with a regular succession of bishops for their superintendence, of whom seventeen are named in the sagas. This colony, strange to say, was obliterated, no one knew how or when, and its very existence was forgotten by the civilised world. It was chronicled, however, in the Icelandic sagas and brought to light by antiquaries of the highest authority. The statistical details given by the sagas have been corroborated by the actual discovery in Greenland, in the eighteenth and nineteenth centuries, of vast ecclesiastical and other buildings. These are facts which do not admit of reasonable doubt — so writes Samuel Laing in his translation of "The Heimskringla, or Chronicle of the Kings of Norway," vol. i. p. 141.

That free and easy individual could not understand the dreamy moods into which his master fell, still less could he comprehend the gleams of quiet humour and expressions of intense seriousness, with other contradictory appearances, which occasionally manifested themselves in Leif's visage and demeanour. It was plain that there was much on his mind, and that much of that was gay as well as grave. Anders made several attempts to find out what was the matter, but was met at one time with grave evasion, at another with quiet jocularity, which left him as wise as before.

Towards the Scottish brothers Leif maintained an unvarying aspect of reserve, which filled them with uneasiness; but with the female members of his household, and the children, he was all gentleness, and often playful.

"Leif," said Karlsefin to him one day, "it appears to me that something weighs on your mind, or else ye have left some of your wits in Vinland."

"Think ye not that the cares of such a large and growing colony are sufficient to account for any new wrinkles that may appear on my brow?" replied Leif, with a peculiar smile, and a glance from the corner of his eye.

"Well, I daresay that might account for it, and yet things are swimming on so well that these cares do not seem to be much increased."

"Sometimes domestic cares trouble a man more than public ones, Karlsefin. Look at thy friend Thorward, now. 'Tis little that he would care for a mountain of outside troubles on his broad shoulders if he might only drop them when he crossed the threshold of his own door."

"That is true," returned the other; "if a man have not peace in his own house, there is no peace for him on earth. Nevertheless my friend Thorward is not in such a bad case. Freydissa has improved vastly of late, and Thorward has also grown more amiable and less contradictions — add to which, he and she love each other dearly. But, Leif, there can be no domestic troubles in your case, for your household is well ordered."

"Thank God there are none," said Leif seriously. It was the first time that Leif had used that expression, and his friend heard it with some surprise and pleasure, but said nothing.

"Still," continued Leif, "I am not destitute of troubles. Has not that thrall Hake overturned the peace of my sweet kinswoman Bertha? The girl loves the thrall — I can see that, as plain as I can see the vane on yonder masthead — and there is no cure for love!"

Karlsefin looked earnestly at his friend as if about to speak, but observing the stern frown on Leif's countenance, he forbore.

In a minute or so Karlsefin remarked quietly that Hake was a faithful thrall.

"I'm not so sure of that as ye seem to be," returned Leif, with increasing sternness, "but, whether faithful or not, no thrall shall ever wed Bertha."

"What is that you say about Bertha?" asked Biarne, coming up just then.

"Nothing of moment," replied Leif. "What news bring you, Biarne? for that ye bring news is plain by the glance of your eye."

"My eye is an incorrigible telltale," cried Biarne, laughing. "However, it has not much to tell at present. Only that you are about to receive a visit from some old friends, and that Anders will have to keep his kettles full for some time to come. A band of Skraelingers are — . But here they come to speak for themselves."

At that moment a troop of the Greenland savages came round the point — the identical point where they had received such a terrible shock some years before — with Flatface dancing joyously in front of them.

Flatface had heard of their coming, had gone out to meet them, had found several of his relations among them, and was now returning, scarce able to contain himself with delight, as he made their mouths water by dilating at great length on the delicious things contained in Anders's capacious kettles.

While Leif and the others went to meet the Skraelingers, Heika and his brother sat in their own sleeping-closet, talking in a low tone, and making the final arrangements for their flight.

"Now are ye sure that all is on board — nothing omitted?" asked Hake, "for it will be hard to obtain anything once we are out on the sea, and we can't well return to fetch what we have forgotten."

"All is ready," answered Heika sadly. "I cannot tell how much it grieves me to go away in this fashion; but freedom must be regained at any price. Now remember, meet me exactly when the moon shows its upper edge above the sea tonight. Not later, and not sooner, for the longer ye can remain about the hall the less likely will any one be to inquire after *me*."

"I will be sure not to fail you; but, Heika, is that not a little too late? The flood-tide will be past, and if there is any sea on, it will be ill passing the skerries, many of which are but little covered, even at high water."

"Trust me, Hake; it will not be too late. Be sure that ye come no sooner — else evil may ensue."

"My heart sinks when I think of Bertha," said Hake, with a deep sigh. "It will seem so cold, so hard, so unaccountable, to leave her without one word, one farewell."

"Think better of it, brother," said Heika eagerly; "I am prepared to start alone even now!"

"Never!" exclaimed Hake, flushing. "What? shall I draw back like a coward at the last moment, after pledging my word to go? and shall I leave you to face this enterprise alone? Nay, Heika, we have suffered for many years together, we shall triumph now together — or perish."

"My poor brother," said Heika, grasping Hake's hand, and kissing it with deep feeling. "But go now to the hall, and leave me; I hear them laying the tables for supper. The window is easily removed; I will hasten at once and get things ready. Take good care not to reenter this closet after leaving it, for the carls are moving about the hall, and may chance to observe that it is empty. Be circumspect, brother."

They squeezed hands again, and Hake went into the hall, where he mingled with the house-carls, and chatted carelessly about the events of the day.

The instant he was gone Heika rose and removed the parchment window, took a billet of firewood and laid it across the bed, then, leaping out, he walked smartly towards the west end of the village.

It was beginning to grow dark, and few of the people were about. To those whom he passed Heika nodded familiarly, but did not stop. The moment he had rounded the cliff which hid Brattalid from view, he ran westward at full speed.

Meanwhile supper was laid in the hall, and all were awaiting the entrance of the master of the house and Karlsefin, but there was no appearance of either. After a quarter of an hour had passed, and they were beginning to wonder what had become of them, the door opened and Biarne entered, saying that Leif had sent him to say that as he had business which would keep him out late, they were not to wait supper for him.

Hake began to feel somewhat uneasy at this, and when supper was finished he resolved to leave the house a little before the appointed time. For that purpose he entered the sleeping-closet, intending to pass out by the window.

The first thing that caught his eye was the billet of firewood lying *across the bed!* His heart almost stood still at the sight, for this, coupled with Heika's display of deep feeling, and their recent conversation about signs, caused the truth to flash upon him.

With one bound he passed through the window and flew westward like the wind – round the point, over the ridge, and down towards the appointed rendezvous at the skerries.

But, to return to Heika. When he neared the inlet he changed his pace to a rapid walk, and glanced cautiously from side to side, to make quite sure that he was not observed by any one who might chance to have wandered in that direction.

Now, it is a well-known fact in the affairs of this world, that many strange things occur in a most unaccountable manner. Who can tell how it was, or why it was that, just a few minutes before Heika approached the inlet from the landward side, a small boat entered it from the seaward side, out of which stepped Leif Ericsson and Karlsefin? They drew their boat into a corner in deep shadow, and then, going to another corner, also in deep shadow, sat down on a ledge of rock without uttering a single word.

They had never been in that inlet before; had never seen it, probably never thought of it before, yet there they were, quietly seated in it – and, just in the nick of time!

From the place where they sat neither their own boat nor Leif's could be seen – only the landward opening of the inlet.

Presently approaching footsteps were heard. The two friends rose. A moment later and Heika stood before them. He stopped abruptly on beholding them, and his eyes blazed with astonishment, rage, and despair. Suddenly he looked round as if in search of a weapon, or of a way of escape.

"Be wise, lad," said Leif, kindly yet very gravely; "no evil will come of it if ye are wise, and take your misfortunes like a man."

Heika was subdued by the gentle tone. He crossed his arms on his heaving chest, and stood erect before them with his head slightly drooped, and a look of profound sadness, rather than disappointment, on his countenance.

"Come hither, Heika," said Leif, pointing seaward, "I have somewhat to show thee."

They went down the beach till they stood beside the boat, which was ready for sea.

"This is a strange sight," he continued; "here is an excellent boat, well found, well loaded, well busked in every way for a long voyage. Knowest thou aught in regard to it, Heika?"

"I know," answered the Scot, bitterly, "that if ye had come hither only half an hour later, that boat would have been on its way with me to Scotland."

"What, with you *alone*?"

"Ay — with me alone."

"That is strange," said Leif, somewhat perplexed; "I had fancied that you brothers loved each other passing well; but I suppose that a man who can be guilty of ingratitude is not to be much depended on in the matter of affection."

Heika winced at these words — not that the charge of ingratitude affected him, but he could not submit calmly to the unjust supposition that in his contemplated flight he had been actuated by selfish indifference to his brother. At the same time he would not condescend to give any explanation of his conduct. Drawing himself up, he looked Leif full in the face.

"Norseman," he said, "small is the gratitude I owe to thee. 'Tis true, ye have treated me and my brother kindly since we came hither, and for that I owe thee thanks, and would gladly have paid this debt before leaving, had such been consistent with flight; but kindness, however great, is not a worthy price for liberty, and when King Olaf Tryggvisson sent me to thee, I made no promise to sell my liberty at such a price. But in regard to Hake —"

"Ay, in regard to Hake, go on; why dost thou stop?" said Leif, in a stern tone. "There is some truth in what ye say about gratitude; but what of Hake?"

The Scot still remained silent, with his lips compressed, and dropped his eyes sternly on the ground.

"This seems to me a bad business," said Karlsefin, who had hitherto listened with an expression of anxiety and disappointment gradually deepening on his countenance. "I had thought better of thee, Heika. Surely Hake's longing to be free and in his own native land must be to the full as strong as thine. I am puzzled, moreover, for two were better than one in the mad voyage ye thought to undertake."

Heika smiled at this.

"Truly," he said, "my brother loves his native land and freedom, nevertheless he prefers bondage to freedom, and Greenland to his native land. And yet would he fain have sacrificed his preference, and resigned his bondage out of love to me, if I would have allowed him."

"Resigned his bondage, Heika!" exclaimed Leif. "Ye speak in riddles, man; what mean you?"

Instead of replying the Scot looked at Leif with an intelligent smile, and held up his forefinger as if to call attention. At the same moment the sound as if of some one running at full speed was heard faintly in the distance.

Leif and Karlsefin looked at the Scot in surprise.

"It is my brother," he said, sadly.

In a few seconds the steps were close at hand. Leif seized Karlsefin by the arm, and dragged him swiftly under the deep shadow of the cliffs just as Hake came through the narrow opening with such a rush that on seeing Heika he could not avoid plunging violently into his extended arms.

"Was this right in thee, brother?" he cried, laying his hand on Heika's shoulder, on recovering himself; "was it wise to treat me thus like a child?"

"It was kindly meant," said Heika, much perplexed as to how he should act in existing circumstances.

"Kindly meant!" exclaimed Hake, vehemently. "Ay, well do I know that, yet it was not wisely kind to forsake me after promising to take me with you, when ye knew that I did but leave Bertha for a time, and meant to come back and win or demand her from – ."

"Hush! brother, hush!" cried Heika, laying his hand on the other's mouth. "Whatever I thought or meant to do matters little now, for I have found it impossible to undertake this voyage after all."

"Impossible!" echoed Hake; "why, what craven spirit has come over thee? Is not the boat ready? am not *I* ready, and is not the opportunity favourable?"

"All is ready, no doubt," replied Heika, hesitating, "but –"

"But the truth is," cried Leif, as he and Karlsefin issued from their place of concealment, laughing heartily, "the truth is, that the opportunity is *not* favourable, for I have some objection to either of you leaving me at present – though the objection is not so strong but that it might give way if ye desired it greatly. Come hither, all of you."

He went a few steps towards the boat, and pointing to it, said – "Tell me, Hake, for thou art not a bad counsellor at need, dost think that vessel there is a sufficiently large one to venture a voyage in it on these northern seas at this time of year?"

"It is large enough for men who would be free," replied Hake moodily, for his astonishment on first beholding his master had given place to deep mortification, now that he perceived his brother's hopes and plans were frustrated.

"Nay, as to being free," returned Leif, with a laugh, "thy brother hinted not long ago something about thy preference for thraldom, in regard to which I now perceive some glimmering of reason; but I ask thee for a matter-of-fact opinion. Dost think there would be much risk in the voyage thy brother contemplated?"

"There would be some risk, doubtless, yet not so much but that we would have run it for the sake of freedom."

"H'm! In my opinion it would have been a mad venture," rejoined Leif. "What say you, Karlsefin?"

"A useless venture, as well as mad," he replied; "for death, not freedom, would have been the end of it."

"So I think," returned Leif, "and that is my only objection to your undertaking it, Hake. Nevertheless if you and Heika are still willing to venture, ye may do so. There lies the boat; a fair wind is blowing outside; get on board, shove off, hoist the sail and away to bonny Scotland if you will, for *I grant you freedom to go!*"

"It is ill to jest with thralls," said Heika, looking sternly at his master.

"Nay, I do not jest — nor are ye thralls," replied Leif, assuming a look and tone of unwonted seriousness. "Give me your attention, friends; and thou, Karlsefin, take note of what I say, for I care not to talk much on this subject until my mind is more clear upon it. My opinion is that this new religion which we hear so much of just now, is *true*. It is of God — not of man, and I believe that Jesus Christ, my Lord, has come in the flesh to save His people from their sins. Many things have led me to this opinion, in regard to which I will not speak. I have thought and heard much for some years past, and woefully have I been staggered, as well as helped on, by the men who have been sent to Greenland with the Good News. Some have, by their conduct squaring with their profession, led me to believe. Others have, by their conduct belying their profession, hindered me. But the Lord Himself has led me into a certain measure of light; and there is one law of His in particular, which just now comes home to me with much power, namely this — 'Whatsoever ye would that men should do unto you, do ye even so unto them.' This law, I am persuaded, is of God. Long have I lived, and never before have I seen it acted on till these Christians came amongst us. They do not, indeed, always practise as they teach; but they are imperfect, therefore they cannot practise *fully* as they teach, because they teach *perfection*. This law I shall henceforth follow as I best can. I follow it today. If I were in thraldom to *you*, Heika, just now, I would wish you to set me free, therefore I now set you and your brother free. The rule is very simple of application. It only wants a willing spirit. And let me add — ye have to thank the Lord, not me, for your freedom."

The brothers stood speechless with surprise on hearing this, but Karlsefin grasped Leif's hand and said very earnestly — "Ye have done well, brother. Long have I thought to urge thee to this, and frequently have I asked of Him that it might be as it has turned out. Now, my prayer is answered. But what say Heika and Hake to this?"

"Never mind what they say," returned Leif brusquely. "Doubtless their thoughts interfere with their speech at present. And hark 'ee, all; as I said before, I desire to have no further talk at present on this point. Ye are welcome to tell whom ye please what I have said, and what I have done, and why I have done it — there let the matter rest. So now, Heika and Hake," he added, in a gay tone, "I mean what I say. There lies the boat, and ye are free to go if it please you. Only, if ye will accept my advice you will make up your minds to spend this winter in Greenland as my guests, and in spring there will be better weather and a more fitting craft to carry you over the sea to Scotland. Meanwhile Hake will have ample opportunity to woo, win, and wed — without demanding — the fair Bertha!"

Need we say that the brothers gladly accepted this generous invitation, and endeavoured, in spite of Leif's prohibition, to express their gratitude in a few earnest though broken sentences.

Great was the surprise that night in Brattalid, when it was made known that Leif Ericsson had given freedom to his thralls out of regard to the Christian religion. Leif afterwards told his friends that it was out of regard to the Founder of that religion, but it was long before many of the people could see a distinction in that. Numerous were the theological discussions, too, which this act of emancipation called forth in every household, and great was the joy which it created in one or two hearts.

To say nothing of the young Scots themselves, it caused the heart of timid little Bertha to sing for joy, while Gudrid, Astrid, and Thora rejoiced sympathetically, and looked forward with pleasant anticipation to the approaching marriage. Even Freydissa opened out in a new light on the occasion, and congratulated her handmaiden heartily, telling her with real sincerity that marriage was the only thing she was fit for!

But it was Olaf who displayed the greatest amount of feeling on the occasion, and it was Snorro on whom he expended himself!

On the morning after the great event, he hoisted Snorro on his back with his wonted care and tenderness, and hurried off with him to the solitude of the seashore — for, alas! there were no umbrageous solitudes in Greenland. There, not far from the spot where Flatface and his friends had once been made to wriggle their coattails with terror, he set Snorro down, and, sitting on a rock beside him, said —

"Now, old man, it is going to have a talk with me."

"Iss," replied Snorro, very contentedly.

"Does it know what has happened to Hake and Heika?"

Snorro shook his head.

"Well, my father has set them both free."

"Bof f'ee?" repeated Snorro, with a puzzled look.

"Yes, both."

"W'at's f'ee?" asked Snorro.

Olaf was greatly perplexed, for he knew not how to convey an idea of the meaning of that word to his little friend. He made various attempts, however, by means of simple illustrations and words, to explain it, but without success — as was made plain by Snorro's usually intelligent countenance remaining a perfect blank.

At last he seized the child by both wrists and held him fast for a few seconds.

"Snorro," he said, "you are *not* free while I hold you. Now," he added, releasing the wrists, "you *are* free."

Snorro's countenance was no longer blank, but, on the contrary, extremely perplexed.

"Leif," he said, "no' hold Heika an' Hake by e *hands*!"

"No," replied Olaf, "but he holds them by the spirit."

"W'at's spiwit?" asked Snorro.

Olaf was in despair!

"Well, well," he cried, after stroking his chin and pulling his nose, and knuckling his forehead in the vain hope of hitting on some other mode of explaining his meaning; "it don't matter, old man. They are free, and that has made them very happy; and oh! I am very glad, because I am so fond of Hake. Don't you remember how he came to save us from the Skraelingers, and nearly did it too? And he is going to be married to Bertha. Isn't that nice? It knows what married means, don't it?"

"No," said Snorro.

"Well, no matter; it's what seems to make everybody very happy; and Bertha is very happy, and so am I, for I'm fond of Bertha, as well as of Hake; and so is Snorro, isn't he?"

"Iss," replied Snorro, with a very decided nod.

"Well, that's all very pleasant," continued Olaf, running on with the subject until it led him into another subject, which led him into a third and fourth, and so on, with the ever-varying moods of his gay and fanciful mind, until he was led in spirit to Vinland, where he and Snorro remained lost in the woods, perfectly contented and happy, for the remainder of the day.

And now, patient reader, we must lead you in spirit away from the scenes on which we have dwelt so long, across the wide ocean to Scotland.

There, on the heights of a lionlike hill, stand Heika and Hake. A precipitous crag rises behind them. In front towers a rock, from which Edwin's castle frowns down on the huts of an embryo city. The undulating woodland between resounds with the notes of the huntsman's horn. Away in the distance lie the clear waters of the fiord of Forth, and the background of Scotia's highland hills mingling with the sky.

The brothers stand in rapt and silent admiration of the scene, as well they may, for it is surpassingly beautiful. But they do not stand alone. Bertha leans on Hake's arm, and a tall girl with dark hair leans on Heika's. Beside them stands a fine-looking though somewhat delicate old man; whose benignant gaze seems to be more attracted by the young people than the scenery.

Need we say that this is the Scottish Earl, the father of our fleet-footed thralls, and that the dark-haired girl is Emma? We will not violate your sense of propriety, gentle reader, by talking of Mrs. Heika; nor will we venture to make reference to the little Heikas left at home!

But these are not all the party. Karlsefin, Biarne, and Thorward are there — on a visit to the Earl — with Gudrid and Freydissa; and away on the fiord they can see their two Norse galleys towering like quaint giants at rest among the small craft that ply and skim about there.

Shall we listen to what our friends say? We think not. Too long already have we caused them to break the silence which they have maintained for the last eight hundred years. Let us rather bid their shades depart with a kind farewell.

But before the memory of them is quite gone, let us say a word or two in conclusion.

Whether the Norsemen ever returned again to Vinland is a matter of uncertainty, for the saga is silent on that point; and it is to be feared that Snorro, the first American, did not return to take possession of his native land, for when the great continent was rediscovered about five hundred years later, only "red-skins" were found there; and the Pilgrim Fathers make no mention of having met with descendants of any colony of white men.

What ultimately became of Snorro and Olaf is, we regret to say, unknown. This, however, is certain, that Karlsefin, according to his oft-expressed intention, retired to Iceland, where he dwelt happily with Gudrid, Leif, Biarne, and Thorward for many years. It is therefore probable that Snorro and Olaf took to a seafaring life, which was almost the only life open to enterprising men in those days. If they did, they distinguished themselves — there can be no doubt whatever upon that point.

As to the other personages who have figured in our tale, we can only surmise — at least hope — that they lived long and happily, for the saga relates nothing as to the end of their respective careers. But of this we are quite sure, that wherever they went, or however long they lived, they never failed to retain a lively recollection of that romantic period of their lives when they sojourned in the pleasant groves of Vinland — that mighty continent which, all unsuspected by these men of old, was destined, in the course of time, to play such a grand and important part in the world's history.

Thus ends all that we have got to tell of the adventures of the Norsemen in the West, and the Discovery of America before Columbus.

THE END.

www.ingramcontent.com/pod-product-compliance
Lightning Source LLC
Chambersburg PA
CBHW020334260626
47156CB00004B/1514